is grammar s̶c̶... ̶-̶p̶a̶p̶e̶r̶,
market res̶... ̶a̶n̶d̶ flying background.

A frequent traveller to all points of the compass, the author's favourite country firmly remains Thailand.

Writing is a new activity, to be added to longer established pursuits, notably photography. Work on a sequel to *The Killing of Innocence* is at an advanced stage, to be followed by a story about intrigue within an international corporation.

When not en route to some far flung outpost of the planet, J C Sinclair lives in rural Oxfordshire.

J C Sinclair

THE KILLING OF INNOCENCE

The Romance Club
R.001

Aspire Publishing

An Aspire Publication

First published in Great Britain 1998

ISBN 1 902035 03 8

Printed and bound in Great Britain by
Mackays of Chatham Plc, Chatham, Kent.

Typeset in Palatino by Kestrel Data, Exeter, Devon.

Aspire Publishing – a division of XcentreX Ltd.

Part One
Youthful Encounter

Chapter One

Quick-tempered maybe, intolerant sometimes, impulsive often, but aggressive rarely. Yet the glint in Robert Stone's eyes, as he strode purposefully home, was because he was bent on delivering a metaphorical kick to somebody's bottom – either his mother's or Melanie Bishop's.

Robert should have been feeling on top of the world. End of term exams were finished and the results had exceeded even his parents' expectations. He had just led the under-15 football team to victory over their toughest rivals, scoring the winning goal himself and, to cap it all, in a few days he would be leaving for the holiday of a lifetime. If it had not been for Melanie, his horizon would have been free of cloud.

As he approached his fifteenth birthday, Robert's attitude towards girls was already undergoing a fundamental change. Until recently, they had rated as rather silly creatures to be avoided at all costs. Hardly any of them were interested in football, cars, video games, or the Internet. Instead, they seemed to be content to fritter their life away on non-activities like listening to rap, dancing to techno, and trying on clothes. But now, in spite of these lamentable characteristics, he was slowly coming to the conclusion that there was something else about girls that perhaps he had previously overlooked. He had not exactly fathomed what it was yet, but he at least recognised that they could no longer be dismissed out of hand. This was still mega miles from actually associating with them, of course, which was why Melanie weighed so heavily on his mind.

The problem came out of the blue a few days earlier when, for some inexplicable reason, she decided that she fancied Robert and persuaded her friend, Denise, to ask him if he would like to be her next boyfriend. A tallish, good looking boy, with lightly-waving blonde hair and grey-blue eyes, he had lately become the focus of attention for more than one early teenage miss. But to a lifelong Chelsea supporter, it was like being asked if he would change his allegiance to Arsenal. Ridiculous.

Not that there was anything wrong with Melanie. Indeed, she was regarded by the *cognoscenti* among Robert's pals, as one of the most desirable girls in the school, whatever that meant. All he knew was that if his pals even suspected that Melanie Bishop had designs on him, they would rib him mercilessly.

To make matters worse, he had failed to communicate his true feelings on the matter to Melanie and she, misreading his feeble response, had invited him to her birthday party, hinting that he would be the guest of honour. This had not bothered Robert too much, since the party was to be held after he had left for his holiday. By the time he returned, there was a good chance that her unwelcome attentions would have been re-directed towards some other unsuspecting mug. It had proved to be a forlorn hope and a short reprieve.

Melanie's birthday party invitation had come through her mother to Robert's mother. Knowing how her son would react, Mary Stone had responded with typical adult insincerity and walked straight into Melanie's trap.

'I'm sure Robert would love to come, thank you.' Then a deep sigh of regret. 'Wait a minute, did you say the 30th? What a pity, I'm afraid we leave for the States on the 27th. He will be so disappointed . . .'

Polite, no offence, and she had got Robert off the hook without his even becoming involved.

'Don't worry, Robbie, I took care of it,' she had assured Robert later.

The fateful words now grated like the scratchy soundtrack of an old movie, for fourteen-year-old Melanie had just demonstrated that there is no age limit to the devilish cunning of females. As he left the station this particular afternoon she had been waiting to inform him that she had managed, after a great deal of trouble, to persuade her parents to bring the date of her party forward. In his honour. Now it would be held just before he left for his holiday, so he would be able to come after all. Wasn't that *wonderful* news?

On reflection, perhaps the bottom kicking should be more than just metaphorical . . .

Events took a turn for the worse when Robert arrived home. 'Is that you, Robert?' Something in his mother's voice spelled bad news, and his spirits sank further. Had she got him into another fine mess?

'Yes, Mum.' He pushed open the kitchen door and saw she was busying herself over the preparation of dinner with studied haste. A bad sign.

'How did the match go?'

'We won, but . . .'

'Well done, Robbie, I'm so pleased.' Mary Stone turned to face her son, wiping her hands vigorously on a tea towel. In looks and temperament, her son favoured her. Even now, only a few years short of her fortieth birthday, her shoulder-length ash blonde hair and elegant figure were still capable of turning male heads.

'Er . . . your father telephoned this afternoon,' she said, with a certain amount of trepidation.

That was hardly news to set his pulse racing. His father often phoned home from the office.

'I'm afraid there's been a change of plan for the holiday.'

'Oh, no!'

Even Melanie Bishop at her most devious could not have dropped such a bombshell. The holiday had been planned for ages and in the past few weeks they had talked of little else. Surely nothing could stop it now.

'You mean we aren't going?'

'Well, not to America. Something has come up at your father's office. There's some sort of financial crisis at one of their overseas branches and they want him to go over there to sort it out. Apparently it's very urgent and he has to go next Wednesday. But don't worry, we're still going with him.'

'Going *where*, Mum?'

'To Bangkok. I'm sure you'll enjoy it as much. It will just be . . . er . . . different.'

'Do they have Disney World there and Universal Studios and a Cape Kennedy and . . . ?'

'No, probably not, but I expect they'll have other attractions you won't find in America.'

'What other things?' Robert threw his bag down in disgust. In an instant his castle of dreams had crumbled. 'How could they be so mean, this close to the holiday?'

'They wouldn't have asked your father to change his plans at this late stage if it hadn't been an emergency.' His mother had been thinking up some counter arguments before he came in to try and soften his disappointment, and she went on: 'It's quite a compliment that he's been chosen to do it. They've even offered to pay the travel costs and hotel expenses for all three of us.'

'Some compliment,' Robert retorted bitterly. He was not interested in economic considerations.

'Your father and I are just as disappointed as you, Robert, and remember it's far worse for him. At least we'll be on holiday, enjoying ourselves, while he will be working most of the time.'

He had not thought of that, but it still wasn't fair.

'What will I tell the boys at school? After all the talk about going to America, I'll look a right prat.'

'Tell them the truth. Explain that your father's been given an important assignment, which means that we'll be going somewhere completely different. Remind them that lots of people have been to America, but how many have been to Thailand?' It was the first plus point since the news had broken. His mother saw she had struck a chord and hastened to build on it.

'Look, Robbie, I know it's a bit of a shock, but try to think positively. I don't know anything about Thailand, but we could be pleasantly surprised. Let's give it a chance, eh?'

Robert knew she was right and he would have to try and put his disappointment behind him. His eyes lit up when a thought suddenly struck him.

'What is it?' his mother asked, noticing the change of expression.

'I've just thought of something.' He was feeling better already. 'Did you say we would be leaving on Wednesday?'

'That's right, three days before we were due to go to America. Why?'

'Melanie's birthday party is on Wednesday. That means I won't have to go to it after all.'

Robert's father, Brian, worked for InterProm, an international advertising agency based in London. Now in his late thirties, Brian Stone was rated by his bosses as sound middle management material. All the portents for the future suggested a steady path of consolidation, with no risk-taking, through his forties to probable early retirement on a comfortable pension by his middle fifties. It added up to a secure if unspectacular career. Until out of the blue, this chance to make a name for himself in Thailand had landed in his lap. He was determined not to be found wanting and was currently spending most of his leisure hours working on his brief.

Perhaps, against the odds, his career might yet take off.

Robert's mother also had her work cut out to complete the domestic preparations for their journey. There was a last minute appointment with their doctor for inoculations. Visas, travellers cheques, airline tickets, travel insurance and hotel all had to be organised; milk and newspapers cancelled, and arrangements made for the dog, cat, two hamsters and a lizard to be cared for.

Despite his immediate resentment at the change of

destination, Robert was soon caught up in the excitement of the preparations and a growing anticipation of the unknown that lay ahead. He read several guide books on Thailand and even tried to master a few useful phrases, such as "I do not speak Thai."

The length of the flight too would be a new experience for him, many times longer than the hops over to Majorca or the Costa del Sol that were all he had ever done so far. The obvious route was south east across the width of Europe which they would leave behind at the Bosphorus. The length of Turkey and Iran would keep them clear of some of the more politically sensitive countries in the region. Then over Pakistan, the Indian sub-continent, Bay of Bengal and Burma, now Myanmar, before crossing the Thai border and descending to Bangkok.

By comparison, with only a single stretch of water to cross, the flight to America looked positively dull.

Although Robert's early misgivings were not completely allayed, he began to wonder if going east instead of west might prove to be a lucky break after all.

Chapter Two

Robert's initial chagrin over the change of holiday returned on the taxi ride from Bangkok's Don Muang airport to their hotel. He saw none of the attractions he had read about in the travel books and sensed that his mother and father felt a similar disenchantment as they looked out at grey, uninspiring buildings, an overcast sky, and interminable traffic which slowed to a crawl when they neared the city centre, in spite of the frantic urging of uniformed police at strategic points along the route.

What he did not know was that a certain flat feeling often accompanies long flights which are dominated by boredom, discomfort and for most people an inescapable anxiety. Just as quickly, once he had showered, changed and made a quick tour of the hotel's facilities and the surrounding area, Robert's natural optimism was restored. But as the first day wore on and fatigue asserted itself, both he and his parents began to flag and with the coming of dusk they called it a day.

This did not stop Robert's father from going off to work early next morning. He was determined to lose no time in tackling the problems his company had sent him all this way to resolve.

Without the same spur, Robert and his mother slept late, had a leisurely lunch and sat down with the hotel's travel agent, to plot their itinerary for the next few days. Guided by a smiling Thai girl in a smart green suit, who spoke impeccable English, they considered a wide range of tourist attractions. Later, they discussed these with Brian to determine which ones he would like to accompany them on and which they would take in on their own while he was at work.

The following day was Saturday and Brian Stone's first opportunity to relax with his family since their arrival. Still suffering the effects of jet lag, they decided to take it easy on this first weekend and, in Mary's view at least, what could be more relaxing than a wander round the best stores in the city?

'We don't need to buy anything,' she said casually, 'but it will be nice to get a feel of the shops, and I hear they have some lovely things at Jim Thompson's.'

It sounded innocent enough, but her husband recognised the all-too-familiar spending signals.

During the next few days, Robert and his mother discovered a world that no TV programme or travel book could ever begin to describe. This was the real thing and they were part of it, experiencing at first hand the sounds, the smells, the heat, the food and, above all, the people of Thailand.

In a long tailed boat that left a deep widening swell and a cloud of spray in its wake, they rode down the wide Chao Phraya River of Kings that bisects Bangkok from north to south. Less frenetically, they stuttered their way up the narrow *klongs*, or canals, that splinter off the main river, past the rusting tin roofs, dark windowless rooms and crowded washing lines of poor shanty dwellings. If the colour of the water raised doubts about its crystal purity, it did not seem to worry the children who cavorted naked in the shallows and waved cheerfully at the passing craft.

More comfortable and sedate was the steady surge upstream in a converted rice barge. While they helped themselves to a buffet of tropical fruits, pretty Thai hostesses in colourful ankle-length dresses plied them with iced drinks.

They visited the Crocodile Farm at Samutprakarn, alleged to house thirty thousand crocodiles, and in a small amphitheatre watched a man walk among the malevolent log-like creatures, haul on their tails and tap their snouts with a stick till they reacted with a spine-chilling clunk of their fearsome jaws. As a finale, he picked one up in his arms and lay down with another, allowing it to nuzzle his face.

Much against his mother's wishes, Robert paid to pose with a chained tiger. It was probably quite safe, but he began to wonder when he placed his hands gingerly on its back. The tremor of undulating steel-hard muscles under its satin-smooth coat conveyed a latent power that was scary. He hoped that the strange grumbling noise emanating from within was just a loud purr.

One of their boat trips took in a Snake Farm, where they watched a youth in bare feet and baggy trousers crouch eye to eye and sway in unison with a cobra. By prodding it with a rolled up newspaper, he angered it into striking only to leap out of its reach with an apparent ease that made the deadly game look perfectly safe. More terrifying still was the arm's length view of a cobra. It was first forced to eject its deadly venom through muslin into a glass jar and then carried round within reach of the wary onlookers. In spite of sharing most people's fear of these creatures, Robert reached out and stroked its dry scaly skin as it passed. Later, he was told it was good luck to touch a king cobra.

More barbaric was a fight staged in a small glass cage between a cobra and a mongoose. Although it was first on the attack, the cobra's strikes succeeded only in hitting the tinfoil floor with an eerie 'thump', as its intended victim leapt aside even faster. The reptile was eventually hauled out of the cage in a sorry state, whether to die or recover to fight another unequal battle, Robert would never know.

At the Rose Garden, they also saw exhibitions of Thai boxing, Thai dancing and a fiercely realistic sword fight that combined exceptional skill, daring and athleticism with the right blend of humour.

These tours were interspersed with further shopping expeditions; Mary Stone was particularly impressed by the many huge department stores. For size and variety of goods they equalled almost anything back home. Robert preferred the ambience of the smaller shops and stalls to be found in the markets of Sukhumvit, Silom and Pratunam. Here, the array of clothes, bags, paintings, watches, music and video cassettes and all manner of other goods was endless, good quality and cheap.

Much of the merchandise bore familiar names, like Gucci and Cartier, Rolex and Dior, Boss and Lacoste; names that conjured up images of style and prestige, only here, being locally produced, they were a fraction of the price in the West.

The people working on these stalls were always cheerful and few transactions were completed without lengthy bargaining and exclamations of feigned outrage. The result was almost invariably a friendly conclusion that left both parties satisfied they had struck the best deal.

Some of the harsher realities of life were uncomfortably in evidence on the busier streets. Robert could never get used to seeing cripples and young women with tiny babies in their arms, seated on the pavements, thrusting plastic beakers at passers-by, more in hope than expectation. In particular, he was shocked by a young girl with twisted legs, little thicker than a hose pipe, and the tiny figure of a young man, truncated by a total lack of limbs.

'Don't they have anyone to look after them?' he asked his mother more than once.

'I don't know,' his mother replied uncomfortably. She felt inadequate to deal with her son's questions about these people. 'There are a lot of very poor people all over the world. We should remember them when we think we have troubles.'

She knew she was repeating the platitudes of the 'haves' of this world. Nevertheless, she was pleased to see that Robert stopped to drop a small coin into many of the proffered cups.

Mary Stone was particularly touched by another incident that occurred one evening when they were walking slowly back to their hotel after a later than usual dinner. It was about 10 o'clock and she was not aware of anyone else beside her until her hand was touched. The little girl could not have been more than seven or eight, and was peering up at her with big serious eyes. When she saw she had Mary's attention, she held up a large card with English writing on it, which read: 'Please buy a flower from my school. Thank you. 10 bahts.'

Brian produced twenty bahts and handed it to the child, receiving a plastic yellow rose in return. The girl acknowledged the transaction with the traditional *wei* and, without having spoken a word, scurried away after her similarly-sized friend, happily flourishing the twenty baht note.

For his part, Robert was beginning to feel that perhaps, after all, Thailand had quite a lot to offer.

Chapter Three

Life in Bangkok was dominated by the traffic. Getting about the city, especially during rush hours, was usually a near mission impossible. The noise, heat and fumes added to the discomfort and sapped the stamina of the most dedicated tourist. After a week of it, Mary Stone was beginning to long for a calmer environment.

'The girl at the tourist desk gave me a brochure on a nice park not far from here,' she told Robert over lunch. 'I thought we might go there today. It'll make a change from the traffic and the noise, and you may find some new things to photograph.'

Visiting parks was near the bottom of Robert's list of favourite activities, but he fell in with his mother's suggestion readily enough.

It was apparent, as soon as they passed through the tall iron gates where the taxi dropped them in mid-afternoon, that Lumpini Park covered a vast area. They hesitated at the entrance, unsure which of the several paths to take. Then, spotting a glint of water through the trees, they headed off towards it. As they penetrated further into the park the traffic noise re-ceded to be replaced by a welcome hush, disturbed only by the murmer of voices and chaff of birdlife.

They strolled along paths of packed-earth, between closely trimmed lawns and well-stocked flower beds, kept fresh and moist in the intense heat by water sprays playing gently over them. Some of the blooms, like roses and petunias, were familiar, but most of them they had never seen before. Their perfume filled the air with a blend of fragrances. Spaced at intervals along the path were metal carts, tended by young girls and old women, dispensing cold drinks, sweets and ice cream from under faded umbrellas.

They reached the lake at a point where small boats were available for hire. It proved to be a large expanse of water, roughly circular in shape, with a fountain in the middle pumping water high into the air. At the far side of the lake were two stone bridges. Later they discovered that these linked the main park to an oval-shaped island. The slight breeze coming at them from across the water was welcome on their faces. Mary Stone sank gratefully onto one of the shaded benches by the water's edge.

'Isn't this pleasant?' she said, surprised to find this idyllic oasis in the heart of the crowded, fume-sated metropolis. 'Let's rest here for a few minutes.'

'Do you mind if I go round the lake while you wait here, Mum?' Robert was still bursting with energy. 'I might get some good shots looking back from that bridge.' Something of a camera buff, he was ever on the lookout for photo opportunities.

'Of course not,' his mother agreed. 'You go ahead. We'll have a drink when you get back.'

Robert sauntered along the path that faithfully followed the lake's contours, stopping from time to time to watch the people in the rowing boats, canoes and pedalos. Nearer the bank, small groups of ducks weaved their effortless, aimless courses with just as much enjoyment within their small world.

He reached the stone bridge and leaned over the

low balustrade. Looking back across the water he could just make out his mother's white dress under the trees. He waved but she didn't appear to see him. He decided this would be as good a spot as any from which to capture a few scenes on film, and was reaching for his camera when a soft voice spoke to him from behind.

'You drop this?'

"Drop" sounded more like "dlop," but the meaning was clear enough. Robert turned sharply in surprise to face a young Thai girl, holding something out to him. He had not been aware of her approach, thinking himself to be alone on the bridge. The girl was about his age, perhaps a little younger, and a shy smile played about her lips, as if she wanted to be friendly but wasn't sure if she should. Especially as he was a foreigner - a *falang*. A quick glance at his camera confirmed that the lens cap was missing.

'Er . . . yes, it is mine. Thank you. It must have fallen off my camera.'

Inexplicably he felt nervous as he took the cap from her and fitted it over the lens.

'You see? It fits perfectly.'

She smiled again, more confidently.

'Where you from?'

'England. I'm on holiday with my mother and father. He's working over here actually.'

'First time you come Bangkok?'

'Yes, first time.'

'You like?'

He nodded emphatically. 'We're having a great time. It's very different from England.'

'What way different?'

'Lots of ways. There's the weather for one thing and . . .'

Melanie Bishop flashed across Robert's mind. Perhaps, sub-consciously, he was making comparisons. Certainly, they could not have been more apart in appearance: whereas Melanie was slim and tall, about Robert's height, this girl was shorter, which was probably why she seemed stockier in build. Melanie was pale complexioned, with curly blonde hair, while the Thai girl was much darker skinned. Like most of her race, her hair was dead straight, jet black and glossy fine as Thai silk; she wore it gathered in a pony tail by a white bow. She had a roundish face with slightly plump cheeks, the snub button of a nose and a small mouth that made her lips seem thicker, as if set in a permanent pout.

But it was her eyes that captivated Robert. Wide-set and arched by thick eyebrows, they were deep brown, virtually black in the shade, with high inner curves that slanted towards the corners giving them the distinctively attractive shape of southern Orientals.

She wore a blouse of duck-egg blue, pulled in at the waist by a black belt, and a plain navy blue skirt of demure knee-length. White ankle length socks and black low-heeled shoes rounded off the classic school uniform.

Robert, arch-avoider of the female sex, made an instant judgement that this girl's face was the most beautiful face he had ever seen.

'It's much hotter here than England,' he said, continuing the trite talk and wishing like mad he could think of something more inspired to say to her.

'What your name?' she said, perhaps sensing his confusion and trying to ease his path.

'Robert,' he blurted, grinning uneasily in his relief.

'Lobut?'

'No,' He trilled the first "R". 'Rrrrrrobert.'

'Lobut. I never hear that name before.'

Robert gave up on the pronunciation. 'What's your name?'

'Doungjai.'

He repeated it slowly. 'I've never hear that name before either. It's a nice name.'

'You like?' His approval seemed to please her. She indicated his camera. 'Nice camera. How much it cost?'

'I don't remember,' he said, mildly taken aback by her directness. 'I was just going to take a picture of the lake.' He suddenly had an inspiration. 'Can I take a photograph of you?'

'You take photograph of me?' She looked startled.

'If you don't mind. You're the first Thai girl I've really talked to.'

'No mind.'

'OK. Would you like to sit on the wall over there?'

She backed uncertainly to the wall and perched on it tentatively, as if she thought it might be red-hot. Looking straight at the camera, her features set in a serious unnatural expression. Robert knew it would not look right on film, but he was at a loss how to deal with it, so he clicked the shutter and wound on.

'Can we try another one - and how about smiling this time?' he suggested.

The second effort was no better, her attempt to look happier only emphasising her camera-shyness. As he captured the stiff smile, Robert wondered if he should abandon here and now a cherished ambition to be a professional a photographer. His mind worked over-time, wondering how he could get her to relax for just one shot.

Still peering through the viewfinder, he became aware that she was no longer looking at the camera, but sideways, towards the lake. The tension had vanished and she was smiling naturally. Robert followed the direction of her gaze and saw she was watching a straggling line of tiny ducklings waddling across the path by the bridge behind their mother.

'*Pet!*' she exclaimed.

With great presence of mind, Robert snapped her in profile, looking happy and relaxed, and again in mid-turn, as her gaze swivelled back towards him. Satisfied with this stroke of luck, he put his camera away.

'They go for swim,' she said, pointing at the ducks, as if this were a unique event.

'Do you like ducks?'

'Like all animals.' Her eyes were gleaming. 'One day I like to work with animals, like doctor, but Mama say no can.'

Mention of her "Mama" reminded Robert of his own. He had completely forgotten her.

'I'm sorry, but I have to go. My mother is waiting for me and she'll be wondering where I am.'

'You go now?' She looked genuinely disappointed.

'I'm afraid I must. Thank you again for finding my lens cap.'

'You welcome. Maybe see you again?'

To his ears it sounded more than a mere conventional parting remark.

'I come here often on way home from school,' she went on.

'I . . . I don't know. I'm not sure what our plans are. You see we're only on holiday in Bangkok.'

It was a pure reflex response. His old awkwardness with girls had reasserted itself and he was instinctively backing off, unwilling to let himself become even marginally involved.

'Maybe you come here again before you go home?' she suggested hopefully. No mistaking now her earnestness. The dark brown eyes were serious in her young, slightly sad face.

'Maybe.' Robert hated himself for his offhand response, but it was too late to correct it. Yet he was just beginning to realise how much he had enjoyed talking to Doungjai. In the end, the faintheart within him won.

'It was nice to meet you. Goodbye.' He was already backing away.

'Goodbye, Lobut,' she called after him.

His mind was in turmoil as he walked rapidly back along the path by the lake. It was not eased when he shot a quick glance over his shoulder and saw her small figure still sitting alone on the bridge wall.

'You were a long time, Robert,' his mother greeted him. She was still where he had left her, but her observation was casual, and she showed no concern.

'I met someone on the bridge and got talking.' He did not elaborate.

'Did you take any photos?'

'One or two.'

'How about that drink now?'

Robert was silent as they sat with their drinks. His mother could see he was preoccupied and she did not intrude. Perhaps it was the "someone" he had met; he kept glancing across the lake towards the bridge. She noted, too, that he seemed in no hurry to return to the hotel. Even so, she would never have dreamed that the source of his abstraction was a *girl*.

Chapter Four

The late afternoon sun was slipping away rapidly when Robert descended to the hotel pool. Most of the poolside promenaders had already collected their belongings and drifted back to their rooms, and he was able to swim without fear of collision.

As he swam, in his rather uncoordinated fashion, his mind returned to the girl on the bridge. In the space of a few minutes that afternoon, something had happened to him. He felt unhappy and thoroughly mixed up. Back home, he went out of his way to avoid girls. The chief attraction of the change in their holiday plans had been missing Melanie Bishop's birthday party. So why was he sparing this girl a second thought?

Apart from being about the same age, they had nothing in common. Although she spoke a sort of English, her conversation was limited; she couldn't even pronounce his name properly. As for seeing her again, it was quite true that his time was limited. He still had a lot to see on this holiday, so why use up valuable sight-seeing time by entering into some sort of relationship with her? Even if he did manage to meet up with her again, where would it lead? A big nowhere. No, far better to forget all about her and focus on enjoying the holiday.

Only who was he kidding?

Even as he tried to nurture and sustain these dismissive thoughts, he knew they were false and, furthermore, they were ineffectual. Put simply, she had got under his skin in a way no girl had ever done. She intrigued him, not least on account of her air of naive innocence. She had a wistful, rather sad smile and she spoke a funny kind of English. Most of all though, those magical dark eyes haunted the hell out of him. She had even expressed the hope that they might meet before he went home, but he had crazily, clumsily dismissed the idea out of hand. He had no idea where she lived or which school she went to. The only solid item of information he possessed was that she went through the park on the way home from school sometimes. Perhaps if he were to be on the bridge at the same time tomorrow, he could contrive to bump into her. No sooner had the hope arisen when it turned to frustration. Tomorrow was Saturday and there would be no school. Or would there? For all he knew, they went to school on Saturday in Thailand. Well, if they didn't, there was always Monday.

The more these thoughts crowded in, conflicting and confusing, the more he felt angry with himself. For the first time in his life, he was learning that the most important human relationships were usually a hotchpotch of contradictions, in which doubts and fears rubbed shoulders with hopes and fulfilment. Straightforward, they were not.

So immersed was he in his thoughts that he did not notice the onset of dusk. The pool lights came on suddenly, bathing the water in an aquamarine glow. He was alone there. He climbed slowly from the pool and retrieved his towel. His mind was made up. Come tomorrow, come Monday, come hell and high water, he would seek out Doungjai. And then we would see.

For Brian Stone, it had been a tough first week in unfamiliar surroundings after a long and tiring journey. His bosses in England had been right. The local company's finances were in a mess and needed to be dealt with speedily. Yet by the end of the first week, most of his doubts were behind him. There was still a lot to be done, but now he was certain of his ability to put the books in balance. Thankfully, it was a question of incompetence rather than dishonesty. Consequently, he sat down to dinner with Mary and Robert on the Friday evening, feeling at ease and satisfied.

While his parents discussed his father's work, Robert's thoughts were elsewhere and he gave a start when his father shook his arm.

'I hear you enjoyed the park this afternoon, Robert,' his father repeated.

'Oh, er . . . yes, it was OK, Dad.'

'I gather you met someone by the lake. Were they on holiday as well?'

It was an opening Robert chose not to seize.

'Well no...actually . . .' He picked his words carefully. 'I dropped my lens cap and this person picked it up.'

'That was lucky.'

'Then we just got talking and . . .' The soup arrived at that moment and a relieved Robert spooned into the hot limey Tom Yam Gung. 'This is jolly good,' he enthused with exaggerated approval, hoping the subject of his activities would die a natural death.

'So who was this person?' his father probed. He had already been primed by Mary and was curious why Robert was being so unusually reticent.

'It was just a . . . er . . . sort of schoolgirl.' Robert said, casual as could be as he imbibed another lengthy spoonful of soup. 'They certainly put in plenty of prawns.'

'What did you talk about, darling?' his mother asked gently, intrigued, but anxious not to embarrass her son.

'Nothing much. She was on her way home from school and asked if I liked it here.'

'So she spoke English, obviously?'

'A bit. I could understand her and she seemed to understand me, but she had a funny way of saying things.'

'Was her English as good as your Thai?' his father teased.

Robert smiled and relaxed a little. 'Er . . . a bit better actually. But she couldn't say my name properly . . . kept calling me Lobut.'

'They do seem to have a problem pronouncing their "r's",' Brian Stone agreed gravely.

'What was her name?' His mother asked, between spoonfuls.

'Doungjai.' Then, after a slight pause: 'I took her photo.'

With some difficulty his parents refrained from looking at each other.

'She didn't mind?' His mother kept a solemn face somehow.

'No, she seemed quite pleased. I thought I might give her a print when I get the film developed. You know, as a kind of thank you for finding my lens cap.'

'That would be a gentlemanly gesture,' his father approved, smoothing his thinning brown hair. 'So you've arranged to meet her again?'

'Not exactly arranged. You see I didn't think of it till afterwards and that's a bit of a problem, because I don't know where she lives, only that she goes through that park on her way home from school.' He looked up from his soup. 'I wondered if we could go back tomorrow and see if she's there.'

This time his parents did look at each other.

'It's Saturday tomorrow, Robert,' his mother reminded him. 'Do they go to school on Saturday?'

'I don't know, Mum, but we can easily find out.' He tried to maintain his nonchalant pose, as if it were of no consequence. 'Even if they don't, she might still go to the park for a walk.'

'Don't forget we're going sightseeing tomorrow. Your father hasn't seen anything of Bangkok yet outside of his office.'

'That's no problem,' Brian quickly interposed. 'We've got the morning and all of Sunday for sightseeing. A walk by the lake in the afternoon will do me nicely.'

'Thanks, Dad,' Robert said gratefully.

Maybe the door was not closed after all.

Robert was up an hour before his parents next morning, but he was still a few minutes behind them in reaching the restaurant for breakfast. He looked pleased with himself.

'I've had a busy morning,' he explained in response to their unspoken questions. 'I wanted to finish off the film in my camera so I've been out taking shots around the hotel. Then I took the film to the photographic shop to have it developed. They can have it ready by lunchtime.'

'Well done,' his father said, suppressing a smile.

The Stones took a taxi to the River City Shopping

Centre and, after wandering through the multi-storey arcades, stood watching the many different kinds of craft plying their busy way up and down the Chao Phraya. After lunching at the Sheraton, they took a taxi to the park, making a detour to collect Robert's prints en route.

Sitting in the front beside the driver, Robert studied the results of his handiwork, flicking through the views till he came to the pictures he had taken of Doungjai. As he suspected, she looked stiff and uncomfortable in the first two. He was relieved that the third one in profile was in focus, for he had snapped it hurriedly. It captured her happy smile as she spotted the ducks and she looked altogether more natural. But it was the fourth photograph that caused him to stare for long seconds. It was probably a fluke, but he knew he could not have produced a better composition had he used the whole film. It could not have been bettered by a pro with five thousand pounds worth of equipment. Her face was glowing and happy, her eyes sparkling and lips parted. The black silkiness of her hair reflected the late afternoon sunlight and, as the picture had been taken a split second before she realised the camera was pointing at her, her expression and posture were not marred by self-consciousness.

As he continued to dwell upon Doungjai's lovely features, he knew why he had thought of little else but her since yesterday, and why he was so desperate to see her again.

'What are they like, Robert?' His mother touched him on the shoulder 'Did the one you took of your friend come out?' She was curious to see what this schoolgirl, who seemed to have made such an impression on her son, looked like.

'They're not bad, quite good really.'

'May we see?' his father asked.

Without even thinking, Robert slipped the last photo he had taken of Doungjai to the back of the pile and passed the other three to his mother.

'The one where she was looking away is the best,' he remarked casually. 'She looks a bit camera-shy in the others.'

His father and mother studied the photos in silence.

'Well,' his mother said at last, 'she certainly is a pretty girl, isn't she, Brian?'

'Yes, indeed.'

'This is the best one.' Robert handed the last one over.

'Yes, *indeed*,' his father repeated, with real enthusiasm. 'She's not just pretty, she's beautiful.'

Robert experienced a flush of pride, as if she were his private possession.

'I only want to give her the photo as a kind of thank you,' Robert hastened to explain, anxious that his motives would not be misunderstood. Or understood.

'Of course.' His mother understood perfectly. 'It's a very kind thought and your father is right – she is beautiful. You've taken some lovely photos and I'm sure she'll be thrilled when you give them to her.'

They arrived at the park about the same time as the previous afternoon. Robert was out of the taxi and through the gates almost before the wheels ceased to roll. He looked back at them impatiently, as his father paid off the taxi.

'Do you mind if I go on?'

'It's a big place, Robert,' Brian Stone cautioned. 'We

don't want to lose each other.' The park was much more crowded than on Robert's previous visit and he acknowledged his father's concern.

'Let's meet by the lake where you waited for me yesterday, Mum. I shan't be long.'

'All right, but be careful.'

Brian and Mary Stone watched their only son trot away across the grass until he was no longer in sight.

'Do you think he'll be all right, Brian?' Mary looked to her husband for reassurance. 'I don't like him going off on his own like that.'

'He can't come to any harm in here,' he assured her. 'I'm more concerned about how disappointed he's going to be. You know how he builds up his hopes. There's no school today so he's relying on seeing her by chance.'

They took their time strolling to the lake. They found a shady spot near where Mary had waited for Robert the previous afternoon. After an hour spent soaking up the sights and sounds of the park and the people, they proceeded along the lakeside for a couple of hundred yards and then back the other way, always keeping the bench where they were to meet Robert in view. Back at the rendezvous point, Brian bought two Fantas and they sat watching and waiting while the sun began to dip towards the top of the trees.

'Here he comes,' Brian exclaimed just when they were beginning to feel the first stirrings of anxiety. The boy's face was gloomy.

'He didn't see her,' Brian murmured to his wife, who had already reached the same conclusion.

Although disappointed, Robert was not too devastated by Doungjai's failure to show up. The possibility of her being here on a Saturday had always been pretty slim, since there was no school. On reflection, it had made little sense to look for her today. Monday would be a different matter though.

On Sunday, the Stone family took a tour to Ayuthaya. A minibus transported them to the river departure point where they boarded a large cabin cruiser, the *Oriental Queen*, and chugged up the river towards the place that had been Thailand's capital until 1767. They lunched on the boat, then left it about fourteen miles short of the old capital to explore the Bang Pa-In Summer Palace. The exquisite little Thai pavilion in traditional green and orange, which sits in the centre of a small lake, was another subject for Robert Stone, ace photographer.

Robert's parents raved over it, and his father fired off his own camera from every conceivable angle. Yet to Robert, it was no more than a time filler until his next meeting with Doungjai.

If there was to be a next meeting . . .

Chapter Five

Robert stood on the bridge and scrutinised every young girl who came by. It was Monday afternoon and he knew this was his last chance to meet Doungjai again. If she did not come today, it would be hard to justify more visits to the park. His father was back at work and, as before, his mother had accompanied him. Only this time she had gone off to explore other parts of the park on her own.

As this was his third visit to the same spot in four days the surroundings were becoming familiar to Robert. He even recognised some of the women selling drinks from their metal box trolleys. The duck and her family were still there too. It felt almost like a homecoming.

As each minute ticked away and his chances of ever seeing her again gradually receded, a cloak of hopelessness settled on him. The afternoon edged towards evening and he realised with resigned certainty that she was not going to appear. It was well past the hour when they had met before, and the shadows were quickening their pace across the grass. His mother would be waiting for him. He decided to stay five more minutes. In the event he stayed for ten. He gave the whole area a last despairing scan before retracing his steps round the lake to where his mother was sitting patiently. She had no need to enquire as to the outcome of his vigil.

Few words passed between them on the way back to the hotel. Mary Stone could not remember when she had seen her son so despondent and there was little she could contribute to make him feel any better. Gone was his last chance of ever seeing the girl again, and that was that.

Coming to terms with the events of the past few days was for Robert a trial unlike any other he had endured. Meeting Doungjai had changed his whole perspective of the holiday, of girls, of life even. The excitement and thrill of discovery that had characterised their first days in Bangkok had been replaced by a kind of emptiness. Somehow, he had to rise above it, if only for the sake of his parents. After all, this was their holiday too.

For the sake of something to do, he went over to Reception to pick up the latest issues of the Bangkok tourist journals.

'I'm sorry.' The receptionist shook her head. 'They haven't arrived this week yet. They may be late because yesterday was a public holiday.'

Robert stopped in his tracks. 'Public holiday?' he echoed. 'Yesterday?' The adrenalin was suddenly pumping. 'Were the schools on holiday as well?'

'Yes, schools always close for public holiday.' The receptionist looked puzzled, and doubly so when Robert beamed at her, showered her with thanks, and dashed for the lift.

Some people chose not to use the *tuk tuks* that were such a common sight on the streets of Bangkok. They tended to view these brightly coloured three-wheelers, with their handlebar controls, as unstable and their drivers as speed fiends. And it was true that for the passengers, perched high behind the driver, there was scant protection in the event of a collision, and none at all from the toxic fumes of the massed traffic. Scurrying along on the two-stroke engines, from which their name is derived, the *tuk tuk* did at least create a refreshing rush of air around the open canopy. They could also wriggle through gaps in the traffic that deceive the eye and defy the laws of physics.

In the hope of making better time Robert rode one of these conveyances to the gates of Lumpini Park. Aware that he was later than on previous days, he ran along the now familiar path towards the lake.

He was out of breath and a good hundred yards away when he saw a small figure in a white blouse crossing the bridge. He slowed, the better to focus. Could it be her? It *looked* like her, but then schoolgirls in uniform were plentiful in Bangkok. Another anxious thought struck him, incredibly for the first time. Would she want to see him again? Their short conversation was hardly the basis on which to build such ambitious hopes. Why should she say more than a polite hello, followed immediately by a polite goodbye?

But it was too late now for such negative thoughts. He broke into a sprint.

She was some distance beyond the bridge when he reached it. His heart was hammering, and not only because of his exertion. Now he was closing fast, just a matter of yards . . . feet . . . He reached out and touched her.

'Doungjai? he wheezed.

The girl turned.

'Lobut!' she exclaimed, and those incredible limpid eyes lit up in recognition and pleasure.

'Hello, Doungjai.' His legs suddenly felt like rubber. 'I . . . I thought it was you. It's good to see you again.'

'This big surprise for me also. I think already you no come here again.' The words tumbled out fresh and natural; no artificial coyness, only unaffected delight.

Robert Stone, captain of the under-15 cricket and football teams, macho fifth form student and disdainer of the fair sex, was completely overwhelmed now that he had at last tracked down this small female creature from the far side of the planet.

'I . . . I . . .' After all the chasing, uncertainty and disappointment, he was speechless. A stinging behind his eyes posed another threat.

She sensed his disarray, even though she didn't attribute it to her effect on him.

'You look hot, Lobut, you like a drink?' Her words steadied him and he was grateful for her down-to-earthness.

'That's a good idea.' He dug into his pocket but she stopped him.

'I get them,' she insisted.

He followed her over to one of the trolleys and watched her forage for some coins in an old purse. She had just enough for two drinks.

'Please let me,' he protested, but she was adamant, holding up a single remaining coin after she had paid.

'Still have five bahts,' she proclaimed as if it were a pot of gold.

Although he had helped to reduce her liquidity to a few bahts, Robert felt more pleasure than guilt in the knowledge that she was prepared to spend what little she had on him.

'Shall we sit over here?' he suggested, his thoughts

now turning to how he might consolidate their re-
union.

'Drink OK?' she asked him when they were seated,
slightly awkwardly, beside each other.

'It's fine, thank you.' He took a long sip on the
straw to give himself a few extra seconds of preparation time.

'I've got something to show you.' He reached into
his shirt pocket and produced three of the photos.
The last and best one he had deliberately left at the
hotel.

'Photos you take of me?' She gave a little self-
conscious laugh and studied them solemnly and carefully before seeking his opinion. 'What you think?'

'I think you look very nice.' His composure had
now returned and he was functioning normally
again. More or less.

'No look funny?' She indicated the first two.

'Perhaps a little bit serious, but that doesn't matter.'

She held up the third one and looked at him questioningly.

'I like that one best,' he admitted. 'You were looking at the ducks.'

She nodded and smiled at the recollection.

'You can have them if you want.'

'For me?' She clutched them to her, obviously
delighted; then as an afterthought: 'You no want?'

'Oh, yes, but I can get copies from the negatives.'

'Thank you very much, Lobut.'

She inspected them again before placing them carefully into the wallet section of her well-used purse.

'Lucky we meet again, first Friday and now today.'

If Robert was going to come clean, this was the
moment. 'As a matter of fact it wasn't just luck. I came
here specially today, hoping to see you again.'

She looked as if she did not understand. 'You come to see me?'

'That's right. I was here on Saturday and yesterday as well.'

'Saturday, no school, I work in shop. Yesterday, holiday, I go shopping for mama and help look after my brothers and sisters.' She still looked confused as if she found it unbelievable that Robert had deliberately sought her out. 'You come back every day to see me, Lobut?'

'That's right, I enjoyed talking to you when we first met, but I had to rush away because my mother was waiting. I thought if we met again, we could talk some more.'

When she did not respond, he reminded her of their previous conversation.

'You said last time that maybe we could meet again before I go home. Do you remember?'

'Remember.' She nodded thoughtfully.

'I also wanted to give you the photographs as a thank you for finding my lens cap.'

Her silence made him wonder if he had overplayed his hand. Had he alienated her by revealing his repeated attempts to see her again?

'No boys try to meet me like this before,' she said seriously, after a long pause. Then her face lit up in a huge smile.

'Can I send you a postcard when I go home to England?' he ventured, eager to make up ground.

'You write postcard to me?'

'If you don't mind giving me your address.'

'No mind.'

He produced a pen and gave her the paper wallet that had held the photos. 'Would you write it on this, please?'

She took them, but the pen remained poised.

'No can write English,' she admitted reluctantly.

Damn! He had forgotten that the Thai script was unlike that of any other country. Even many Thai people who could speak English could not write it. Similarly, few foreigners could read Thai. Then he had an inspiration.

'I know – if you write your name and address in Thai, I'll get someone at the hotel to put it into English.' He was not sure how successful he would be, but it was worth a try. Another obstacle to communication occurred to him. 'If I write to you in English, you won't be able to read it.'

'No problem,' she said confidently. 'I have friend who knows someone who read English. He read your postcard, and if I give him fifty bahts, he write to you in English for me.'

It sounded like a good arrangement, apart from the cost.

'Isn't that a lot of money to have a letter written?'

'Never mind. I work more time in shop and make money to write to you.'

The relationship seemed to be progressing in great bounds. They swapped addresses though neither of them could read the other's.

'You know time?' Doungjai asked.

'Nearly five o'clock.' He showed her his watch to make sure she understood.

'Sorry, I have to go, Mama worry.' She stood up and hesitated. 'I see you again before you go home?'

'I would like that very much.' There was no equivocation this time. 'Look, you bought me a drink today, so tomorrow I'll buy you one. OK?'

She nodded eagerly. 'Here? Same place?'

'How about somewhere different?' He thought

quickly. 'Do you know McDonalds in Silom Road? It's not far from here.'

'My school near Silom Road. I go to McDonalds sometimes before already. They sell very good hamburgers, but expensive.'

He smiled at her jumbled syntax. 'If you like I'll buy you a hamburger as well.'

'And French fries?'

'And French fries.' Robert felt very grown up. He had never bought a meal for a girl before. 'Perhaps you can stay longer tomorrow and we will have more time to talk.'

'What time we meet?'

'How about 4.15 at McDonalds?'

'I tell Mama I come home late tomorrow. She have big surprise when I say I have boyfriend from England. Never have boyfriend before.'

He was glad to hear that. It was barely a fortnight since Robert's status had been under threat when Melanie Bishop determined to make him her boyfriend. Now, but a few days later, he was accepting, even welcoming, a similar fate without a second thought.

'I'll see you tomorrow then,' he said, and self-consciously shook her hand.

'Goodbye, Lobut. Thank you for photographs.'

'Goodbye, Doungjai.'

He stood and watched her hurry away and did not move from the spot until she was lost from view.

Chapter Six

Robert's *tuk tuk* made an efficient job of negotiating Bangkok's peak hour traffic and he was back in the hotel before dark. His initial euphoria at catching up with Doungjai eased slightly when he began to consider how his parents might react to his absence. He expected them to be less than enthusiastic about his plan to meet her again, especially in one of the city's busiest streets and some distance from their hotel.

He had not over estimated his mother's concern. She was aghast when he broke the news that he had been back to the park on his own.

'But the *tuk* . . . er, taxi took me right from the hotel to the park gates,' he protested, prudently amending his mode of transport, in case his parents had heard scare stories about the *tuk tuks*. 'I didn't even have to cross any road.'

'But in all that traffic. What if the driver had taken you to the wrong place, or . . . or?' She searched vainly for an endless list of disasters that might have overtaken him, but could not immediately think of any, apart from the unthinkable which she preferred not to voice.

'Oh, Mum, you're worrying about nothing. The main thing is I made it there and back without any problems, and I met her.'

He gathered himself to deliver the second piece of

news. 'Er . . . I've also arranged to see her again tomorrow.'

'You're going back to the park?' His mother sounded even less enthusiastic.

'No, I thought we should try somewhere else, so I suggested McDonalds.'

'The one we went to the other day?' His mother's tone remained sceptical.

'Yes, it's near her school and we can sit there and have a Coke and . . .' he shrugged, '. . . talk for a while.'

'Robert . . .' When his mother started a sentence with his name, in that certain tone of voice, it always boded ill. 'I don't know what's come over you. Sneaking off on your own without letting your father or me know where you were going. What if something had happened to you? We wouldn't have known where to start looking for you. It was very thoughtless of you. And now you want to go off again to an even busier part of the city to meet a . . . a stranger.'

'She's not a stranger,' Robert protested heatedly. 'We're the strangers. We had a great chat today, and she bought me a drink. I thought it was only polite for me to offer to buy one for her in return.'

'There's nothing wrong with that, but you're not at home now, Robert. You simply can't go running all over the place meeting people, whoever they are and whatever the reason.'

'You make it sound as if I do it all the time. I wish you would stop treating me as if I were still a child.'

'But you *are* still a child.'

Being referred to as a child was guaranteed to infuriate Robert.

'I'm nearly fifteen. In some countries, people have been married for years at my age.'

His mother glared, not impressed by the analogy.

'Now you're being silly.'

'*I'm* being silly?'

What had been an unexpectedly good day for Robert was rapidly turning sour.

'Look, Mum, I said I'd meet her. What would she think if I didn't turn up?' He tried another tack. 'You and dad have always stressed how important it is not to let people down and to keep promises.'

'This is different.'

'How is it different?'

Mary Stone was rarely stumped for words.

'Because you made a promise without being sure you could keep it. And now you're blaming me for stopping you. That's cheating, Robert.'

'Well, I think you're over-reacting.'

His mother's expression said clearly that she disagreed, although inwardly she felt less confident of her case. She had long since realised that bringing up children was as much a learning process for the parents. Teenagers especially needed delicate handling.

One thing she had learnt was always to leave room for manoeuvre and compromise.

'Robert, you're our only son . . .' No, that wouldn't do, she decided. Start again. 'It's not that we don't think you can look after yourself, but this is a big and very busy city in a strange country. Things can . . . happen to chil . . . to young people. Really bad things, I mean. You could be . . . well, abducted. Doesn't that prospect bother you?'

Robert shrugged. Of course it would bother him to be abducted.

'It just seemed like a good idea to meet her somewhere different. That was the fourth time I'd been to the park and I couldn't think of anywhere else on the spur of the moment. McDonalds is about as safe as you can get.'

'Suppose I came with you?' she suggested, brightly, a last desperate throw.

His response was predictable.

'Come off it, Mum. It would look as if I wasn't allowed to go anywhere on my own – which isn't far from the truth it seems. What would she think?'

'You could explain that I wanted to meet her, which is true. I would like to.'

Robert hesitated. 'She would still think you were there to keep an eye on me.'

'What if I just say hello, then go off to do some shopping? I could come back later and meet you when she's gone home.'

'That might work,' Robert conceded grudgingly. 'But if she saw you come back, I'd feel like a little boy being collected from school.'

'I wouldn't return until she'd left,' his mother promised. 'You won't want to sit in McDonalds for more than an hour, surely. If she does look like staying longer, you can say you have to get back to the hotel because you're going out in the evening.'

Robert had another thought. 'Are you sure you'll be all right on your own, Mum?'

'I don't think I'll get mugged if that's what you mean. I'll keep to the busy areas.' She smiled. 'Besides, Jim Thompson's shop is only a short walk away. I wouldn't mind going back there to browse for a while.'

By a tortuous route, they had reached a compromise that was acceptable to both of them.

Later in the evening, Mary related the events of the afternoon to her husband. 'I don't want to be a gooseberry, Brian, but what was I supposed to do?'

Brian covered her hand with his.

'I think you handled it very well in the circumstances, sweetheart.'

'I never thought I would be involved in some subterfuge to help Robert meet his girlfriend,' she confessed ruefully.

'At least not on this trip,' Brian agreed. 'She must be something out of the ordinary to have this effect on him.'

The taxi ride to Silom Road took no longer than usual at that hour of the afternoon, but to Robert it seemed never-ending. He fidgeted and fretted at every traffic light and hold-up. After two changes of lights, the taxi at last swept across Rama 4 into Silom Road and, a few hundred yards down on the left, swerved into a space outside McDonalds. Robert surveyed the restaurant's large picture windows anxiously as they got out, and almost pushed his mother into the bustling air-conditioned world of fast foods. He stood just inside the door, his eyes sweeping the interior, fearful that Doungjai may have changed her mind. Then he spotted her at an empty table by the window and his heart leapt. She saw him at the same time and waved cheerfully.

'There she is,' he said to his mother, and led her between the tables.

Doungjai stood up as they approached and came towards them. 'Hello, Lobut,' she smiled, while her eyes flicked uncertainly towards Mary.

'Hello, Doungjai. It's good to see you again.' He half turned. 'Er . . . I'd like you to meet my mother.'

The girl brought her hands together and bowed over them.

'I'm very happy to meet you, Doungjai.' Robert's mother was a little unsure how to respond to the Thai *wei*.

'Thank you, I happy to meet you too.'

'Mum's going shopping,' Robert was quick to explain. 'So we came down in the same taxi.'

'Silom Road is very good for shopping,' Doungjai volunteered eagerly. 'You been to Silom Village before? Nice shops and good restaurants, only about ten minute walk, or taxi cost forty bahts.'

'No, we've not been there,' Mary responded. 'I might give it a try.'

'You have drink and hamburger with Lobut and me first?' Doungjai suggested, backing towards the table.

Mary hesitated.

'You don't have much time do you, Mum?' Robert hinted heavily. The grand plan was already threatening to unravel.

'Not take long to have coffee and hamburger,' Doungjai insisted.

'Perhaps just a coffee,' Mary conceded, not wishing to appear unfriendly. 'And then I must go. Why don't you go and order, Robert, while Doungjai and I sit here and hold the table?'

Robert raised his eyes to the ceiling. 'What can I get you, Doungjai?' he asked.

'I like fishburger, Lobut please,' she said, fixing him with her huge dark eyes, 'and some French fries?' adding quickly: 'Is that all right?'

49

'Yes, of course. And how about a milkshake?' he suggested.

'Milk shakes expensive,' she sighed.

'A milk shake it is,' he said decisively. 'And a coffee for you, Mum?' Robert stumped off towards the counter. While he waited to be served, he observed that the conversation seemed to be flowing freely at the table. The musical lilt of Doungjai's laughter greeted him as he returned with a laden tray.

'What's the joke?' he enquired, when he had laid out the food and sat down beside his mother.

'I was asking Doungjai what her mother thought of the photos you took of her, Robert.'

'My mama think they good.' Doungjai laughed again. 'But my sister, she say my face is like . . . like . . . stone person?'

'A statue,' Robert supplied.

'Yes, like statue.' Doungjai set her face stiff and expressionless and then became serious as she took up her fishburger. 'Like fishburgers very much, but no have for long time.'

As she bit into it, Mary noticed how the girl's eyes remained on her son, and his on her. They were certainly keen on each other. She hastened to drink her coffee.

'I must be going,' she announced, 'or I'll never get my shopping done .'

Robert slipped quickly out of his seat to facilitate her exit. 'See you back at the hotel, Mum?' he said pointedly.

'All right, Robbie.' His mother played along. 'It was very nice to meet you, Doungjai. I hope I'll see you again.'

'I very happy to meet you too, ma-dam.'

Mary could well understand how Robert was so

smitten by this girl, with her bubbling personality and natural, unadorned wide-eyed beauty. An idea occurred to her.

'Perhaps if you aren't doing anything on Saturday, you would like to come over to our hotel in the afternoon,' she suggested. 'You can swim in the pool and meet Robert's father.'

Doungjai looked questioningly at Robert as if for guidance. 'Thank you,' she replied, a little uncertainly.

'That would be great.' There was no uncertainty in Robert's mind. 'Will you come? Do you like swimming?'

'Swimming?' She was still hesitant, as if translating the word in her mind. After a small pause she nodded eagerly. 'Yes, like . . . swimming very much, thank you.'

After Mary Stone's departure, Robert and Doungjai chatted non-stop. He told her about his life in England and the conversation flowed until he got on to his favourite summer game. But after trying, and failing, to answer a stream of questions mostly prefaced by 'why', he decided that explaining the game of cricket to a teenage Thai girl was beyond him.

In turn, Doungjai told him about her home and family. Unlike Robert, who was an only child, she had four brothers and two sisters. As number three behind two brothers, it fell to her to help run the household, and look after the younger children. What with her studies and working in a shop to contribute to the family budget, her leisure hours were restricted.

This, their first real date, went well. Even the timing of Robert's mother's return was flawless; she arrived while he was watching Doungjai's tuk tuk plunge into the river of traffic.

'Everything all right' she asked him, flapping an arm at a taxi.

'Couldn't be better,' he said smugly.

Chapter Seven

As Saturday approached, Robert's thoughts became increasingly concerned with Doungjai's perception of him as . . . well, as a man. Contemplating himself in the mirror, trying to decide which swimming trunks to wear, he was sure she would consider him too skinny. Actually he had a good physique for his age, but whereas girls of fourteen seemed to be pretty mature, physically-speaking, he still looked more like a boy than a young man. He was painfully aware, too, that although he had worked on his suntan since their arrival, he was bound to look almost anaemic next to her.

Then there was his prowess in the water: ironically, while he excelled at ball games he was an indifferent swimmer and always made a point of keeping within his depth. She was bound to be able to swim like a dolphin. Instead of being impressed by him, which he wanted so much, she would see him as a puny wimp, unworthy of her attentions. Too late though, for a body building course. Even Schwarzeneggar hadn't pumped himself up in half a day.

One of Robert's fears was dispelled on the Saturday morning. As on every day since they had arrived, the sun broke through the early morning cloud and quickly hoisted the temperature from the all-night low eighties to the high nineties. Rain was never a possibility. Robert kept an eye on poolside space during the morning and when a few of the hotel guests began to appear, he laid claim to four of the sun loungers, by draping a towel over them. He would not be popular, but to smooth the path towards a perfect day with Doungjai he would have commandeered the pool itself.

Back in his room, he packed a holdall with two extra towels, suncream, camera and spare film, Walk-man, sweets and comb. He decided to wear his swimming trunks underneath his shorts, and even remembered to pack underpants to change into after swimming. Somewhere he had read that thorough preparation went a long way towards successful exe-cution. Here at least he was determined not to be found wanting.

He considered at length his parent's role and con-cluded that it would be more appropriate if they joined him and Doungjai after they had settled by the pool. In this way she would not be obliged to walk round the pool to meet them. It was a considerate touch. Well aware of the importance of the occasion for their son, Mary and Brian accepted their son's dispositions with deadpan expressions.

Robert went down to the lobby twenty minutes early and alternated between sitting in the adjoining lounge, where he could keep the entrance in view, and pacing the length of the reception area with in-creasing frequency as the digital clock clicked towards 2.00. The magic hour came up and moved on, with no sign of Doungjai. His disappointment mounted with each passing minute. Five past, ten past . . . that was it. She had cried off. He slumped miserably into a cane chair. Fifteen minutes past, six-teen, seventeen . . . a compact figure, carrying a small

54

duffel bag, emerged through the revolving doors. He sprang from the chair and checked an urge to break into a run.

'Hello, Doungjai.'

'Very sorry I late, Lobut,' she gasped, clearly out of breath. 'Traffic bad. Everything stop so I leave *tuk tuk* and walk.'

Right then Robert would have forgiven any lapse.

'Never mind, you've made it. That's all that matters.'

The excitement of seeing her made him slow to take in the change in her appearance: her hair was no longer constrained by a bow but hung loose and soft on her shoulders. Gone too was the staid school uniform; she looked several years older in a tight-fitting top and full flowered skirt. The small diamond earrings and necklace of multi-coloured stones, though no more genuine than the black Cartier watch on her wrist, added a subtle touch of sophistication, while the white shoes with small wedge-shaped heels added a couple of inches to her height. Standing at arm's length to study her, Robert tried to find the words to express his approval.

'You look really nice,' was finally the best he could do.

'Thank you.' The anxiety of the journey had already drained away and that now familiar wide smile took over. 'Bring swimming suit and towel – OK?' She indicated the duffel bag.

'Of course. Shall we go on out to the pool?' He guided her towards the lift and when they emerged into the sunlight on the second floor, he was relieved to see that no one had usurped his loungers. As they skirted the pool, he noticed the covetous glances cast by other male guests in the direction of his lovely companion.

'My parents will be joining us in a few minutes,' he said by way of explanation of the two additional sun loungers. 'Before we settle down, would you like to put on your swimsuit? The Ladies changing room is over there, where we came in.'

He watched her retrace her steps round the edge of the pool. As soon as she was out of sight, he quickly slipped off the locally bought Boss T-shirt and stepped out of his shorts. As the heat of the sun struck his bare skin he knelt and squirted generous dollops of suncream on his shoulders.

'Can I help you, Lobut?'

In his preoccupation, he had been unaware of Doungjai's return. Now, when he looked up at her, all thoughts of sunburn were forgotten.

Her navy blue, one-piece swimsuit was the height of modesty. It was held high at the front by broad shoulder straps with only a slight cut out scoop at the back. But it fitted her like a wetsuit and accentuated with stunning effect pubescent curves that any pin-up girl would have been proud to display.

She misinterpreted Robert's appraisal and looked down at herself with concern.

'Not all right, Lobut?'

'Oh yes!' he enthused and jumped to his feet. 'Very all right. You look terrific. I do like your swimsuit.'

'Very old,' she said dismissively. 'It too small for me now.'

'I think it fits you perfectly.' Then, conscious that his appraisal might be embarrassing her: 'Here, come and sit down.'

'Thank you, I sit in shade. No like sun.'

It was another reminder that the local people in hot

climates have the good sense to avoid the sun, unlike their Western visitors.

'You like to sit under umbrella also?' She moved over to make room for him.

'Just for a few minutes,' he conceded offhandedly, though secretly pleased to have the opportunity to get closer to her. As he perched on the edge of her lounger, his arm came into contact with her thigh. It felt soft and warm and exciting.

'Is that OK?' he asked hastily.

'OK.'

Neither of them made any effort to move apart and when Robert looked down at her, he caught her watching him, the lids of her huge dark eyes slightly lowered. At that moment, the hotel could have collapsed into rubble around them and he would not have noticed it. Instinctively, he sought and found her hand and she returned his tentative squeeze. He wanted to say something, but his tongue seemed to be stuck to the roof of his mouth.

Unfortunately, the moment was short-lived for Brian and Mary Stone appeared just then. As his parents approached, Robert reluctantly drew his hand free, and the two youngsters stood up. Robert introduced his father.

'I've been looking forward to meeting you,' his father smiled, and he wasn't just being polite. 'Robert has told us all about you.'

'Thank you, I very happy to meet you, and also to meet ma-dam again. You like to sit where no sun?' She indicated the shaded loungers.

Mary and Brian accepted the offer thankfully. The walk round the edge of the pool had been enough to convince them that they were never going to be able to stand the afternoon heat without some protection.

'Care for a swim?' Robert suggested to Doungjai after his parents had exchanged a few pleasantries with her. She nodded eagerly and, as he followed her to the poolside, he noted how the swimsuit clung to the contours of her rounded buttocks.

Brian had also appreciated her rear aspect, and when she slipped into the water, he gave a small sigh.

'Brian Stone,' Mary accused with mock seriousness. 'I hope you're not thinking what I suspect you're thinking.'

He grinned. 'Let's just say I can see now why Robert has been such a pain in the neck these past few days. She's a little corker.'

While Robert thrashed about in the water, largely using brute force as a substitute for finesse, Doungjai glided up and down the length of the pool employing a steady economical breast-stroke without apparent effort. She was still going strong when he finally emerged panting, to sit on the edge of the pool, legs dangling in the water, content to watch her glide back and forth. Her swimsuit, tight and glistening, reminded him of the pelt of a young seal.

Ten lengths later she scrambled out of the water and returned with Robert to the loungers.

'Very nice.' She beamed at Robert's parents, patting her face with a towel. 'You like swimming?'

'We're not great swimmers,' Robert's father admitted. 'But we like to take a dip to cool off. You swim very well, Doungjai.'

She shrugged modestly. 'Very slow. Granpapa say I like baby whale. Him very rude to me because him good swimmer. Learn in navy, but no swim now, too old.'

'What work does your father do, Doungjai?' Mary Stone enquired.

'No have papa. Him killed in road accident two years before.'

'Oh, I'm sorry,' she said hastily, and her husband made suitable murmurs of condolence.

There was a momentary silence, broken by Robert.

'Would anyone care for a drink?' he ventured.

'May I have orange juice?' Doungjai said.

'That's a good idea,' his father agreed. 'We'll all have one.'

As Robert went off in search of the poolside waitress, he heard his mother say, 'Where do you live, Doungjai?'

When he returned, the conversation seemed to be in full spate, for which he was thankful.

'Mama was angry when I go home,' Doungjai was saying, 'because I have big hole in my jeans.' She turned on one hip and unselfconsciously presented a plump round bottom cheek to Brian Stone's gaze. 'Right here on this ass.' She pointed and gave her now familiar tinkling laugh. 'You call him ass?'

Robert and his father could scarcely contain their amusement; Mary Stone pretended not to hear.

'That's one of several words you might use,' Brian grinned.

'Then I get angry with Granpapa,' Doungjai continued. 'Him say my ass too fat, say I eat too much.' She looked at Robert appealingly. 'You think I eat too much, Lobut?'

'Of course not,' Robert denied gallantly, avoiding his parents' eyes.

The afternoon flew past. Doungjai used the pool twice more, obviously glad to have the opportunity, and spent the rest of the time chatting non-stop to Brian and Mary, while Robert just slipped in the occasional contribution and ensured the drinks kept

59

coming. He was content to sit and listen and observe this shapely, little brown-skinned girl, who seemed to have enchanted his parents as much as himself. He was further encouraged when she occasionally glanced towards him with that wonderful warm smile that told him she was thoroughly enjoying herself and was glad to be here with him.

She asked Robert what he was going to do when he left school. He shrugged.

'He keeps talking about wanting to be a photographer, but I'm not sure if that's a very secure career,' his father replied. 'His mother and I want him to take up something with a more certain future, advertising perhaps like me, or something in the City.'

'My brother work in the city,' Doungjai said cheerfully. 'Him drive a bus, very good job.'

She told them she would be leaving school soon and was planning to work full time in the shop in Sukhumvit Road, where she already helped out at weekends. She was supposed to be working there today.

'But I ask my friend to tell my boss I not come today.' She put her hand to her mouth to suppress a giggle. 'I tell her to say I have to go doctor because I sick'

'Wouldn't you like to do office work?' Mary Stone queried.

'Like to work with animals, but cannot, no have money for study.' She shrugged dismissively. 'Never mind, I happy to sell and bargain with tourists. Make good commission. Maybe one day I do something better.'

Her innocent optimism about the future struck a note of sadness in the Stones. Even Robert, with little

60

knowledge of the hard world outside home and school, was touched by Doungjai's fatalistic acceptance of her limited horizons. She seemed resigned to an endless verbal battle on the busy thoroughfares of Bangkok, trying to extract a few extra bahts from a stream of well-heeled tourists.

'You OK, Lobut?' She looked anxiously towards him.

'Yes, I'm fine,' he replied robustly and forced a grin. 'I was just wondering if I come and buy something from your shop, will you serve me personally?'

'Of course.' Doungjai beamed. 'Perhaps you come tomorrow? Have nice T-shirts and sweaters. I give you good price.' The familiar catchphrase broke the spell of despondency and they all laughed. Robert promised to visit her shop the next day if she would agree to join him for another fishburger on Monday after school. He looked sideways at his parents for their reaction, but they gave no sign of dissent.

'I show you another McDonalds,' Doungjai enthused. 'We take the bus, only three bahts.'

Mary Stone looked at her husband with an expression that said, 'I give up.' He just grinned.

When the time came to leave the pool, Doungjai expressed fulsome appreciation for a 'very happy afternoon.' She agreed to have a drink with Robert in the hotel coffee shop before going home and his parents were taken aback when she dug into her duffel bag and produced a brooch, in the shape of a spray of flowers, 'for ma-dam', and a leather wallet, 'for Mister Brian.'

'Small present,' she explained. 'I hope you like.'

They thanked her, deeply touched. Goodbyes were exchanged and Doungjai and Robert left the party, pausing to wave before entering the hotel. When

Brian turned to speak to Mary, he saw her eyes were moist.

'I know, please don't say anything,' she said with a sniff as he took her hand.

In the coffee shop, Doungjai insisted that she was not hungry. Even so she still managed to demolish a large slice of raspberry cheesecake and a glass of milk, while Robert settled for a coffee. They sat talking for nearly an hour yet, after he had seen her off in a *tuk tuk*, he could not recall a single word of their conversation.

When she was with him, it was akin to inhaling a powerful drug – his senses were sharpened and he felt alive and happy as never before. Then, when she left, an emotional void opened up and the feeling of euphoria vanished, leaving behind an emptiness and, worst of all, a lingering dread that he might never see her again.

Chapter Eight

The next day, the Stone family visited the Grand Palace, Bangkok's number one tourist attraction. Robert only agreed to join the expedition when he was assured they would be back at the hotel by lunchtime. He had already formulated his plans to visit Doungjai's shop in the afternoon and mere sight-seeing could not be allowed to interfere with that. He could not understand why she had to work on a Sunday as well as attending school all week, but at least he would see her.

He set out on foot at 2.15 and after a few minutes emerged into one of the busiest streets in the city. He picked his way over and round the potholes and other obstacles littering the pavement until he came to the strange conjunction of traffic systems where Ploenchit Road becomes Sukhumvit. Here, the road is confronted by a railway line which carries goods trains of interminable length. When they choose to rumble through, an extra dimension is added to the term 'traffic jam'. If this were not enough, one of the city's expressways ran above the railway line, with a toll booth entrance and slip road exit leading into Sukhumvit Road. This coming together of so many diverse and overburdened traffic systems was the stuff of motoring nightmares and yet somehow, against all logic, it worked.

Passing under the stressed concrete expressway and stepping carefully over the railway lines, Robert crossed the road by one of the overhead pedestrian bridges.

Many of the small side roads or *sois*, branching off the main streets of Bangkok were little more than narrow lanes, but each was numbered, making it easy to locate any address in the city. The shop where Doungjai worked was between Sois 7 and 9 in Sukhumvit Road. In theory then, finding it would be a walkover.

Robert walked along the teeming thoroughfare, peering into each shop. There were no doors or windows, just open spaces piled high with goods. At night, many of the shops were only protected by canvas sheets or strips of bamboo matting, secured with pieces of string.

When Robert at last spotted Doungjai, she was in full negotiation with two young tourists. He edged closer, feeling slightly guilty to be listening in without her knowing he was there, but intrigued to see how she handled the situation. Unlike many of the shop keepers, who bargained with the aid of a pocket calculator, Doungjai's English was proficient enough for her to argue the prices verbally.

The couple were shaking their heads. 'Too much. Up the road they are selling purses like this for one twenty,' the girl insisted. She had some sort of Nordic accent.

'But these real leather,' Doungjai protested. 'Look, look.' She opened the flap to show the inside, then took a cigarette lighter and applied a flame to the purse to demonstrate it was genuine.

'I don't think so,' the man declined. 'Maybe we'll come back later.'

'Why not buy now?' Doungjai pressed as if her life depended on the sale. 'Very cheap for leather.'

It looked like a lost cause to Robert, but he was underestimating Doungjai's selling skills and persistence.

'Make very nice present,' she went on. 'Why not buy one more, and have three for special price?'

The couple hesitated that fatal second and Doungjai pounced. She looked around as if afraid of being overheard and said in a dramatically loud whisper. 'No tell my boss. I give you special discount, three for four fifty.'

This was the clincher. A brief nod from the girl settled the transaction. Doungjai took the money and wrapped the goods. Her face was gleaming with perspiration, but she could not have looked more pleased if she had just successfully wound up a multi-million pound deal.

As the couple took their leave, she spotted Robert and her face lit up anew.

'Hello, Lobut.' She looked towards the other girls in the shop as if to say, 'I told you so and here he is to prove it.'

Robert wanted to grab and hug her but, under the curious gaze of several spectators, settled for a brief handshake.

'I see you're busy.'

She shook her head. 'First sale today. Very quiet, not many tourists.'

'Well, I'm a tourist. Can I look around?'

'Soon. First you sit down. You my guest today' He was introduced to Doungjai's friends, given a small stool to sit on and a bottle of Coke was pressed into his hand. While he drank it, Doungjai and her friends stood round him, swapping comments and giggles among themselves and plying him with questions. His newly purchased Rolex watch quickly came under investigation.

'How much you pay?' he was asked and favourable nods confirmed that the five pounds he had parted with was not a ripoff.

'She like you,' one of the girls informed him when Doungjai had to go and serve a customer. 'She good girl.' Firm nods all round.

That was another thing Robert had always disliked about girls. They were all born matchmakers. Only now, he didn't mind being matched.

Another sale concluded, Doungjai rejoined Robert.

'Now you choose something?' she said.

Owing to frequent interruptions while Doungjai served other customers, he took half an hour to choose a sweatshirt. Having run out of excuses to hang around, he took his leave.

'I see you tomorrow,' Doungjai said, accompanying him to the entrance.

'You bet.' He was reluctant to go. Tomorrow was a whole day away. 'Will you be all right going home tonight on your own?'

She giggled. 'I go home alone every Saturday and Sunday. I catch bus.'

'Oh . . . yes, of course. That was stupid of me.' He gave a helpless gesture. 'So . . . goodbye, then'

'Goodbye, Lobut.'

'Goodbye, Doungjai.'

But she was already heading back into the shop, homing in on another prospective buyer.

Chapter Nine

Although Patpong was not exactly recommended viewing for young teenagers, it was there where Robert and Doungjai chose to stroll on their first evening together. Patpong consisted of two short parallel roads, linking the main thoroughfares of Silom and Surawong. By day they were quiet and ordinary, even dull, but every evening an amazing transformation took place and they became the most remarkable stretches of road anywhere in the world.

On Patpong One, between the rows of bars and clubs that sported names like 'Firecat', 'Pussy Galore', 'Butterfly', 'Lipstick' and 'Super Girls', and along the adjoining Silom Road, a whole town sprang up around dusk. Laden carts and trestles popped up from nowhere. Metal rods were slotted together and the frameworks covered with transparent plastic sheeting, tarpaulins or bamboo matting, held in place with string. Strip lighting, fed by old car batteries, portable generators or long leads from the surrounding permanent buildings, was plugged in and switched on to illuminate an unimaginable range of merchandise. Crowds appeared and bargaining began in the sauna-stifling heat, the touts intensifying their efforts to entice the bemused tourists into the dark interior of the bars, where attractive girls gyrated on small mirrored stages to mind-numbingly loud music.

In some of the bars the girls preserved their modesty with tiny bikinis; in others they went naked. As well as dancing, an amazing repertoire of specialty acts were performed in some establishments. These involve the female anatomy and an array of props, including candles, darts, cigarettes, balloons, crayons and bottles.

Many tourist guides tried to describe Patpong, but none had succeeded in capturing its unique ambience. Although it had bars, girls and sex in unashamed abundance, to write it off as an exercise in erotica would be to do it an injustice. It was essentially a friendly place, lacking tension or malice. So if the touts and stall owners were ever keen to pull in the customers and swoop on the slightest show of interest, a smiling shake of the head was all that was needed to decline. Rarely was there any rancour at a non-sale.

Such was Patpong, which came to life from dusk until the early hours, when it melted away, Cinderella-like, until the next evening.

After a lengthy chat over Big Macs and Coke, Robert and Doungjai crossed Silom Road for a look around Patpong before parting to go their separate ways. Robert had no intention of buying anything, but he was tempted by one of the many T-shirts on display. It bore a slogan that epitomised the very essence of Patpong – its mixture of sex and sleaze, of frivolity and fun, spiced with the need to be careful – 'AIDS kills don't be silly put that condom on your willy'.

Doungjai saw Robert smiling as he re-read the slogan. 'What it say, Lobut?' she queried.

'It's a bit rude.' His smile thinned slightly. 'Are you sure you want to know?'

'Sure.' She pulled at his arm impatiently. 'You read for me.'

Robert read it slowly and clearly and watched her face closely to see how she would react.

'Willy? No understand what is willy?' she asked, after a long thinking pause.

Not for the first time, her lack of guile had him floundering. With some circumspection he worked round to an explanation through the word, condom, which she understood. Enlightenment suddenly dawned on her face.

'Ah,' she smiled, without embarrassment. 'Willy, you call him willy? I never hear that name before. I thought English word is cock.'

'There's several names you can use. That's just one.' Robert wished he had never started this.

'Like ass? Your papa tell me you have other names for ass,' she informed him seriously.

'Much the same,' he nodded.

She shook her head doubtfully. 'I think cock easier remember than willy,' she decided at last.

Chapter Ten

During the next week, Robert met Doungjai every day. He was not to be deterred or dissuaded, and his parents resigned themselves good-naturedly to the inevitable. Their earlier fears for his safety in the city's streets, if not dispelled, were at least lulled, though they still insisted on retaining one sanction – that Robert should be back at the hotel in time to join them for dinner. Since Doungjai could not stay out late either, this did not create conflict.

Although they continued to frequent McDonalds, Doungjai initiated Robert into some of the delights of traditional Thai food and especially the fruit. The likes of *gloo-ay* (bananas), *sapalot* (pineapples) and *ma-pow* (coconuts) were no strangers, but many of the shapes and colours, piled on the carts along the streets, were unknown to him. Under Doungjai's guidance, he made the acquaintance of the vaguely familiar *ma-moo-ung* (mangos) and *ma-la-gaw* (papaya) and *som-oh* (pomelos).

He reciprocated by introducing Doungjai to some traditional British cuisine when he took her to the pub environment of Bobby's Arms in Patpong's multi-storey car park. Doungjai saw off a large individual steak-and-kidney pie, followed by a generous helping of bread-and-butter pudding and pronounced them 'velly good'.

On the way out of the pub, Robert spotted a dart board beside the bar and challenged Doungjai to a game, which he explained as they went along. He discovered his mistake too late, for the darts proved to be deadly weapons in her hands and the only safe place was behind her.

Late one afternoon, they took a long-tailed boat across the Chao Phraya to the Thonburi side of the river and climbed Bangkok's most famous landmark, Wat Arun, the Temple of the Dawn. High on the steep, narrow steps above the river, they watched the sun go down. It was a romantic setting. Later, on the boat back, they vowed that one day they would return at dawn and see the sun rise over the city.

At Doungjai's request, Robert had brought some photos of his home village, his house and one of himself. She became very quiet as she slowly scrutinised each photograph in turn. Suddenly, he regretted showing them to her. Views of their large stone-built house, with the two cars parked in the wide gravel driveway, smacked of affluence. But when she passed the photos back to him there was no envy in her face, although there was a touch of wistfulness in her voice when she said, 'You have lovely home, Lobut.'

She studied for many minutes a photograph of Robert himself, astride his bike, and seemed reluctant to part with it. He told her she could keep it if she liked. With a delighted grin she tucked it away in the old purse.

That same evening, she sprang a surprise by saying she would not have to go to school the next day and she could spend it with him if he liked. Robert did not ask whether this was a genuine school holiday or if she was playing the Thai version of hookey. He couldn't have cared less. He was just grateful for the gift of a few more hours in her company.

They met at ten o'clock the next morning and caught a taxi to Makkasan Station in Petchburi Road, where Doungjai bought tickets for the train to Chachoengsao. The accomodation was crowded and hot; there was no air-conditioning and the temperature was only slightly relieved by the draught through the open windows and the small, sweeping electric fans spaced at intervals along the carriage walls. In spite of these petty discomforts, Robert was kept entertained by the frequent halts at primitive wayside stations, most of which consisted of a shack and little else. Between times, he had the opportunity to study Bangkok commuters at close range. In sartorial taste at any rate, they had little in common with their opposite numbers in London, he decided.

From Chachoengsao Station, where an old engine stood sentinel as a solid reminder of the age of steam, a five minute *tuk tuk* ride transported them to Sawton Temple. This was one of the lesser known temples as far as tourists are concerned, but was very popular with Thais. Robert appeared to be the sole European there, but with Doungjai at his side he felt very much at home.

When they returned to the city, they had a late lunch at the City Food Centre in the Ambassador Hotel complex. The spring rolls, cooked and cut while they waited and served with an orange coloured sauce, followed by a plate of fresh fruit, were delicious and cheap. Even Doungjai did not quibble over the price.

Afterwards, they crossed the car park to see the exotic birds on display there. As they read the captions, Doungjai shook her head and pursed her lips in disapproval.

'Very beautiful, but I no like to see them in cages.'

Most poignant of all were the two lovebirds, resplendent in their pastel shaded plumage of green, orange, yellow and grey. Sitting tight against each other on their perch, they might have been telling the world that they would endure their captivity in stoic silence as long as they had each other.

The most unforgettable event for Robert in a week of memorable moments was their visit to the Erawan Shrine. It was set in the heart of the city on the corner of Ploenchit and Rajdamri Roads, and pervaded by the smell of burning incense. The table in front of the shrine was laden with fruit, coconut drinks and other edible offerings, while the fence around the bronze image was festooned with garlands of multi-coloured flowers. In one corner, strange sounding instruments played Thai music as an accompaniment to dancing girls in their colourful costumes and distinctive, high-pointed head-dresses.

Robert and Doungjai sat on a marble bench running along the inside of the heavy, iron railings while some of Bangkok's heaviest traffic surged past only feet away. A blind man sat beside them, holding a display board of lottery tickets.

As Robert soaked up the intense atmosphere of this most unlikely place of worship, Doungjai left him and went across to the stall by the gate. She made a purchase, approached the Brahma image in the centre and placed some objects on the table. Lighting a candle and joss sticks, which gave off a scented smoke, she pressed them into the bed of sand and knelt with head bowed and hands together in prayer.

'What did you buy?' Robert asked when she returned and sat beside him.

'Four elephants.'

'What for?'

'I give to Buddha.'

'Why?'

She turned to him, her small mouth set and her eyes deadly serious. 'I thank Buddha for bringing you to Bangkok, Lobut. I ask him to keep you safe and come back one day to see me again.' She took his hand and squeezed it. 'Lobut, I very happy when I with you.'

'I'm happy too,' he affirmed and turned his head away as he felt his eyes fill. It was not the first time he found himself overwhelmed by her childlike certainty. The newfound emotions she inspired in him were sometimes more than he could handle.

She was still looking at him with that serious gaze when he hastily brushed a tear that had escaped down his cheek and turned again to face her

'That smoke is strong,' he said brusquely and stood up. 'Shall we go?'

Outside the gate, he saw women sitting under the trees on the pavement with what looked like small red boxes beside them. They proved to be more bird-cages: inside were tiny, sparrow-like birds. One of the women called to him, and he looked towards Doungjai for an explanation.

'It good luck if you let them go free,' she explained.

'How much?'

She fired off an unintelligible question at the woman and received an equally unintelligible response.

'Ninety bahts for six birds,' she relayed to Robert.He took out a one hundred baht note and gave it to the woman who handed him one of the cages, containing the six birds, and his change. The birds, called *krajoks*, Doungjai informed him, became more agitated as he peered at them through the thin wooden struts. Doungjai watched him with approval as he lifted the trap door arrangement and let the tiny creatures flutter from their prison. One could not find its way out and he tapped the side gently until it followed the others up over the traffic and into the night sky. He returned the cage to the woman. It was a gesture, no more. The pavement was lined with similar cages, all of them occupied. It was a cruel way to buy good luck, he decided.

It was almost dark when they walked the few yards down Ploenchit Road to McDonalds, beside the pedestrian road bridge which spans the road to the Meridien President Hotel opposite. Doungjai insisted on paying in spite of all Robert's objections.

'But I have the money right here,' he protested and flourished some notes.

'I have money also,' she responded firmly. 'Have good day at the shop on Sunday.' Her irrepressible laugh bubbled up. 'Many good customers.'

She dug into the old purse and withdrew an assortment of coins and well-worn notes which she laid carefully on the counter as she placed their order for milk shakes and hamburgers. There seemed to be little left though, by the time she had settled the bill. It made no sense for her to fritter away her hard-won spoils, but Robert had come to accept the resolute streak that lurked behind the girlish giggle and those big dark eyes. He knew it had something to do with pride and self-sufficiency, and he would never try to rob her of these, even if it left her purse empty. Unknowingly, he was learning about values that had no price tag.

When they ate, she normally chatted non-stop, but tonight she was unusually quiet. He loved to watch her with head bent over the table sucking up the milk shake through a straw, all the time with her eyes up-raised to him in a kind of quizzical expression.

'Is something wrong, Doungjai?' he asked her at last.

She answered with a question of her own. 'You happy, Lobut?'

'Of course, why do you ask? Aren't you happy?'

'I happy if you happy, only . . .'

'Yes?'

'Monday, in two days, you go Chiang Mai.' She forced out the words as if she felt she had no right to say them. 'I miss you, Lobut.' She turned her head away. 'I sorry.'

This was the first time she had mentioned his impending trip out of Bangkok with his parents. As the weekend had drawn near, the prospect had become increasingly less attractive to him too. He had pushed it to the back of his mind and tried not to think about it. Not only that, the more depressing prospect of his departure for England the following weekend was looming ever closer.

He reached across the table and took her arm to pull her back to face him. 'I'll miss you too, but I'll only be gone a few days.' For her sake he put on a brave face, trying to sound cheerful. 'I'll be back on Friday and, if you want me to, I'll meet you from school, OK?'

'OK.' She nodded and smiled, but the usual enthusiasm was missing.

'And don't forget, we still have tomorrow.'

That seemed to perk her up, but a thought struck him. 'You don't have to work in the shop do you?'

'You want to see me tomorrow?'

76

'Now what sort of question is that? Of course I want to see you.'

'Then I no work.'

'Are you sure you won't be seeing another boyfriend when I'm not here?' he teased in a playful effort to dispel any residual gloom.

'No have other boyfriend.' She gripped his hand. 'Only you, Lobut.'

'What would you like to do tomorrow?' he asked her, slightly embarrassed.

She was usually so sure, so positive in her responses, but now she hesitated. Her expression said she had an idea, but was not sure how he would react.

'Doungjai?.

'You like to come to my house, Lobut? she blurted, then: 'Meet my mama and grandpapa?'

She regarded him anxiously. The suggestion took Robert by surprise. Until this moment, the thought of visiting her home had never occurred to him and he would not have suggested it himself. In a way it would have seemed like encroaching on the privacy of her family. But Doungjai was inviting *him*, so no reason at all to feel uncertain.

She misunderstood his silence. 'If you no want to come, no problem. We do something else.'

'No . . . no, I would love to. It's a wonderful idea, but are you sure your mother won't mind?'

'She no mind. I tell her about you and show your photograph.' She smiled impishly. 'She say you handsome man.'

While Robert floundered for an answer, she followed up with: 'And I think so too.'

'Now you're pulling my leg,' he parried weakly, unused to such flattery and lacking the skills to deal with it.

'Pulling leg?' She looked mystified.

'Teasing me. It's a saying we have in England.'

'No tease, Lobut. I think you very good looking and you have kind heart.'

As he sat high up in his *tuk tuk* on the way back to the hotel, Robert's head was unashamedly in the clouds. Not only did the most wonderful girl in the world think he was good looking and had a kind heart, but she had just invited him home to meet her mother. The ultimate seal of approval.

Chapter Eleven

Life had become much more complicated for Doungjai since that chance meeting on the bridge in Lumpini Park. Studying all day at school, helping her mother to bring up a large family and working at the shop weekends meant that her days were already full, so finding extra time to meet Robert had not been easy. Far more stressful was the emotional strain that had built up with her new friendship. This was a completely new experience in her young life and was creating new internal conflicts.

In spite of this, she would not have changed a single minute of it. Where it might lead to was tomorrow's problem. Her philosophy was to enjoy today and take care of the future when it became the present. At least this had been her philosophy until now; now even that was under attack as, increasingly, she found herself dwelling on her next rendezvous with Robert. Indeed, she thought of little else.

Her mother dwelled upon the relationship from a different viewpoint. Doungjai had talked eagerly of her boyfriend and, like any parent with a teenage daughter, her mother was not surprised. It would probably have happened sooner had the girl spent less time helping at home. Her mother had felt considerable qualms, though, on learning that the boy was English and only in Bangkok on holiday. The potential problems were all too obvious, but short of appearing repressive, she could only caution her daughter to be careful and sensible and remember that he would very soon be gone and she would probably never hear from him again.

Doungjai's school friends had been far less circumspect and vicariously enjoyed every detail they could extract about her meetings with Robert. But, using somewhat earthier language than her mother, they also repeatedly reminded her of the all the implications of associating with a young *falang*.

As so often in the past, Doungjai had turned eventually to her grandfather for advice. He was a wise old man who had had much exposure to the vicissitudes of life. She told him about Robert and her fears – fears that had been heightened by the ribald comments of her schoolfriends. Her grandfather, who loved all his grandchildren dearly, had a special affection for Doungjai. Her father had often been away from home for lengthy periods and so even before he was killed, she had usually turned to him for help and advice.

'I think my greatest pleasure in this life was watching our only daughter, your mother, grow up,' he once told Doungjai. 'Seeing her change from a little girl into a lovely young lady, day by day, before our eyes, was a very special experience for me. But I have been doubly lucky, because it has happened twice in my lifetime. You are so like your mother when she was your age and watching you grow up has allowed me to see it happen all over again.'

Now that he was too unsteady on his legs to leave the house, he was never happier than when his grandchildren gathered round his old battered armchair – on the arms, at his feet, on his knees. Sometimes he reminisced about the past while they listened attentively for as long as he cared to go on. At other times, he would counsel them when they brought their troubles to him and share their happy moments. When Doungjai asked for his guidance on Robert, he was as direct and uncompromising as ever.

'Always follow your instincts, Doungjai,' he said simply. 'You obviously like him, or you would not be asking what I think, so that is a good sign. Just remember this: true friendships are all too rare and too special to toss aside lightly. If you do make a mistake, put it down to experience and try to learn from it.'

His eyes became distant and he smiled weakly at a long ago memory. 'I remember an old shipmate who came from Scotland. He drank whisky like other people drink water and yet he was the fittest man and the hardest worker I've ever known. He used to have a favourite saying: "When you see a stick, cut it." In other words, if you see something you like and you think it's for you, go after it, because if you wait and return for it later, it might not be there.'

Ironically, her grandfather then precipitated the next minor crisis in Doungjai's relationship with Robert by suggesting she invite him to their home.

'But, Grandpapa, he lives in a lovely house in England with a big garden. What will he think of our small place?'

'Never be ashamed of your home, Doungjai.' The old man's voice took on a severe tone. 'It is maintained by honest money and hard work and never forget, in this house your mother and father raised a fine family. If your English friend is the person you think he is, when he sees your home he will think more of you, not less.' He shrugged weakly. 'In the end, you will both make up your own minds about each other, whatever I or anyone else tell you.'

But it was his final words that would stay with her forever, for they encapsulated exactly her feelings for Robert.

'Doungjai,' he went on, 'if you are still not sure about this English boy, ask yourself this: does it hurt every time you say goodbye and when you are not with him, do you miss him?'

He saw the answer in her face.

Chapter Twelve

Robert handed the piece of paper, containing Doungjai's address, to the taxi driver. She had written it in Thai script for the benefit of the taxi driver, few of whom read English. 'Only pay fifty bahts,' she had told him. The taxi driver's opening bid was seventy and, after some face pulling, Robert settled for sixty. He was in no mood for hard bargaining today, there was too much on his mind.

Within minutes, the familiar streets around the hotel were left behind and they were driving through a part of Bangkok that was completely new to him. He had thought of trying to follow their route on a map of the city, but the street signs, such as they were, were difficult to read from a bouncing taxi.

Although it was Sunday afternoon, the traffic seemed as heavy as ever, the weekday workers giving way to the weekend shoppers. The taxi driver tried to start a conversation, but neither his English nor Robert's comprehension was equal to the task and the journey lapsed into silence. This suited him because, for once, the eager anticipation of seeing Doungjai again was tempered with trepidation about meeting her family.

Suppose Doungjai's mother took a dislike to him. She probably wouldn't show it – the Thais were too polite for that – but she might discourage Doungjai from seeing him again. Or even forbid it, if she were especially strict. After tonight, he would be apart from her for a few days, more than long enough for the relationship they had developed to cool and the tenuous link to be broken.

The taxi turned off the main thoroughfare. The narrow rutted *soi* was clogged with cars, motor bikes, hand carts and pedestrians, but the taxi drive drove on as serenely as if it were an open country road. By mounting the walkways and squeezing through seemingly impossible gaps, they progressed at a respectable pace for nearly half a mile before emerging into an open area surrounded by small single-storey dwellings. Footpaths ran between these to other buildings behind, but they were too narrow for a vehicle. The driver indicated that they had reached their destination and a slightly anxious Robert forked out the sixty bahts and dismounted, clutching a bunch of flowers and another small package.

Collections of children were playing in front of their homes, the air full of their childish chatter. As he stepped forward, Robert was conscious of questioning stares from beneath the shaded verandahs and the open doorways all around. It was stiflingly hot, not a breath of wind, and when the taxi had swung round and disappeared up the *soi* he suddenly felt very much alone.

There was no sign of Doungjai and another worrying thought gripped him: that the taxi might have brought him to the wrong place. He had no idea which part of Bangkok he was in, and it was doubtful if anyone in these houses spoke English.

'Lobut!'

His anxiety vanished the instant he heard her call.

There she was, running towards him along one of the footpaths between the houses. As she approached, she slowed to a walk, then stopped, as though unsure how to greet him before her neighbours. The children had fallen quiet, watching intently. In the end she put out her hand and, awkwardly laden as he was with gifts, he shook it.

'You wait long time?' she asked.

'No, I've just arrived. I was a few minutes early.'

'Pretty flowers.'

'I brought them for your mother. Does she like flowers?'

Doungjai nodded eagerly. 'Always we have flowers in our house. Please, this way.'

Watched by the silent children, she led him along a footpath, between rows of small dwellings, most of them with low, shallow verandahs. Overall, there was a calm air of inactivity, although Robert was conscious all the time of the inhabitants peering curiously out at him as they passed.

After about a hundred yards, Doungjai stopped in front of one of the houses and led the way through a gap in the low fence that cordoned off the front of the dwelling. Under the sloping roof, a low table and an old armchair occupied most of the area beside an open door. An old man was seated in the chair and appeared to be asleep.

'This Grandpapa,' Doungjai explained softly. 'You like to come inside?'

She kicked off her sandals and pushed them beside several other pairs that were scattered round the doorway, following the Thai custom of removing shoes before entering a house. Robert took somewhat longer to untie the laces of his trainers and lever them off.

The room was L-shaped and had a Spartan appearance, due mainly to the shiny linoleum floor and the pale blue walls that were almost bare. There was no air conditioning, only a large fan that circled overhead churning up the air just enough to give an illusion of cooling. A small image of Buddha stood on a low cupboard. In front of it, on a tray, were a bunch of flowers, an opened coconut with a straw sticking out of the top and a glass of water. The far right hand corner was occupied by a gas cooker, fridge and other culinary accessories beside a door leading to another room. There was a further door to the left, which Doungjai later explained was the shower and toilet, while the other arm of the L was occupied by a double bed. A small girl and boy, about six or seven years old, sat on the floor in front of the bed.

'My brother and sister,' Doungjai explained.

They both stood up, placed their hands together and greeted him with a solemn *wei*. Robert, who was about to shake hands, returned the gesture, albeit rather awkwardly.

'Hello,' he smiled, and gestured to the books on the floor. 'What are you reading?' Doungjai translated and their serious expressions became animated as they got back down on the floor and held their books for Robert to see. He placed the flowers and the other package on the bed and went to sit with them, while Doungjai looked on with an amused smile. The children showed Robert their books, although neither side could understand a word the other was saying. Occasionally, Doungjai intervened with a word of explanation, until at last Robert was rescued by the arrival of her mother.

'Lobut, my Mama,' Doungjai said, as he clambered to his feet and took the woman's small, warm hand.

'I'm pleased to meet you,' he said in the time honoured English fashion.

Doungjai said something to her mother who
replied briefly without taking her eyes off his face. He
felt her scrutiny far more than any words.

'Mama no speak English,' Doungjai explained. 'She
say she happy to meet you too and would you like a
drink?'

'Thank you, a cold drink would be nice.'

'You like Coke?'

'That would be fine.'

'I get in special for you,' she grinned. 'You always
drink Coke at McDonalds.'

'Oh, just a moment, Doungjai.' Robert lifted the
presents from the bed. 'Would you please tell your
mother I brought these for her?'

Doungjai translated and Robert was rewarded
with a look of pleased surprise. First she admired the
flowers, before handing them to Doungjai, and then
started to open the package. For the first time, Robert
was able to take a good look at her. She was not
quite as tall as Doungjai, but somewhat stouter under
the loose fitting, dark green dress. Her hair, drawn
tightly back from her face, was still jet black, but her
face was that of a somewhat older woman. That she
and Doungjai were mother and daughter was very
apparent. For Robert, it was as if he were seeing
Doungjai as she would be twenty five years or so
from now. He was not disappointed, for despite the
wrinkles, Doungjai's mother was still a very attractive
woman.

'Mama say to thank you, but she not expect present.' She laughed. '*Two* presents.'

When her mother had opened the package, she
stared for long moments at the framed photograph of

87

her daughter. Her expression was of delight blended with incredulity, as she showed the photograph to Doungjai.

'Photograph of me!' Doungjai exclaimed. 'I not know you have this one.'

'I took it at the same time as the others,' he told her. 'I thought it was the best one so I kept it back to have it enlarged and framed as a surprise. I was going to give it to you, Doungjai, but when I knew I would be meeting your mother, I thought I would give it to her instead. I hope you don't mind?'

'No mind. You make Mama happy, I happy too.' She took the picture from her mother and gave it further appraisal. 'You think it good, Lobut?'

'I think you look very beautiful,' he said with relish. 'Will you tell your mother that I think she has a very lovely daughter?'

'Oh, Lobut, me no lovely. Now you make me shy.'

'Go on, tell her,' he insisted.

Her mother nodded enthusiastically in agreement with Robert when Doungjai explained with a giggle, and took back the photograph to show it to the two children who had gathered round to look.

'You like sit outside, Lobut,' Doungjai suggested, 'while I get you coke.'

Robert dutifully stepped out to the verandah, where he found that Doungjai's grandfather had woken up. They looked at each other for a moment before the old man spoke.

'You must be Robert. Doungjai said you were coming to see us. I hear you are from England.' His English, though strongly accented, was fluent. He leaned forward, stuck out his hand. It was bony, dry and felt fragile; Robert shook it tentatively.

'Excuse me not getting up but it takes a big effort these days.'

'I'm pleased to meet you. Doungjai has told me a lot about you.' Robert stood a little uncertainly until the old man gestured to the other chair.

'I hear you were in the Navy,' he said conversationally.

'A long time ago.' The old man settled back in the leather-bound armchair that looked as if it was made to fit him. 'But I still have the memories now that I cannot get about any more.' For a moment his eyes lit up and a smile hovered on his lips. 'As you get older, and your time begins to run out, memories become more important, especially if you have lived a full life.' There was no hint of regret in his whispering voice.

'Doungjai told me you taught her to speak English.'

The old man nodded. 'She was a good pupil and could speak the language before they started to teach it at school.'

His head began to droop a little with the effort of talking, but he found a new energy when Doungjai appeared with Robert's Coke. 'Here she is, my little inspiration.'

'You awake, Grandpapa? This is my friend, Lobut, from England.'

'We have already introduced ourselves,' the old man said gravely.

'Lobut give Mama flowers and a big photograph of me.' Doungjai smiled happily at Robert while she took her grandfather's hand and held it in a childlike gesture of affection.

'Let me see it.' He waved his free hand imperiously, and Doungjai retreated back into the house, without a word, returning with the picture.

'I cannot see properly without my glasses,' he complained after a quick glance at it. 'I think they are beside my bed.'

Doungjai went off again and fetched the missing glasses. As he hooked them onto his ears, Robert saw that one of the arms had broken off and was held loosely to the main frame by a piece of wire. For a long moment, the old man gazed at the picture.

'You like, Grandpapa? Mama think it very good.'

'Did you take this?' The old man looked towards Robert.

'Yes, the first time we met in the park.'

'It *is* very good. She looks beautiful and just the same as her mother when she was her age.'

Doungjai clapped her hands with delight

'You really think so?'

He nodded. 'But more important, beautiful here as well.'

He put his hand over his heart. Now Doungjai really did blush. She sat on the arm of the chair beside her grandfather and placed her arm round his shoulder. He patted her arm and looked at Robert. 'I hope one day many people will see her as I see her. I just wish . . .' He struggled for the right words. 'I wish you were both a bit older because then . . . ' He left what he was thinking unsaid and after another long look at the picture, passed it back to Doungjai.

'I must go inside for a moment.' He tried to pull himself to his feet and Doungjai was quick to get her shoulder under his arm in a way that showed she had had a lot of practice.

Robert rose to help and was surprised how light the old man was. When he was steady, they drew back to let him walk unaided, which he clearly preferred.

With slow hesitant steps he negotiated his way into the house.

'Has he lived with you long?' Robert asked, when he judged the old man was out of earshot.

'Long time, since I was little girl. He come stay here when Grandmama die. I no remember when he not live with us.'

'I can see you're very fond of him.'

'Love him very much. He teach me many things. Always help when I have trouble. Now him not so well. Not walk good and has bad cough. Mama tell him he smoke too much, but him not listen.'

They stood together under the verandah in silent reflection until Doungjai's grandfather rejoined them. He managed to sit down without assistance, easing into his chair, like a slowly deflating balloon.

'I think I have left my cigarettes inside,' he announced when he was settled. Doungjai departed on yet another errand.

'You smoke too many cigarettes, Grandpapa,' she scolded, as she held the lighter for him.

He took no notice until he was safely lit up. Then he screwed up his face and aimed a conspiratorial wink at Robert.

'You are still very young, Robert, but I expect you have already learned that what women enjoy most is trying to deny us men the pleasures of life.' He gave a hoarse chuckle. 'The trouble is, they also make sure our lives would not be worth living without them.'

Robert smiled and for some reason Melanie Bishop flashed across his mind while he mentally struggled with the old man's proposition, trying to decide whether or not he agreed, or even understood it.

'Take this one.' The old man brushed his hand weakly against Doungjai's leg. 'She's always telling

91

me what is good for me and what is bad for me.' He chuckled again. 'But I get my own back. Now she is growing up, I tell her she eats too much and is getting a fat ass.'

'Grandpapa.' Doungjai affected outrage, but not very convincingly. 'You very bad man, tell Lobut like this about me. Make me shy.' She took his hand and pretended to smack it, while Robert looked on and enjoyed the family interplay.

'If I say I am sorry, will you get me a cup of coffee?'

Doungjai went to attend to her Grandfather's latest whim.

'Coffee helps to keep me awake during the day,' the old man explained when he and Robert were alone. 'Then I sleep better at night. I do not suppose you have such a problem at your age, but the longest and most wasted hours in life are those spent lying awake in the middle of the night.'

The longer they spoke, the more Robert recognised a kind of inner strength which compensated for the old man's physical frailty. At times his eyes almost closed and he seemed to be dozing off, only to suddenly flare into life again when it seemed that something stirred within him, like an ember fanned by an intermittent breeze. Without realising it, Robert found himself listening closely to the little gems of wisdom that flowed forth during the old man's periods of loquacity.

As the afternoon sped by, Robert was repeatedly conscious of the willing way in which Doungjai's family, even the youngest, catered for her grandfather's every need without question. They drew him into their conversations and activities, even though he never rose from the old battered chair. Robert could not help reflecting the contrast between this close-knit relationship and the way his parents regarded his grandparents back home. Although their occasional visits to each other's homes were cordial enough, there was always the feeling that both parties were relieved when it was time to take their leave.

After a while, another brother and sister appeared. They were perhaps two or three years younger than Doungjai, and settled down at once on the arms of their grandfather's chair to regale him with some long story, to which he listened mainly in silence, occasionally nodding his head or asking a mono-syllabic question. Then he decided to read his news-paper, sparking an immediate search. Eventually it was found tucked down the arm of his chair. It was the *Bangkok Post*, an English language news-paper, which surprised Robert.

The old man read his mind. 'I try to get this as often as I can,' he explained. 'It is about the only chance I have nowadays to keep up my English.'

Doungjai's mother stayed in the background for most of the time, content to leave her father and daughter to entertain Robert. Perhaps over-sensitive of the language barrier, she was happy to busy herself inside the house, although she favoured Robert with a smile whenever their eyes met.

Doungjai volunteered to give Robert a grand tour of the house, which did not take long as there was only one other room he had not already seen.

'This is the bedroom for Mama and my sisters and me,' she explained.

It was simply furnished with one double bed, an old wardrobe, a couple of wooden chairs and a mirror on the wall above a low cupboard that doubled as a dressing table. Doungjai opened the wardrobe door. It was packed full of the family's clothes, some hanging on the rail, others piled in bundles on the shelves and the floor. At one end of the rail, slightly separate from the women's clothing, a single garment hung, protected by a plastic cover. Doungjai lifted it carefully, almost deferentially off the rail, and held it in front of her.

'Papa's army uniform. Mama keep good for memory.'

The olive green jacket was neatly pressed and in immaculate condition.

'It looks very smart,' he remarked.

She nodded solemnly. 'Papa always very smart in his uniform. Mama and me and my brothers and sisters, we all very proud of him.'

Robert felt slightly uncomfortable and shuffled his feet.

'Miss Papa,' Doungjai said simply as she closed the wardrobe door, and her dark eyes glistened. She directed Robert towards the far side of the room where an old blanket, hanging from a length of cord, stretched from wall to wall. About head high, it formed a curtain and partially blocked off what lay beyond. Doungjai held up the blanket.

'My bedroom,' she announced with a flourish and sat down on the brightly coloured, patchwork blanket that covered a narrow strip of foam on the floor. She patted the blanket for Robert to join her and bounced up and down.

'Comfortable bed,' she said enthusiastically. 'I put up blanket to make my own room, give me privacy now I grown up.'

'Brilliant idea,' Robert enthused.

The foam bed took up most of the floor space behind the blanket, leaving just enough room to step round it. Another cord reached across a corner and some of Doungjai's clothes hung from it. But it was the low cupboard in the other corner by the head of the bed that caught Robert's attention. A couple of paperbacks lay on the top and in front of them stood a small picture frame. It contained the photo of himself that he had given her a few days before. She saw the direction of his gaze and smiled shyly.

'Very handsome man I know,' she informed him. 'He come from England and watch me every night when I go to sleep.'

Robert could hardly bring himself to speak. He had already been mentally comparing his own bedroom back home, with its TV set, video and hi-fi, a desk with a personal computer, a wardrobe full of clothes, a cupboard full of sports and other leisure gear; and its large picture window that looked out over prime English countryside. The lowly nature of Doungjai's 'bedloom' shook him, especially since she seemed so proud and contented with it. The final straw was seeing his picture by her bedside and her accompanying chirpy comments.

'Well I think he's very lucky to have his photo beside the bed of such a lovely young lady,' he responded gallantly, adding: 'I like these colours.' He turned away from her to indicate the blanket on the bed, buying time to reinstate his composure. 'Mama and Grandpapa give me for my birthday,' she told him. 'Like bright colours.'

Before they returned to the other room, Robert gave a final backward glance towards the blanket that concealed Doungjai's own personal little world. He wondered what dreams and hopes evolved there in the long night hours.

Back in the living room it was uncomfortably hot,

for the overhead fan had been switched off. Doungjai turned it on again to get the air circulating.

'Mama switch off. Electricity very expensive. One day Mama say we get air con. Maybe.'

The guided tour continued as she pointed out the gas cooker. 'For cooking.'

'Are you a good cook?' he asked, concealing a smile.

She laughed. 'Sometimes, when Mama busy, I cook little bit for brothers and sisters. Cook good rice. You like something to eat now, Lobut?'

'Not at the moment, thanks,' he declined. 'I was hoping you would let me take you out for a meal tonight, since I'm going away tomorrow. My mother and father have been invited to dinner by the people at his work, so maybe we can stay out just a little longer than usual.'

Doungjai looked thoughtful while his words slowly sank in. 'Where you like to eat, Lobut?'

'I thought we would go to a restaurant I was reading about in my guide book.' He felt in his pocket for a piece of paper. 'It's called Tum Nak Thai. Do you know it?'

'I hear about it, but never been before. I ask Mama.'

Robert stood awkwardly while Doungjai and her mother discussed his suggestion.

'Mama say we can go eat, but she want me come home by ten o'clock, OK?' She delivered the parental edict a little tentatively. 'I go change now.'

'Right. I'll wait for you on the verandah.'

The old man seemed pleased to have another opportunity to practice his English and encouraged by Robert, reminisced about his stint in the Navy and in particular the voyage to Britain. He recalled the grey chill and mean buildings of Glasgow, the pubs of Liverpool and the red double-decker buses of London. He had worked down to Portsmouth when Doungjai emerged, her heels clopping on the boards, causing him to break off what had become almost a soliloquy. His jaw dropped, while Robert simply stared in dumb appreciation at this new version of Doungjai. She was wearing a pale lemon, cotton suit, with dark blue piping along the edges. The jacket was wide-shouldered, nipped in at the waist and then flared to mid-thigh; the skirt was shorter than any he had seen her wear, revealing a shapely pair of legs in low-heeled pumps. Her hair hung heavy and shiny on her shoulders, and her make-up was understated: just a smear on her eyelids, cheeks and lips. She could easily have stepped out of a fashion magazine.

'Is it really Doungjai?' Her grandfather echoed Robert's thoughts.

'You not like?' she asked, her smile fading when he did not speak.

'You look terrific,' Robert gasped.

'Never wear before.' She relaxed and indicated her suit. 'I keep for special time. Tonight special with you, Lobut.'

'Is this really my little girl?' her grandfather repeated, shaking his head doubtfully. 'You are growing up far too fast.'

'Oh, Grandpapa, I nearly fifteen and soon leave school.'

Doungjai turned to her mother who had just appeared in the doorway. She contemplated her daughter with undisguised approval. Words were exchanged.

'Mama say she has been happy to meet you,' Doungjai translated. 'She thanks you for lovely flowers and also photograph. We go now.'

97

Robert shook hands with Doungjai's mother and waved farewell to the children. 'Please thank your mother and brothers and sisters for their hospitality and say I hope to see them all again. Oh, and say I will make sure you are home by ten o'clock.'

Last of all before leaving, he turned to Doungjai's grandfather who, with a mighty effort, pushed himself half out of his chair. As he clasped Robert's hand, he leaned forward to speak softly in his ear.

'Take care of her. I will not always be here to give her advice.' His voice trembled as he spoke and Robert had to strain to catch his words. 'Tonight she looks a very grown-up young lady, but she is still only a child and thinks good of everyone. Today, in this world, that can lead to disappointment.'

Robert was unsure how he was expected to respond to this caveat.

'She'll be safe with me,' he said stoutly.

The old man nodded, smiled, and sank down onto his chair.

'Ready, Lobut?' Doungjai called.

'Yes, ready.' Then to the old man: 'It's been a great pleasure meeting you. I've enjoyed talking to you very much and I'll remember what you said.'

All of a sudden Robert felt an unaccountable sadness. The afternoon had already proved to be the most memorable of his holiday so far, but in the last few minutes particularly he had come to realise, with a deep certainty, that this Thai adventure would be much more than a memory when their aircraft took off for home, little more than a week from now.

Disneyland seemed a long way away and very insignificant.

Chapter Thirteen

In the confined environment of the taxi Robert became aware of Doungjai's perfume. It may not have been Chanel, but whatever the brand it added a further heady stimulus to his already overloaded senses. It also added to the feeling that he was a shade underdressed for the occasion.

'Do you mind if we stop at the hotel for a few minutes?' he asked. 'I'd like to have a quick shower and get changed.'

'OK,' Doungjai said, easygoing as ever.

He would not be able to match her sophisticated appearance, but he felt he had to improve on the jeans, sweatshirt and sneakers he had been wearing all afternoon.

As he was crossing the hotel foyer an idea occurred to him, literally in mid-stride. He faltered, his brain racing. It was a daring, even dangerous idea, and though it had come out of the blue it took root immediately. Still deep in thought, he collected his room key at the hotel desk and returned to where Doungjai stood waiting by a bookstand.

'Would you like to come up to my room to wait while I change?' He tried to sound casual and matter of fact.

'Come to your room?' She repeated his words as if she had misheard them.

'I shan't be long, but it would be better than waiting down here.'

'Your Mama and Papa no mind?'

'They have their own room, but anyway they will have gone out by now.'

'Hotel no mind?'

'Why should they?' He had not even considered the hotel's views on the subject. In any case, what business was it of theirs?

'OK?' he urged, and guided her towards the lift before she could think up any more objections.

It was a matter of a few steps, but he was convinced the entire hotel desk staff, as well as every guest seated in the hotel lobby, were watching them, putting the worst interpretation on their actions. By her silence and her stiff carriage, he suspected that Doungjai shared his feelings. Naturally both lifts were in use and their respective lights seemed to take ages to work their way down, stopping at almost every floor. By the time the bell rang and the doors slid open to disgorge its occupants, several other guests had gathered and followed them into the lift.

Leaning against the side, as they ascended in silence, Robert wondered what his friends back home would say if they could see him now – heading up to his hotel room with an exotic female in tow.

Thankfully, the corridor on his floor was empty and Robert felt a distinct sense of relief when his bedroom door swung open and he and Doungjai stepped into the room. While she stood by the closed door, as if keeping her escape route to hand, panning the room with anxious interest, he went around switching on all the lights and pulling the cords to close the heavy velvet curtains.

'Very nice,' she approved, looking slightly more relaxed as she ventured further into the room.

Robert sat on the edge of the bed and patted the space beside him. 'Come and sit down while I get ready.'

She lowered herself tentatively onto the bed, as if it were a bed of nails, and they sat side by side in an awkward silence.

'Like TV?' she queried, pointing to the set on the table in front of them.

'Yes, but I can't understand a lot of it here in Bangkok. Most of it is in Thai, although there are some channels in English. I watch video films mostly. There's a special channel for them. Do you like TV?'

'Like, but no have. Sometimes I go visit my friend. Her Mama have TV so I watch with her.'

Robert leaned forward and pressed the ON button. 'Why don't you watch it while I'm having a shower? You change the programmes here.' He pressed a succession of buttons and scrolled through a succession of channels.

He collected clean clothes and took them with him into the bathroom. When he looked back from the bathroom door, Doungjai was already riveted to some game show. When he emerged a quarter of an hour later, fresher and smarter, she had not moved.

'Would you rather stay here and watch television than go out?' he asked half seriously.

For a second she looked as if she were considering the suggestion. Then she smiled and shook her head. 'No good for you, Lobut, you no understand TV here.'

'I don't mind.' He warmed to the idea. 'I could sit and look at you while you look at the television. I would much rather watch you anyway.'

'Oh, Lobut, you always saying nice things.' She stood up and looked back at him in the large wall mirror beside the television. 'You talk too much to Grandpapa. He say same about me.'

He stepped up close behind her, put his arms round her waist and drew her back against him. She might have turned and pushed him away, or demanded he keep his hands to himself. Instead, she sank back into his embrace, her head beneath his chin.

Any lingering doubts he had were swamped by her nearness and the scent of her hair against his face. His hands slipped under her jacket and his excitement rose several notches when his fingers encountered bare skin above the waistband of her skirt. Their eyes met in the mirror as one hand released the single button holding her jacket closed and rested on the gentle swell of her belly over her skirt. The other crept upwards over her ribs and kept climbing until it reached the edge of the well-filled bra, her sole garment under the jacket.

As he gently fondled her breast through its lacy covering, the blood surged in his veins. He had never touched a girl there before, but he knew that it was a very sensitive part of the female body and should be handled with great care. He eased his hand up to the cleavage until he was touching the top of her breasts, where they swelled above their confinement. Slowly and carefully, hardly daring to breathe, and expecting her to resist at any moment, he edged his fingers inside.

The flesh was warm and full and firm, yet resilient enough to absorb his questing fingers. He wriggled his hand still further southwards, and suddenly her nipple was there, under his fingertips. The tiny nub felt hard and the skin was rougher than the surrounding flesh. He pressed it gently and was rewarded with a small sigh from Doungjai. She lifted her hand and placed it over his, squeezing it harder against her.

Robert felt he could stand there all night with her bottom pressing into his loins, and her breast cupped firmly in his hand like a small trapped animal. Now he wanted to see as well as feel it, but he had heard that girl's bras were notoriously complicated contraptions. While he pondered his next tactic, his other hand assumed a mind of its own. It probed at the waistband of Doungjai's skirt and tried to find a way underneath. To ease his path she drew in her tummy, either involuntarily or as an invitation. No matter. Like a blind man fumbling his way, his hand slid down ever so slowly over the smooth tight skin of her belly, while Doungjai thrust her bottom backwards ever more aggressively, creating a further space problem below Robert's waist. The blood was pounding behind his eyes when he encountered outlying strands of pubic hair.

Every new discovery was proving more wonderful than the last and this one especially so. Robert had not been sure if girls of Doungjai's age grew hair on their bodies – there – and now here he was, actually touching it. It had the gentle texture of the softest down, not at all crinkly and coarse like his. Nor was it abundant: it thinned out almost to nothing as he came into contact with that holy of holies, her vagina. This he probed with great circumspection and deference, his forefinger sliding down the deep groove in the centre, parting the pliant lips.

Doungjai gave a little gasp and her grip on his hand tightened. 'Lobut,' she murmured. Was it approval or reproof?

Her eyes encountered Robert's in the mirror. For several seconds she stood frozen, accepting Robert's clumsy, intimate fumbling, neither of them sure how to progress to the next stage. For Robert, the only thing in the world that mattered at this moment was to extend his exploration of her adolescent anatomy. For Doungjai, it was a question of when to cry halt.

The answer came from an unexpected quarter in the form of a loud knock on the door.

'Bloody hell!' Robert gasped.

A momentary paralysis was followed by a frantic attempt to disengage. Robert tried to wrench his hands away from Doungjai's bodily treasures, his panic increasing when his wrist became trapped in her waistband as she tried to turn and face him. He finally managed to tug free and, red faced, tiptoed over to the door, leaving Doungjai to restore order to her clothing.

He peered through the spyhole and his relief was a palpable thing

'It's the maid,' he hissed.

Keeping the safety chain on the door, he opened it a couple of inches and failed in his efforts to look nonchalant as he smiled at the girl standing there in her neat hotel uniform.

'May I turn down the bed, sir?' she asked cheerfully.

Chapter Fourteen

Robert and Doungjai had the lift to themselves on the way down. They stood with their backs against opposite walls, staring at each other, neither of them inclined to talk.

Robert was quite certain that the incident had shortened his life expectancy by several years. He had stalled the maid, asking her to come back later. He watched her down the corridor and as soon as she turned the corner, he and Doungjai dashed for the lift. They felt no inclination at all to carry on where they had left off.

Robert felt slightly more relaxed when they reached the lobby, helped by the partial anonymity provided by other milling guests. Doungjai, though, remained keyed up, and even in the taxi she was unresponsive to Robert's rather clumsy attempts to stimulate conversation. It was something of a relief for both of them to reach their destination.

Tum Nak Thai Restaurant, on Ratchadaphisek Road in the north-east of the city, was not a run-of-the-mill eating place. The tables, many cordoned off into cosy alcoves, were mainly grouped round a lake well-stocked with carp. There was a stage in the middle of the lake, where Thai music and dancing entertained the patrons while they ate. Above the stage a notice, in brightly lit lettering, proclaims the restaurant to be the biggest in the world – a claim supported by the Guinness Book of Records. To cope with the obvious problem of transporting the food from the kitchens to the diners' tables, with the least delay, the waiters and waitresses wore rollerblades and communicated using walkie-talkies.

It should have been the perfect choice for Robert and Doungjai to share their last evening together, before he and his parents left for Chiang Mai. Only it was not working out that way.

Even after they had been shown to their table, over-looking the lake, Doungjai remained withdrawn. Ominously for one whose appetite was prodigious, she only picked at the simple rice dish she had ordered and uncharacteristically left it only half-eaten. Her mood rubbed off on Robert who found he had little appetite either. His desultory efforts at small-talk eventually dried up altogether.

It was obvious that his fumbling sexual advances had upset her. To Doungjai it must have seemed that he had set her up by inviting her up to his room. It was true she had not protested or struggled, but maybe she was afraid of making a commotion in case it brought the hotel management down on their heads. Or maybe – perish the thought – she had been scared of *him*.

Less than an hour earlier her grandfather, who thought so much of her, had specifically asked him to take care of her. He and the rest of her family trusted him. Yet scarcely had an opportunity arisen when he had betrayed that trust. What kind of lowlife did that make him?

Now that her ordeal was over, he surmised, Doungjai was obviously just going through the polite formalities for the rest of the evening. She was probably hating every minute of it and longing for it to end, so that she could return to the safety of her home, never to have any truck with him again. In a few mindless moments, he had ruined a very special friendship. All the pleasure and happiness they had shared in each other's company over the past few wonderful days had turned to ashes. Now he would have to live with his conscience.

But he wasn't going to meekly let her walk out of his life. Perhaps there was still time to limit the damage. Doungjai was gazing out over the lake, her face in profile, her expression drawn. He reached for her hand. It lay in his like a block of wood, stiff and lifeless. At least she did not pull it away, he consoled himself.

'Was the food all right? You haven't eaten much,' he said softly.

'Yes, thank you. I not very hungry.' She turned to face him and the look of hurt in her eyes was devastating.

'Er . . . about this evening, Doungjai, at the hotel . . .'

'I know . . .' Now she did withdraw her hand, turning away to look out over the lake once more. A small sob shook her shoulders and, when she looked at him again, he could see huge tears welling up in her eyes before running slowly down her cheeks.

'Lobut, I very sorry,' she cried and, reaching for his hand, held it to her face.

He goggled.

'*You're* sorry?'

'I never did like that before.'

'Did what before?' His bewilderment was total.

'I never go to room with boy before. I know you angry because you no speak tonight.' Now she had started the words came tumbling out as though, having been bottled up for too long, they had to escape as quickly as possible. 'You think I bad girl because I come to your room and let you touch me in my places. You think I do all the time with boys, but I promise I never before. I never have man touch me before like you, Lobut. I not bad girl.'

She turned away from him again and began to cry softly, her head bowed. Still hardly believing his ears, but relieved to shed the mantle of sex monster, Robert got up and went to sit beside her. Heedless of the other diners, some of whom were openly watching developments between the young couple, he wrapped an arm around her shoulders and hugged her to him.

'Hey, you silly goose, I never thought anything bad about you. If I haven't talked much it's because I thought you were angry with me.'

She twisted sideways, her face soaked in tears, but the hurt look in her eyes had given way to hope. 'You not angry with me, Lobut?'

'Of course I'm not angry, why should I be?'

'Because I let you do bad things and I worry you think I make love with other boys, like street woman.'

'The thought never entered my head.' He felt the tears of relief building up in his own eyes now. 'I asked you up to my room without any intention of touching you, I promise. But then I . . . I suddenly felt I wanted to. I've never done anything like that before either, but somehow tonight, it . . . it just happened. Afterwards, I was worried in case you thought I had planned it all and had been trying to take advantage of you.'

She gave him a tearful smile. 'So we still friends?'

'If we're not, I'm going to jump into that lake right

now.' He pretended to move past her and climb onto the rail, but she caught him and pulled him back.

'No, Lobut, no.' The relief and joy in her tear-streaked face was a sight he would never forget, and her gurgle of laughter was the sweetest music in the world. 'I thought you never want to see me again.'

'And I thought the same.' He had never known a greater relief as he sat down beside her. Even now he could hardly believe the turn-around that had taken place in the last couple of minutes.

'Look, you've hardly eaten a thing,' he scolded playfully. 'So I'm going to order you the biggest fruit sundae in the place, and I'm going to have one as well.'

She made no protest and proceeded to prove that everything was back to normal by polishing hers off spoonfuls ahead of him. Afterwards, as they worked their way leisurely through a pot of coffee, Doungjai looked at him as if she had something important to say, but was afraid to.

'Lobut,' she began tentatively at last. 'If I tell you something, you promise you not be angry with me?'

'You can say anything you like as long as you promise to meet me on Friday when I get back from Chiang Mai.'

'Of course I meet you.' She still hesitated and then plunged in. 'Lobut?'

'Yes?'

'You know when you touched me in your room tonight?'

'Yes?' Oh-oh. What was coming now?

'It . . . it feel nice. I like it. You no mind I tell you?'

He smiled and shook his head, his deflated confidence returning in a rush.

'I'm glad you told me, because I liked it as well. I

think you're beautiful and . . . and I would like to touch you all over.' He was surprised by his boldness, but no longer cared.

Her eyes lit up. 'I like that too, Lobut.' Then seriously. 'But I think maybe Mama no like.'

'Maybe not.' Robert deflated slightly. He was absolutely sure her mother would not like. 'Perhaps you shouldn't tell her,' he suggested.

'I think maybe that good idea,' she agreed. 'Oh, and Lobut . . .'

'Yes?'

'What is goose?'

Chapter Fifteen

For the Stones, Chiang Mai should have been an ideal change of pace and scenery after weeks in the hectic cauldron of Bangkok. But for one family member, it was an irritating interruption to his budding romance just as it was about to enter a critical phase.

Since the episode in his hotel room, an extra dimension had been added to Robert's emotional merry-go-round. In spite of the subsequent attack of conscience, he could not forget the feel of Doungjai's body under his hands. He had re-lived those unique and special moments a thousand times: the moulding together of their bodies, the malleable flesh of her breast with its small hard tip, the exciting discovery of her pubic hair . . .

Now he understood why other boys called it 'pussy,' often accompanied by a snigger. But pussy was no sniggering matter. It was serious stuff. It was the entrance to heaven on earth. Or something like that.

Chiang Mai lay about four hundred and fifty miles to the north of Bangkok and an hour's flying time from the capital. Although Thai International ran a service nearly every hour, the Monday morning flight carrying the Stone family was full.

They landed at just before noon. The huge Airbus taxied towards the parking apron, and even before the whine of the massive engines had died into silence, refuelling vehicles were converging on it, while hatches opened to disgorge its load and take on new supplies and passengers.

The flight was met by an army of local people crowding round the exit, many of them holding up signs with the names of arriving passengers. Among them was a representative of the Chiang Mai Plaza Hotel and, since they only had hand luggage, the Stones were on their way out of the airport by minibus, less than fifteen minutes after touching down.

Chiang Mai was less than one fortieth the size of Bangkok and almost rural compared with the capital. It had little traffic congestion; the air was crystal clear and the environment generally much more relaxed. Robert's parents at least welcomed the change of pace.

A tour of the city filled the Stones' first afternoon, and the next day they went on a short safari which took in an orchid and butterfly farm, a demonstration of elephants at work and an hour's ride alongside a wide river on the back of one, followed by another ride this time in an ox cart. And that was only the morning.

In the afternoon they went on a short river cruise which entailed being poled down a wide, sweeping river between undulating, tree-capped slopes, on a bamboo raft. Their minibus met them downstream and on the way back to Chiang Mai, they visited a Mao village where the children, in their distinctive, brightly coloured clothes, were just coming out of school.

On the second full day, they made the almost obligatory trip to the temple high above the city on Doi Suthep. After they had strolled around this most serene and lovely treasure in Thailand's north, they looked out through the haze at Chiang Mai three thousand feet below.

During the days that followed, other memorable visits took place, but curiously, Robert's most lasting impression was of the signs, in Thai and English, pinned to trees in the small wood near the entrance to the U Mong Temple. Among the plethora of profound pronouncements were:

'One today is better than two tomorrows.'

'When money speaks truth is silent.'

'Poverty with dignity is better than wealth based on shame.'

And, more cryptically:

'Do try to do good, but not to be great. Otherwise you will be in danger.'

Robert exposed a whole film recording them. Perhaps he would impress Doungjai by trotting out a quote or two.

It seemed to Brian and Mary Stone that they had barely arrived at their hotel in Chiang Mai when they were packing again.

'We should have arranged to stay longer,' Robert's father commented over dinner on their last night. 'There's so much to see up here and we've barely started.'

'It's been a nice change, though,' his mother pointed out. 'You've had fun here, haven't you, Robert?'

Robert nodded. They had crammed a great deal into a few days and he had enjoyed their short stay in the north – up to a point. He would have enjoyed it much more if his thoughts had not constantly wandered back to the lovely little lady who was waiting for him in Bangkok.

Chapter Sixteen

Bangkok was no less frenetic, no less polluted for their absence. Over lunch in the hotel restaurant Robert's parents sprang a surprise on him.

'Your mother and I were talking about how we might spend tomorrow evening,' his father opened. 'Since it's the last night before we go home, we thought it would be nice if we all go out together and have a good meal in typical Thai surroundings.'

Robert fidgeted uneasily. 'Thanks, Dad, only being the last night I thought . . .'

'We would like Doungjai to come as well, dear,' his mother stepped in. 'That is if you both want to.'

'I'll ask her this afternoon,' Robert replied guardedly. He would still have preferred to be alone with her.

His mother was pretty sure what was troubling him. 'We can have an early meal and then if the two of you want to be on your own for a little while before Doungjai goes home, well . . . it is the last night and as long as you aren't too late.'

'And I expect you'll be seeing her on Sunday,' his father teased. 'By the time we leave, you'll probably be fed up with the sight of each other.'

Robert smiled his appreciation. Until this moment he had not realised how much his parents understood his feelings. Not only did they understand, but they were prepared to back his romantic aspirations to the hilt. Parents were always full of surprises.

'Thanks, both of you,' he acknowledged. 'I'm sure Doungjai would like that. The fact is we do have a lot to talk about. I want to tell her all about Chiang Mai and we don't have a lot of time and . . . '

'I think we get the picture, Robert,' his mother smiled.

Robert had arranged to meet Doungjai from school in McDonalds in Silom Road, where he had first met her with his mother. He marvelled at how far they had advanced since that day of his first real date. The precautions his parents had insisted upon at the beginning now seemed laughable.

He arrived fifteen minutes before the agreed time of 4.15 and sat by the window watching out for her. As the rendezvous time approached, his excitement at the thought of seeing her again mounted rapidly. It had been a whole four days since their evening together at Tum Nak Thai Restaurant. It seemed like four weeks.

A quarter past four came and went. For a few minutes after Robert was not concerned, but by 4.25 a growing impatience began to develop into a deep-down dread. Perhaps she was not coming. By 4.30 he was conjuring up all kinds of reasons why she had not turned up. Illness? An accident? Accidents didn't always happen to other people. Or maybe his visit to her home had not gone down as well as it seemed, and only Thai courtesy and his convenient journey north had delayed the end of their friendship. Or perhaps it was Doungjai herself. Maybe she had had second thoughts about his behaviour in the hotel room and decided he was less of a gentleman than he appeared.

These and other unpalatable thoughts tumbled in his mind as the minute hand moved up towards five o'clock. He bought an orange juice to justify his continued stay at the window table, but only toyed with it before pushing the container away.

By 5.15 he knew it was useless to linger on. He had been there over an hour and in that time the nearby tables had been occupied and vacated several times. It was ironic that, in all his planning for their remaining time together, the only possibility he had not foreseen was Doungjai's failure to keep their date.

Feeling sick with disappointment, he bent down to pick up the gaily-coloured umbrella he had bought for her in Chiang Mai. It had fallen to the floor but, as he reached for it, he sensed that someone was approaching him at a stumbling run.

'Lobut, I here!'

In his relief, he almost fell over the umbrella scrambling to his feet.

'Doungjai!' he exclaimed, moving to hug her, but stopping short as he remembered it wasn't quite the done thing in this part of the world. 'I thought you weren't coming.'

'I very sorry, but . . .' She broke off with a gulping sob. She was breathing hard and looked hot and dishevelled.

'What's wrong,' he said. 'Come and sit down.'

He ushered her into a seat and sat down next to her. Instead of her school clothes she was wearing a dark cotton dress of indeterminate shape. Robert thought she had never looked more appealing. And yet something was clearly very much amiss.

'Oh, Lobut . . .' The tears started to gather like great liquid jewels and she grabbed his hands and squeezed them. 'What is it? What's happened?'

'Sorry I late, but . . . ' She hesitated only for another second. 'Lobut . . . Grandpapa, him dead.'

Robert was genuinely shattered. He drew her to him till her head was resting on his shoulder.

'Doungjai, I'm so sorry.'

She was sobbing now, her whole body shaking. 'Lobut, I love him very much.'

'I know . . . I know.' He had no idea what to say, or how to console her. Aside from which, his own emotions were threatening to overwhelm him. 'Look – er, would you like something to drink?'

'No, thank you.' She pulled away. 'Maybe we go for walk?'

Anyone not privy to their conversation might have supposed them to be making up after a quarrel. As they stood up, Robert held her hand tenderly, trying to convey the extent to which he shared her loss.

The late afternoon heat engulfed them as they emerged from McDonalds and turned left down Silom Road. Crossing the westbound lane was hazardous at any time, but at rush hour on a Friday afternoon, it could be lethal. It was fortunate that their parents were not around to see them dart across to the central reservation behind a bus, inches ahead of a speeding taxi and two racing *tuk tuks*. Robert had no idea where they were going, but sensed that Doungjai had a destination in mind.

As they walked, his thoughts were of the old man he had met for the first and only time less than a week before. He recalled snatches of their conversation, as when he had talked about the importance of memories: '. . . *as you get older and your time begins to run out.*' Did he suspect even then that he had only days to live?

Above all else, what had endeared him so much to

118

Robert, was his patently deep love for his grand-daughter. In this respect above all he empathised with the old man, for he knew now, without any doubt, young though he was, that he too loved this beautiful girl who pattered along at his side.

After about ten minutes, Doungjai slowed and Robert saw they had reached Soi 24.

'Silom Village,' she announced. 'We go in?'

Silom Village was a small complex of stalls, stores and cafes linked by tight passages and winding paths. Robert remembered that Doungjai had mentioned it to his mother, when they first met, and he followed her along a narrow lane until they emerged into a tiny square. Doungjai made for a restaurant that stood back in one corner.

'This place I like,' she stated. 'We sit here for little time.'

'Why not?' Robert said.

The interior was dimly lit, cosy and still empty at this time of day. Robert steered Doungjai towards a table in the corner and sat beside her. They ordered two fresh orange juices.

The walk seemed to have helped Doungjai master her grief, and she was now more her normal self. She clearly wanted to talk but, as she gave Robert more details, her voice grew weepy again.

'It happened Tuesday, three days before today,' she told him. 'I no long come home from school and Mama gone for shopping with my brother and sister. I sit outside with Grandpapa, we talk, him and me. Him very tired and ask me for drink. When I come back, him have problem with breathing.' She made a gasping sound in imitation.

'I very worried, ask him what to do, but he no hear. I take him like this.' She held out her arms in a hugging action. 'I try to hold him because him nearly fall off his chair.' The tears began to gather as she re-lived the painful memory. 'Then he lie back.' She gave a demonstration of going limp and let her head fall to one side. 'I take his hand and he squeeze mine little bit, then . . . then . . . finish. Oh, Lobut, him die very quickly and I no help him.'

Robert felt as helpless as Doungjai must have done seeing her grandfather die in her arms. Until this moment, death had never touched his young life and he could not imagine how he would have reacted in her place.

'It must have been terrible, but try to think of all the happy times you had with him.' Something her grandfather had said gave him a lead. 'When we were talking the other day, he said how important it is to hold onto memories.'

His words seemed to help and she looked at him slightly surprised.

'He say that?' she said, snuffling.

'Honestly, and remember, although it's terrible to lose him, he did not have a painful illness or suffer for a long time. And he was with you when he died. I don't think he would have wanted it any other way.'

'You really think so, Lobut?'

'I'm sure of it, and I'm also sure he wouldn't want you to be unhappy after he had gone.' Robert produced a handkerchief which she took gratefully and mopped her eyes.

'This morning, they put Grandpapa on the fire. He have many friends who come, then after they leave we go home and Mama she cry, so I stay with her. This is why I come late to meet you, Lobut, sorry.'

Robert berated himself inwardly for his insensitivity. Until this moment, it had not occurred to him that Doungjai had left her family grieving and travelled halfway across Bangkok to meet him.

'It's me who should be sorry.' He hastened to explain. 'I was so concerned that you hadn't come to meet me, and then so relieved to see you I didn't stop to think that you ought to be at home now with your family. Please forgive me, Doungjai. I'll take you home right away.'

'Forgive, not necessary. Mama say I must come and meet you because I promise. She OK now, very sad, yes, but OK.'

'I do appreciate that, but I still think you should be at home with your mother tonight, much as I want to be with you.'

'And tomorrow?'

'Yes?' He had made so many plans for their last two days, but now he was not sure how, or even if, he should pursue them.

She came to his rescue. 'You want to see me, Lobut?'

'Very much, but what about your mother and family? Don't you think you ought to be with them?'

'I be with them next week when you gone. Tomorrow I want to be with you, Lobut.'

Not for the first time her decisiveness surprised him, but what about his parents' suggestion that they should all go out together?

'Since tomorrow night is our last one in Bangkok, my mother and father asked me to invite you to join them for dinner. Of course they will understand if you would rather not in the circumstances.'

'They want me to have dinner with them?' She looked astonished. 'Where you eat dinner, Lobut?'

He wondered if she was teasing him. 'I'll be there as well. That is unless you would rather I didn't come.'

The touch of repartee lightened the atmosphere, and she managed a faint smile. 'Perhaps better you no come and then I ask your mama all about your girl friends in England.'

He was pleased to see her loosening up. It reflected no disrespect for her grandfather, more her youthful emotional resilience. Again her expression changed, and a small frown creased her brow.

'Lobut, I no have something to wear for tomorrow night.'

It was the kind of feminine remark that Robert found completely incomprehensible and was a reminder of how complex girls were, even from an early age.

'What do you mean?' he asked.

'I never go out to dinner before with English lady and gentleman. I want to look nice, but no have clothes.'

'What about that yellow jacket and skirt you wore when we went out last week? That looked terrific.'

'But you seen before, Lobut. Tomorrow, last night, is special. I want to wear something different for you but no have.'

Robert could only shake his head in disbelief. 'Look, whatever you wear, I know you'll look just great.'

Over a second orange juice, they arranged to meet the following afternoon early and shop together for souvenirs of Bangkok, for Robert's collection back home. He remembered the umbrella he had bought for her.

'What you look for?' Doungjai asked, when he bent down to check under the seat.

'Your present. It's an . . . oh, *no*! I left it on the seat in McDonalds!'

122

'We go back,' she decided.

'I'll go back,' he said. 'You're going home.'

For once she didn't argue. They walked back up Silom Road towards Patpong, where they hailed a taxi. The usual furious haggling took place as Doungjai insisted on a 'good plice'.

As the wheeler-dealing was concluded, Robert raised his arm in farewell.

'Wait!' she said. This was followed by a barked command to the driver, then she beckoned Robert to bend down so that she could speak into his ear.

'I forget to tell you, but when I with Grandpapa just before him die, we talk about you. He say I very lucky to have nice boyfriend like you.' She stretched up and kissed him lightly on the cheek. 'I think I very lucky also. See you tomorrow.'

Robert watched in a daze as the taxi pulled away and its lights merged into the endless stream of traffic. Quite subconsciously, his fingers touched the spot where her kiss had landed.

Chapter Seventeen

They agreed to meet in the open space in front of the World Trade Centre building which stood on the opposite corner from the Erawan Shrine. Robert had suggested early afternoon, partly to allow Doungjai to spend some of the day at home, partly because he had to make an important purchase and wanted to use the morning to look around.

She was seated under a tree waiting for him when he arrived and, still not entirely at ease in public places, they greeted each other with a rather diffident handshake. She was dressed casually, in a black, long-sleeved blouse, tucked into the almost regulation pale blue denims as worn by ninety per cent of young Thais.

Robert asked after her family.

'All well, thank you,' she said, rather formally. 'You mother and father well also?'

'Er . . . yes, fine.'

No mention was made of the sad event that had overshadowed their meeting the previous evening.

Robert presented her with the umbrella he had retrieved from McDonald's.

'Thank you.' She opened it. 'Can use for sun,' she giggled, spinning it on her shoulder like a geisha girl. 'You very kind, Lobut.'

'It's nothing really,' he said. 'Shall we go, then?'

When she turned and walked ahead of him, Robert couldn't help noticing how the tight-fitting denim outlined the plump cheeks of her bottom. He wondered if she realised just how sexy she looked from this angle.

Doungjai had already earmarked Pratunam Market for their shopping expedition and they wended their way down Ratchaprarop Road after passing under the flyover. Here, the pavements were chock-full of stalls, end to end on the curbside as well as down the inside of the pavement, wherever they did not actually cause an obstruction to the permanent shop entrances. Doungjai and Robert made slow headway, stopping every few yards to look at something that caught their eyes, before moving on towards the complex of stalls in the narrow, crowded alleyways close to the honeycomb walls of the Indra Regent Hotel.

'I think nice lady's dress shop this way,' she said, as they passed the umpteenth clothes stall. 'We go in, OK?'

'You want to buy a dress?'

She nodded. 'Something special for tonight.'

He dutifully trailed along, content just to be with her and observe the things that took her interest. Eventually, in the heart of the market, they came to a stall that specialised in women's dresses and Doungjai began a systematic search, fingering her way through the ranks of different styles, colours and materials that hung from flimsy metal rails. Occasionally she pulled something out for a closer scrutiny and discussed it with the assistant who hovered at her shoulder throughout.

From time to time, she looked across at Robert and smiled before returning to veto yet another candidate. He stood between two racks of dresses with a long-suffering grin pasted on his face. In the narrow passageway a constant stream of shoppers and traders trudged past, many of them hauling trolleys or humping loads that were too wide for the gap, yet somehow they managed to squeeze through.

'No have,' Doungjai was forced to admit at last and looked around, uncertain where to go next.

'Isn't there a department store beneath the hotel,' Robert suggested a trifle desperately. 'Let's see if they've what you're looking for.'

'Department store expensive,' she observed predictably.

'Let's look anyway,' he urged, his patience almost at its limit.

With some reluctance, Doungjai left the stall whose wares she had dissected with such clinical efficiency. The assistant shrugged and attached herself to another browser.

The department store beneath the Indra Regent was air-conditioned. As they entered, a wonderful blanket of cool air enveloped them. Doungjai steered a path round the stocked counters with a sureness that suggested it was not her first visit, expensive though it may be. The store had a much wider selection of dresses than the stall, and they were better displayed, many on lifelike dummies.

'That looks very nice.' He indicated a white creation draped round a stone-faced *papier-maché* model.

Doungjai consulted the price tag and quickly moved on without comment. Several other garments received the same perfunctory treatment and Robert could see they would get nowhere if price were the deciding criterion. He had already made a secret vow never again to go shopping for clothes with a girl.

'What are you looking for?' he pleaded at last.

'Look for pretty dress, but not expensive.'

'I still like that first one we saw.'

'Like, but . . .' Doungjai backtracked along the rail and sought out the price tag again. She presented it to him, as to a backward child. 'Five hundred fifty bahts. I only have three hundred.'

Robert saw a ray of hope at last. 'Then let me pay the extra.'

She shook her head. 'Too much money, Lobut. You pay everything for me.'

'But I want to. Why not try it on? If it fits and you like it, I'll pay the extra. If not, we'll go back and look in the market again.' He mentally crossed his fingers as he spoke.

'But . . .'

'No buts, come on.' He was already signalling an assistant.

Doungjai was ushered into one of the changing rooms while Robert mopped his brow and prayed the dress would fit. To put an end to this torment he would have paid the whole lot.

When she reappeared, smiling shyly and holding out her arms questioningly, Robert could only stare in astonishment. Although the dress was designed for someone older, all the ingredients – colour, style, size – suited her as if it had been tailor made.

She knew it too, but his approval was very important to her.

'What you think?'

'I think it's perfect,' he said without hesitation. 'It looks as if it was made for you.' He turned to the sales assistant who, while not understanding the words was in tune with the sentiment, nodded agreement.

It was tight-fitting and hugged her waist, hips and bottom like a second skin. The hemline came just above her knees and although the neckline dipped to a discreet V, just above the start of her cleavage, Doungjai still questioned it.

'No think this too impolite?' she queried.

Robert shook his head, still amazed. 'I think you look a knockout,' he insisted.

'Knock out?'

'Marvellous.' He was already feeling for the cash in his hip pocket. Decisive action was called for.

'We'll take it,' he informed the assistant before Doungjai could raise any further doubts.

The purchase behind them, they had a coffee and doughnut at the Dunkin' Donut before parting.

'Need time for shower and get hair done,' Doungjai explained.

For once she appeared almost impatient to get away, lured by the prospect of dressing up for the evening ahead.

On his way back to the hotel, Robert reflected on his conversation with Doungjai in the Dunkin' Donut.

'You too kind to me,' she had said almost sadly. 'Always you give to me, but I no give to you.'

'Yes, you do,' he had demurred. 'You give me your company, and I get more pleasure from just looking at you than from any gift you could buy me, whatever it cost.'

'You mean that, Lobut?'

'More than anything in the world.'

'I try to look nice tonight, make you proud of me when we have dinner with your mama and papa.'

'I feel proud every moment I'm with you.'

At the time the words had the ring of a reflex response, but in the taxi on his own Robert realised how true they really were.

*   *   *

For the first time since arriving in Thailand, Robert wore the dark blue blazer his mother had packed. His shirt was new, a pale blue silk made to measure at a few hours' notice by an Indian tailor, a block away from the hotel. The grey flannels were a product of the same tailor, and he even opted for shoes instead of trainers. Doungjai wouldn't know how honoured she was. He fleetingly considered the tie his mother had bought for him at Jim Thompson's, but decided it would be too hot.

To make sure, he took the unusual step of asking his mother to give him the once over, something always avoided at home. A lot had changed since they had left England.

'Very smart,' his mother approved, without gushing. Privately she was impressed. She had never known him to pay so much attention to his appearance.

In a few days, Robert's education had widened immeasurably in a number of ways, not least his understanding of girls, although he had still not come to appreciate their chameleon natures. Apparently without effort, they were able to change their appearance completely by altering the style or colour of their hair, by wearing a new outfit, or applying different make-up. Doungjai was no exception, as she proved when she came striding out of the revolving door, oozing a panache she was probably far from feeling.

His heart missed a beat. He had already seen her in the new white dress in the department store, but without the two butterfly broaches pinned to the bodice, joined by a gold chain, and without the pearl-clustered, pendant earrings and matching necklace.

They had probably only cost a few bahts from one of the many jewellery stalls in Mah Boon Krong or Banglumpoo, but the effect was out of all proportion to their value. Most striking of all, though, was her hair piled high and lush in shiny, jet black coils.

She spotted him at once and seemed to glide across the foyer on her high-heeled pumps which, together with the hairstyle, elevated her to his height.

'Hello, Lobut,' she greeted him happily. 'You look very smart.' She leant closer and whispered. 'And very handsome.'

'And you look . . .' He searched furiously for the right words knowing nothing would be adequate. 'Fabulous.' Adding, more prosaically: 'You've had your hair done.'

'You like?' Her eyes reflected a hint of uncertainty. 'After I leave you, I go see my friend who do my hair for me. Only one hundred fifty bahts. I borrow from Mama.'

'I can't tell you how wonderful you look.' His voice was hoarse.

At that moment his mother and father arrived. They had only seen Doungjai in casual clothes previously and Robert was amused and pleased to note they were as astonished as he was by her transformation.

'You look lovely, Doungjai,' Mary Stone complimented and kissed her instinctively on the cheek, a rare gesture for her. 'Doesn't she, Brian?'

Her husband, looking mildly starstruck, nodded enthusiastic agreement.

'Mama say I have too much make-up and hair too much grown up.' She touched her hair, glowing with the compliments. 'I tell her I must look special for dinner with my friends from England.'

Satisfied with the visual impact she had made, she turned the spotlight on Robert, taking his hand. 'I tell Lobut he look very smart and very handsome.' She gave Brian a wicked smile. 'Just like his papa.'

'Don't encourage them, Doungjai,' Mary warned. 'Men are vain enough without any help from us'.

His parents expressed their sympathy for the loss of her grandfather, which Doungjai accepted with quiet dignity, eyes lowered. But as they chatted away in the lobby like old friends, Robert stood back a little, mentally, and marvelled that this lovely, sepia-skinned girl in white – wide eyed, eager and smiling – was *his* girl; that she loved him. But even as he congratulated himself on his good fortune, his mind turned to a small, barely furnished room a few miles away, with a curtained-off section – a room where this same girl lived and slept and dreamed. The realisation that such beauty, poise and contentment had developed and flourished in that humble home filled him with wonder and admiration.

'Shall we go, Robert?' His father broke into his thoughts and ushered the small party towards the door. Mary and Doungjai led the way, continuing to chat away like two old friends.

'Are you sure she's only fifteen?' Robert's father said to him softly as they brought up the rear.

Robert shook his head. 'Not even that. Her birthday isn't till next month.'

Brian Stone shook his head too, but from disbelief.

Thence by taxi to the Oriental Hotel where, like so many before them, they were impressed by the age-less grandeur and elegance that had echoed to the footsteps of the rich and famous, including the likes of Somerset Maugham, Joseph Conrad and Noel Coward.

Emerging at the far side of the hotel, overlooking the Chaophrya River, they skirted a large open space where an enormous buffet was being prepared and dozens of tables, covered in crisp white linen and gleaming cutlery, waited for the diners to arrive. A path took them down to a tiny jetty and they climbed aboard a small ferry boat that cast off almost immediately. It chugged slowly across to the uniquely-styled building standing on the opposite bank.

In a city where the best of the world's cuisine could be enjoyed at an incredibly low price, Le Sala brought to the tourist a flavour of Thai cuisine and culture in a comfort and style affordable to almost anyone. Some diners sat outside, with a view over the river, but the real Le Sala lay within. Footwear was required to be removed at the entrance. The seating arrangements were unusual: the table tops rose only a foot above the floor and the space beneath them was hollowed out for the diners' legs. So it was possible to sit at the table normally, even though one ate at virtual floor level. The purpose of this plan was to oblige the waiters and waitresses to kneel in traditional Thai style to serve the food.

Le Sala was the perfect setting for the Stones' last night in Bangkok and yet for Robert the occasion, spent in such splendid surroundings in the company of the three most important people in the world, was tinged with sadness. The time for last farewells was rushing towards them and was unstoppable.

During the meal he left most of the talking to the other three, his eyes on Doungjai, subconsciously storing up a picture in his mind to draw upon when they were no longer together. For several days now, something else about Doungjai had been increasingly troubling him, especially since that evening in his room. Seeing her the way she looked tonight only increased that feeling immeasurably.

If she shared any of Robert's dolour, Doungjai gave no outward sign. On the contrary, she appeared to be having a wonderful time, without reservation or restraint. She chattered almost non-stop. She had views on every subject that came up, and was only constrained by the limitations in her command of English. Throughout, she displayed a charm, elegance and maturity that belied her tender years.

Although nothing had been said or planned beforehand, it seemed perfectly natural for Doungjai and Robert to part company with his parents when they stepped off the ferry in front of the Oriental.

'Don't be too late, will you, Robert?' his mother cautioned. 'You want to be fresh to enjoy tomorrow and, remember, you won't get much sleep on the flight tomorrow night.'

As they parted, Mary and Brian Stone again congratulated Doungjai on how lovely she looked and, as the two young people walked away ahead of them, Brian remarked with some pride: 'Now I know our son takes after his father.'

'What do you mean?' Mary asked.

'Simply that he has an eye for beautiful women.'

'Brian Stone, I regard that as a compliment.' She took him by the arm and led him into the hotel. 'For that I'll let you buy me a drink in the bar and then . . .' Her eyes twinkled mischievously, 'you might get a nightcap yourself later.'

As they retraced their steps through the Oriental, Doungjai suddenly asked. 'You OK, Lobut? You no speak much tonight.'

So she had noticed. He stopped and took her

hands, while he came to a decision. 'I was just admiring the most beautiful girl in the whole world who happened to be sitting opposite me during dinner tonight.' These were sincere sentiments. They were also a delaying tactic.

'Oh, Lobut . . .' For once Doungjai was tongue-tied by his flattery.

'As a matter of fact, I was thinking about something else as well.'

She looked at him expectantly, innocently, waiting for him to elaborate.

'The two things are connected,' he added as if that explained everything.

To Doungjai he was talking in riddles.

'What you mean?'

After a quick glance around, Robert guided her towards a couple of easy chairs where they could talk without any fear of being overheard, and began, haltingly at first, then with growing confidence, to explain what he had in mind.

Chapter Eighteen

Robert felt that his head had barely touched the pillow before the 'beep, beep' of his alarm clock was dragging him awake again at an uncivilised five a.m. Knowing his own anathema for early rising, he had had the foresight to place the clock out of reach the night before. To silence it, he was forced to leave his bed. As he lurched across to the chest of drawers, he remembered why he had done this foolish thing.

He staggered through to the bathroom, cleaned his teeth and took a quick shower, but as the tiredness was washed away it was replaced by a rapidly growing sense of unease. It had seemed such a good idea the night before. Risky for sure, and perhaps a bit underhand, but still worth going through with. Now he was less convinced. If there was any way back, he might have been tempted to take it.

The moment of self-doubt quickly passed. He strapped on his watch, which now read 5.09, and drew on a short-sleeved cotton shirt and shorts. He thrust his feet into the trainers that had covered countless miles of Bangkok streets and tugged a comb through his hair. Before leaving the room he cast a last glance round. A few items of clothing were lying about so he bundled these up and consigned them to his open suitcase. His last act was to tidy the bed.

He peered out into the passage and was not

surprised to find it empty. He was about to draw the door closed behind him when he remembered his key was still in the room. To have shut himself out would have put an end to his grand scheme. Tut-tutting under his breath, he retrieved the key from his bedside and used it to turn the lock and soften the sound of the tongue snapping back.

He headed down the passage towards the emergency fire exit at the far end. The locking bar was stiff and needed a sharp smack with the heel of his hand. He winced at the noise and stepped out into a bleak landing that still smelt of recently mixed cement. Bare concrete stairs led up and down. He wedged the emergency door open with a book of matches, to ensure re-entry by the same route, before beginning his descent, two steps at a time.

Outside it was still dark. Mounted lights illuminated the rear and side of the hotel. He hoped Bangkok hotels didn't use closed circuit TV, otherwise he might be taken for a prowler.

A second book of matches was precisely positioned to safeguard his access. Then he was off, trotting the fifty yards to the corner of the hotel, where he stopped and peered up the footpath that ran along the side of the building. This part of the hotel grounds was virgin territory to him, but something else was unfamiliar and it took him a moment to work out what it was: apart from the subdued hum that every sleeping city emanates, all was silent. The never-ending, never-varying boom of traffic that was Bangkok's daytime signature tune, was absent. Even the great metropolis slept some time it seemed, if briefly and fitfully. In less than an hour it would be back to full revs as the countless thousands made their way to work for yet another day.

He looked at his watch: 5.13. He had suggested 5.15 and hoped she would be able to follow his directions. He would have preferred to meet her at the front of the hotel, but to be seen standing around there at this time of the morning would have been a giveaway. He felt guilty putting the onus so heavily on Doungjai, but he had been unable to improve upon his initial stratagem in the short time available and she, bless her, had not minded.

A delivery van swung round the corner and came down the service road just as Robert's watch showed the quarter hour. It chugged past him and pulled into a loading bay beyond the emergency exit. He was glad to see the two occupants disappear into the rear of the hotel, without a second glance his way, and even more relieved when he looked back up the side of the hotel to see a familiar figure appear at the far end.

He waved and Doungjai waved back, and hurried towards him. She wore a white long-sleeved shirt and blue jeans and might have been going on a local shopping trip instead of a clandestine tryst with her aspiring lover.

'Hello, Lobut,' she greeted him in a hushed voice. 'You wait long time for me?'

'Only a couple of minutes,' he whispered back. 'Did you have any problems?'She shook her head. 'Told mama I meet you very early because we have lot to do on last day before you leave Bangkok. She understand.' A nervous giggle. 'I think.'

'Let's go then,' Robert said, casting nervous glances all about.

He guided her towards the emergency exit at a fast walk. The ground floor emergency door was as he had left it and they slipped inside, relieved to be out of sight of inquisitive eyes. They climbed the concrete stairs to the fifth floor in silence. Robert opened the emergency door a couple of inches and checked out the passage.

'All clear,' he hissed.

He took Doungjai's hand and drew her towards his bedroom door. Unlocking it, he pulled her inside, then eased the door shut behind them. He groped across to the bed and switched on the bedside lamp. Phase one of his plan had been accomplished without a hitch. Ever mindful that his parents were sleeping only the thickness of the wall away, Robert touched a raised forefinger to his lip, to warn Doungjai to keep her voice down. She nodded her understanding and their eyes met. The guilt he had felt when he was showering earlier returned. For his own gratification he was putting her through this ordeal, perhaps against her will and better judgement, using their friendship and the imminence of his departure as weapons of persuasion.

'Would you like something to drink?' he asked softly.

'No thank you.' She broke the threatening stalemate with a simple suggestion. 'Can I take shower, please?'

'Yes, of course. There are plenty of towels in the bathroom. Be quiet though. Don't wake the neighbours.'

She didn't understand the joke, but smiled uncertainly and moved to pass him. He restrained her gently.

'Are you sure you're OK?' he asked softly.

The tension in her seemed to ease. 'I fine, Lobut. I happy because I with you.' It was a simple but reassuring statement. 'I only be five minutes.'

As soon as she was out of his sight, Robert's uncertainty returned. Since that first evening she had come up to his room, the memory of her body continued to haunt him. Quite simply, he wanted to see and touch her again, all over. An overnight stay had been out of the question, which was why he had conceived this idea of an early morning rendezvous. It was clumsy, even a little crazy, but it was the best he could come up with in their present circumstances.

The sound of running water in the bathroom spurred him into action. He pulled off his shirt and shorts and kicked off his trainers, leaving only his underpants on. He hesitated, then took the plunge. In for a penny, off with his pants. He dived under the bedclothes. It was one thing to be stark naked, it was quite another to expose himself.

His heart, already beating fast, accelerated when the shower stopped. A short silence was followed by the sound of the bathroom door opening. She emerged, cocooned in his bath towel. The towel was pulled tight under her armpits, tucked in to hold it in place, and hung to below her knees. He had hoped for full exposure and was slightly disappointed, if not surprised. She did not look at him as she walked around the bed and pulled back the covers. As she sat on the edge of the bed with her back to him, he noticed that her arms and shoulders were still sheened with damp.

'It's all right,' he said, in what he hoped was a reassuring voice. 'Don't be afraid.'

He patted the bed by way of invitation. Keeping the towel firmly wrapped round her, she lifted her feet and lay down beside him looking up at the ceiling. She still did not speak, but there was a fragile smile on her lips as her face turned towards him when he eased himself onto one elbow to look down

139

at her. Her expression seemed to say, 'Your move next'.

Rightly, the initiative lay with him. After briefly placing his hand on her thigh over the towel, he pulled back the rest of the bedclothes in a single decisive sweep. Now he was naked to her gaze if she cared to look down. It was another first, for although he had changed and showered at school after gym, he had been among members of his own sex. Now, not only was his penis on display, but it was as stiff as a poker. No one, but no one, had ever seen him with an erection. Perversely, this made him become even bolder and more excited.

If Doungjai saw the evidence of his excitement out of the corner of her eye, she kept it to herself, holding his gaze while his hand crept up to the top of the towel and gently pulled the edge. When he drew the ends of the towel open, her arms lay limply by her sides.

All feelings of guilt, anxiety and doubt fled when he at last surveyed her naked girl flesh, with all its firm peaks, sensuous curves and secret hollows laid out before him. He was instantly certain that his clandestine planning had been worth it a thousandfold.

As he gazed in awe, unsure where or what to touch first, only his erection, jerking and swelling further, betrayed his feelings. Now Doungjai raised her arms, freeing the towel completely. Her breathing quickened slightly when he toyed almost reverentially with her nipples before ever so gently squeezing the incredibly firm and exciting swell of her breasts, almost afraid of damaging them. They were much bigger than he had imagined, and he was entranced by the proud pointed cones.

Growing bolder, he bent lower and prodded at

each nipple with his tongue, until they were moist and rubbery hard, while his hand slid down over her ribs and belly to its inevitable destination. God, how smooth and wonderful her body skin felt – like warm stretched velvet. Doungjai gave a little sigh when his hand reached her pubic mound and moved beyond to her soft, hairless vaginal lips. She seemed as unsure as he in this first male exploration of her body, but instinctively eased her thighs apart, inviting an even more intimate exploration. Simultaneously, she reached for his penis and squeezed it tenderly.

'Willy?' she whispered with a slightly wicked smile.

Robert could not reply. He was speechless in his ecstasy.

Time became a forgotten dimension as they played with each other's genitals, teasing and caressing, completely absorbed in their first brush with sex. Eager to explore even more of her fresh young body, Robert eased his hand under her bottom and carefully rolled her over onto her tummy. He had admired the full, tempting curves that jiggled within the skin-tight constraints of her jeans. Now the plump cheeks of her teenage bottom were at his mercy, to ogle and fondle.

In turning over, Doungjai had released his penis; now she grasped it anew and felt it pulsate in her hand. He shuddered and stroked her ripe buttocks, working his fingers into the deep cleft between them.

Doungjai stirred and gave another little sigh. 'Lobut, you touch naughty place,' she protested without conviction, contradictorily thrusting her bottom upwards enticingly.

'You don't like me touching you there?'

'Like, but naughty.'

'So what?' he breathed. 'I want to touch every part of you.'

'I tell you before, my ass too fat,' she responded in a voice muffled by her position.

'I think it's the loveliest "ass" in the world,' he insisted and continued with his intimate probing.

'Lobut, you make me feel funny,' Doungjai at last protested weakly.

Robert relented and let her turn onto her back again before kneeling between her thighs. She took hold of his erection with both hands this time and, squeezing it gently, rubbed it against the lips of her vagina. Robert lowered his weight and tried to push inside her.

This was completely new territory and he knew only what he had heard and read, backed by instinct. He had not intended to go this far when he asked Doungjai up to his room but he was learning that the process, once started, acquires an impetus of its own, and there was an inevitability about the sequence which followed. Nothing else mattered and Doungjai seemed equally engrossed. This was what men and women were made for and he was going to do it.

Yet when he pushed into the angle of her thighs, nothing moved. Surely he was supposed to slide up inside her? Again he pressed, but still made no headway. There seemed to be no entry. It was impossible.

Doungjai tried to guide him, but with no more success and when she gave a little cry of pain, he retreated. All he was succeeding in doing was hurting her and his passion was giving way to embarrassment.

'I'm sorry, but I can't get it in,' he gasped, unable to look Doungjai in the eyes. 'I thought it would go in easily.'

'Never mind, plenty time,' she soothed.

'But why? What's wrong?' In his frustration his voice shot up.

'I think maybe it more difficult when first time for girl. This my first time, Lobut.'

'It's my first time as well,' Robert confessed, 'But I never thought it would be so difficult.'

'No worry, we try again and I help you,' Doungjai offered.

Robert positioned his lower body with great precision between her thighs. He was determined to get it right this time, but instead disaster struck almost immediately. Doungjai had taken his penis between her fingers and was rubbing up and down the shaft. It felt wonderful, except that her technique was rather more effective than she had intended. With a groan Robert ejected his white, milky sperm all over her belly in great spurts; almost immediately his penis began to return to its normal flaccid condition and his lust slackened with it.

He lay full length on top of her, his head tucked under her chin, partly to recover from his climax and partly to hide his shame. This was one incident that definitely would not be relayed back to his pals.

'I'm sorry,' he apologised weakly when the tension had subsided. 'I . . . I . . .'

'It's all right, Lobut, my fault,' she insisted. 'I squeeze too much, sorry.' She put her arms round him and held him tightly on top of her.

They had never been closer than in these ebbing moments of anti-climax. For all that Doungjai was a virgin, she seemed to know how men performed and how to deal with "accidents" such as had just happened to him. They lay like that for quite a while, content in each other's embrace. Presently, Robert pulled himself up and used the discarded bath towel to wipe the stickiness from Doungjai's belly and his own loins. Then he pulled up the bedclothes and they cuddled up to each other, Doungjai's back pressed against Robert's chest, her bottom snuggling into his stomach. His penis, held trapped between her thighs, began to stir. He looped his arm over her shoulder and held one firm breast lightly in his hand; his other hand combing lazily through her pubic hair making occasional forays along her vaginal lips. In this way, like two spoons, completely relaxed and content, they dozed off.

Robert awoke with a jolt and for a few seconds his mind was a blank. While he slept he had drawn away from Doungjai, although her head was still cradled in his arm. Her gentle breathing showed that she was still asleep. Trying not to disturb her, he eased his head round to check on the time and instantly froze: it was 7.45!

Outside it was bright daylight, and the traffic was going flat out. The hotel would be in full swing – breakfasts being served, rooms being cleaned . . . His movement woke Doungjai. She stirred and opened her eyes. They were sultry from sleep, and comprehending of nothing beyond the nearness of her youthful lover.

'We must get up,' he whispered loudly. 'We've been asleep for two hours.'His mind was now fully functioning and he was already plotting their next move. In a perfect world he would have been content to lay alongside her hot, naked body forever, but the danger of discovery was competing strongly with this physical heaven. He knew it would have to end, and soon, but his will power was weak and the spell of Doungjai's presence too strong.

She sensed his dilemma. 'What time is it?'

'Nearly eight o'clock. I'm sorry, but we really must get up.' To soften the blow, he leaned forward and kissed her lightly on the lips. Words seemed unnecessary to express his feelings. 'I'll go and have a shower and you can lie here a bit longer.'

Without waiting for her reply, he swung himself out of the bed and headed for the bathroom.

His mind was in a whirl as he stood under the hot spray. Notwithstanding the threads of doubt and guilt that threatened to intrude yet again, and his failure to consummate their relationship, the overwhelming sensation was one of tremendous satisfaction. Even without the carnal knowledge, Doungjai had already become the most important thing in his life: the knowledge of her body, its texture, its warmth and all its secret places had been beyond his wildest imagination.

The shower curtain slid back and Doungjai stood there, honey-gold and naked. She was smiling, still a little sleepily, but her intention was clear.

'Can I have shower also?' she asked and climbed in without waiting for his consent.

All shyness and pretence was gone as they soaped each other's bodies from shoulders to knees. Under Robert's eager hands, Doungjai's skin became slippery soft and he missed no part of her anatomy, down from her breasts and their pointedly excited nipples, to her pubic hair and between her legs. Turning her round he lathered her back, working down to the full swell of her bottom and the cleft that bisected it.

Doungjai reciprocated by taking his solid, eager penis in both hands and slowly soaping it until he spurted once more. Satiated and spent, Robert stood still while she directed the shower all over him to remove the soap. He returned the compliment before stepping out and retiring to the bedroom, leaving her to dry and dress.

She had travelled light. No accessories, only the clothes she came in.

'Ready?' he asked, as she came out of the bathroom, zipping her jeans. She nodded. He opened the door and did a swift reconnoitre. No one was about in their passage. Hand in hand, they dashed for the lift. Robert had already decided not to leave by the emergency exit; they were going out via the front door, no matter what.

The lobby was bustling as usual and this worked in their favour. No one gave them a second glance. Robert had already told his parents that he would be meeting Doungjai very early, but had promised to be back at the hotel in good time for their departure. They had not objected, in spite of some concern over his leaving the hotel on this, the last day of their stay. The thought of missing the flight did not bear thinking about.

Hand in hand, they set off from the hotel lobby into the sunlit streets of Bangkok for their final day together.

Chapter Nineteen

The Stone family had a good run to the airport along the expressway and the taxi drew in to the letting-down point at ten minutes before eight. Robert grabbed a trolley and, after checking the TV monitor, his father manoeuvred his party through the fast-growing crowd towards the check-in desk.

'There's Doungjai,' Robert exclaimed, as he spotted her small figure tucked away into a corner by the main entrance.

She spotted the Stones simultaneously and hurried forward to greet them. She was wearing the bright yellow suit with the dark blue piping from the night she and Robert dined at the Tum Nak Thai Restaurant. The outfit would always remind Robert of their first, abortive, sexual encounter in his hotel room.

'I love your suit,' Mary smiled approvingly.

'I think better in bright colour, so you see me,' Doungjai explained, ever logical, ever practical.

Robert wanted to hug her. Instead, he asked: 'Did your brother bring you?'. 'Yes, him wait for me over there. Him shy – same like me.' She gave her infectious giggle and gestured vaguely towards the distant seats.

'Doesn't he mind waiting?'

'No mind.'

Being early at the airport meant they were near the

front of the queue and the formalities of checking in were speedily completed.

'How much time do we have, Dad?' Robert asked when they were left with only their hand luggage.

'I think we should go through to the Departure Lounge by 9.30.' His father looked at his watch. 'In a little over an hour. Your mother and I are going up to the Coffee Shop. Do you two want to come with us?'

Robert shook his head. 'I think we'll go and sit over there if you don't mind. Can we meet you back here?'

'All right, but no later than 9.30,' his mother stressed. 'We can't afford to be late when our flight is called. We'll see you later, Doungjai.'

Robert eased the small zip-up holdall more comfortably onto his shoulder and took Doungjai's hand. Their outwardly calm, unhurried progress through the crowds towards the seats at one end of the building belied their bottled-up feelings. The effects of their long day were also beginning to tell on them, which together with the thought of Robert's impending departure was a further dulling influence on their spirits.

Their final day had been as enjoyable as it could be, given their impending separation. After their early morning endeavours in Robert's bed, they had breakfasted well, without any misgivings or regrets. In fact, they had openly talked about the experience. Doungjai, displaying a tact and sensitivity beyond her years, had even converted Robert's premature release into a virtue by reminding him that a baby could have resulted had he been more successful. What a story *that* would have been for his pals – not that he would ever dare to tell it.

'Better I stay a virgin till you come back to Bangkok, Lobut,' she told him.

When he promised he would get it right next time, she had insisted that he did not seek opportunities to practice back in England.

After breakfast, they had taken a taxi to the Golden Mount, Bangkok's highest natural point, constructed to house relics of Buddha presented by Lord Curzon of India. They climbed the winding path up through trees, graves and shrines to the golden *chedi* house where the relics are kept. Further narrow stairs took them out onto the ramparts for a panoramic view of the city, two hundred and fifty feet below. It was peaceful and cool up here, and there was an air of detachment from reality about the place, as if it were worlds away from the sprawling city below.

But there was only one place to spend their final precious hour together in the city. After a last hamburger in McDonalds, they had strolled slowly, hand in hand, along the paths lined with colour and foliage, to the lake in the centre of Lumpini Park, crossing by the bridge where they had first met. Robert hired a rowing boat and they took turns to row.

All too soon it was time for Robert to return to the hotel. They parted in a flurry of murmured endearments; it was to be their last parting before their meeting at the airport.

Robert recrossed the bridge at a run, stopping once, at the exact spot where they had met, to wave to her. Then he was loping away, and she was alone again and lonelier than she had ever felt in her life.

Would you like a drink?' Robert asked her when they had taken over two empty seats at the end of a row.

149

'You have drink?'

'I think I'll have a coffee.'

'Then I have coffee also, thank you.'

'Anything to eat?'

'No, thank you.'

When he returned, they juggled with the polystyrene cups, sugar sachets, tiny pots of cream and the thin plastic stirring sticks. From the outside, their behaviour was the epitome of normality; in reality of course it was no more than a façade, to keep their emotions in check. Unconscious of the airport activity swirling around them, they sipped at theirs coffees in silence. A few yards away, a TV monitor seemed to mock them as it extolled the virtues of a holiday on the Barrier Reef.

With a rising sickness in his throat, Robert knew he had to break this mutual gloom. 'I've got something for you,' he announced with forced cheerfulness and, delving into his holdall, produced a neatly wrapped package tied with yellow ribbon, and handed it to her.

'For me?' She handled it tentatively, turning it over and over as if she expected it to explode.

'Aren't you going to open it?' he urged.

'OK. I wonder what it is.'

He watched her face closely as she untied the ribbon and unwrapped the parcel, taking care not to tear the gaily-coloured paper.

'Cassette player,' she cried as the display box was unveiled. 'Oh, Lobut, you always spend too much money for me.'

'Rubbish. Here, let me show you how it works.'

For the next few minutes he went over the controls, having previously studied the instructions.

'And its not just for playing back.' He pointed to the

mesh-covered holes on one corner. 'It records as well, so you can record your voice onto a blank tape.'

Doungjai listened intently while he explained this additional function.

'I particularly wanted to get one like this, because I thought you could speak into it and send me messages on tape. It'll be more fun that way. I can make up tapes at home and send them to you too. That way we can still speak to each other. What do you think?' Doungjai shook her head. 'I think it wonderful idea. You very clever to think of it.'

'There are tapes in the box with some of my favourite music.' He drew an envelope from the box. 'And this is for when you want to buy your own tapes and you need new batteries.'

She opened the envelope and took out two five hundred baht notes.

'No can accept this.' There were large, clear pearls of tears in her eyes. 'It too much.' She turned her head away, momentarily too moved to speak.

'Nothing is too much for you,' he declared. 'Here, let me show you how to record.' He performed a demonstration, speaking rapidly into the microphone. 'This is a special gift for my special girl, Doungjai.'

When he replayed it she clapped her hands in delight.

'It very easy.'

'Now you have to promise me to record all your news on this and send me the tape.'

'I promise,' she said solemnly.

This diversion helped to pierce the gloom. But a furtive glance at his watch told Robert that their time was now almost up. At last he could delay no longer.

'We'd better be going.'

'Yes.' Her mouth turned down.

They stood up and retraced their steps towards the giant Departure Information Board which clattered every few seconds to update the status of each flight. Robert's mother and father were already waiting. The anguish on the youngsters' faces was unconcealed, and his parents had no comfort to offer. They all walked the short distance to one of the openings in the high artificial wall that screened off Passport Control. First his father, then his mother gave Doungjai a long silent hug. Robert stood and watched, holding back the tears that threatened to breach his self-restraint.

'It's been a great pleasure for both of us to have met you, Doungjai.' Brian Stone spoke for both of them.

'And thank you for making this such a special holiday for Robert,' his wife added

Doungjai could hardly speak, but she stretched up and gave each of them in turn a big kiss on the cheek. It was a spontaneous gesture that touched the hearts of Brian and Mary Stone.

'Thank you for being so kind,' Doungjai managed in a small, scarcely controlled whisper.

'We'll wait for you inside, Robert,' his father said in a low voice. 'Please don't be too long.' He took his wife's arm. 'Goodbye, Doungjai.'

'Goodbye, Doungjai,' Mary Stone echoed.

'Have safe journey,' Doungjai said and waved to them until they disappeared behind the screen.

Robert drew her to one side and looked down at her, both her hands clutched tightly in his. His heart felt like a huge brick in his chest and the lump in his throat rendered him speechless. Doungjai's face swam in front of him through his tears.

'Please don't cry, Lobut.' She reached up and gently brushed a tear from his cheek.

'Well, this is it,' he managed to mumble.

Everything had been said and done. At any rate, almost.

'Before you go, Lobut, here is small present from me,' Doungjai said solemnly and, reaching into her purse, drew out a package wrapped in tissue paper. She placed it in Robert's hand, holding it there while she explained.

'I want to give you something to remember me, but no have money to buy nice present for you. So I like you to have this.'

She released his hand and he slowly peeled back the paper. Inside was a small square box, of the kind rings were sold in. It was in mint condition, but somehow he could tell it was not quite new. He pressed the stud at the front and it sprang open. In the shaped velvet interior was a tiny golden image of Buddha on a fine gold chain.

Robert lifted it from the box with great delicacy. He knew next to nothing about jewellery, but could tell that this piece was hand crafted and of real value. The figure was heavy for its size, and spangled with tiny precious stones of different colours.

'My grandpapa give to me on my tenth birthday. It belong to his wife, my grandmama. I never wear because I frightened I lose it, so I always keep safe in my room. I want you to have it, Lobut.'

From the very start she had never ceased to fascinate, delight and amaze him, but never more than at this moment.

'I couldn't possibly take this,' he protested, struggling for words. 'It's . . . it's very valuable and your grandfather gave it to you.' But he knew she would insist, and privately he wanted her to; he wanted to keep this memento, which was so precious to her, close to him. It was a symbol of the value she placed on their love.

'Grandpapa no mind if I give to you, Lobut. He like you. I ask mama and she say it OK if I want to give to you, because you very special person. I never so happy before since I meet you. I never forget last three weeks. Now you go home I want you to think about me sometimes. Maybe this help . . .'

'I don't need anything to remember you by,' he said, but it was a token protest.

'Never mind, make me very happy for you to have.'

She took the figure from him and replaced it carefully in the box, wrapped the paper round it and pressed it into his hand. The matter was settled.

'Thank you, I'll treasure it always,' he stammered.

In this most public of places, he took her into his arms and kissed her long and full on the lips. It was a passionate kiss, a summing up of their all too short relationship and their sorrow at this tearing apart. They hugged again, as if their lives depended on it and Robert felt Doungjai's frame shudder.

'I love you, Lobut Stone,' she cried between sobs, in a voice unnaturally high. 'I never forget you.'

'I love you too,' he said, smiling valiantly through his tears.

They broke at last and held hands for the last time, staring into each other's face, weeping openly. Then he gave her a final brief hug and, still clasping the small box, backed towards the opening.

'Goodbye, Doungjai.'

'You come back see me, Lobut.'

'I'll be back,' he promised.

'*Lak sa sook apab* – take care yourself,' she called, and

154

waved frantically until – suddenly – he was there no more.

She stood there a few seconds longer, looking lonely and forlorn. Then she turned away and, head bent, walked slowly on dragging feet to where her brother stood waiting.

Chapter Twenty

Doungjai stood on the bridge that linked the island in the lake to the rest of Lumpini Park. Like most Mondays, the park was quiet after the usual weekend crowds. Several boats sculled lazily out on the lake, while the ubiquitous ducks glided across the water, as if drawn by invisible wires. Park employees, heavily garbed against the sun, crouched over the flower beds, working in silent slow motion to maintain the park's immaculate appearance.

The memories of the past weeks were still so close that almost every act, every sight, brought back some word or occasion she and Robert had shared. They were hurtful memories, yet she felt she must face them. The bridge most of all, because that was where they met; in a way she felt it belonged to them, that it was *their* bridge. But they had visited so many parts of the city together that hardly anywhere did not serve as a poignant reminder of the sweetness of those days, all too few, all too short.

As she leaned on the bridge and looked along the path by the lake, she caught her breath when a fair-haired boy in shorts appeared in the distance. As the boy drew closer she saw that he was older and bigger than Robert, and not at all like him in looks. The split second of hope withered and died almost before it was born.

She looked at her watch: it was four o'clock. By now he would be over Europe, where it was still morning. He would be on the last lap of his journey home, perhaps he was home already. He had promised to write as soon as he arrived, but he would be tired after the flight and most likely would not send a letter until the following day. That meant the earliest she could expect to hear from him would be the beginning of next week. Six whole days. It seemed like half a lifetime. A tape would take even longer to arrive.

She sighed. Here she was already counting the days, and he had been gone less than twenty-four hours. Even if the letters came regularly, she would be on a constant knife-edge, waiting for the next and the next. It would be so easy for Robert to forget her, so easy to write less and less often; so easy to find an English girl to take her place. If ever the gap between his letters became indefinite, she hoped she would understand.

From the beginning, her grandfather had warned her about foreign boys coming to Thailand on holiday and meeting local girls. While it lasted everyone had a good time, but when the holiday was over, the romance was over. To believe anything could come of it was to indulge in self-delusion. Back they would go, to the girls at home – European girls, with whom they had everything in common – and next year there would be another holiday in a different country with a different local girl. Robert wasn't like that, of course. He wasn't shallow and frivolous. Their friendship was special, but was it special enough to withstand the gap of time, distance and culture indefinitely?

But that was only part of her dilemma, for Doungjai was now a changed person from the one who had picked up a fallen lens cap three weeks ago, here on this very spot. It was an old saying, but true: once the genie is out of the bottle, it can never be put back. In the same way, it was not possible for her to go back to what she had been before she had met Robert. With him, she had discovered a new lifestyle and a fresh perspective on her everyday existence. She had dined at Le Sala and Tum Nak Thai, swum in the pool at one of Bangkok's finest hotels and, at barely fifteen years of age, she had shared a bed with a boy from another country, and let him touch her in her most intimate places. Even if she never saw him again, she could not just forget these things, as though they had never happened. They had inspired new appetites and awakened hitherto unknown needs and passions.

She had also learnt an important lesson above all others. The key to all doors in the corridor of life is money. Without money, there is no freedom – freedom to do what you want to do, go where you want to go, be with whom you want to be with. Now that her grandfather was gone, her mother would be relying on her, as her eldest daughter, more than ever before. She would soon be working every day in the shop. But the money she earned would not be hers; it would be used to keep the family fed and clothed, to pay for the necessities of life. There would be nothing to spare for luxuries, for travel. For trips to England . . .

Of course there were ways of earning more money if you were prepared to ditch certain principles. There were the bars and massage parlours, for instance. Girls working there could make real money. When she had first heard about the business of entertaining tourists, Doungjai had not fully understood what was entailed. Her grandfather declined to enlighten her and she would never have dared ask her mother. But over a period of time, from chance remarks and overheard conversations, she came to recognise and accept as true that some girls really did such things for money.

As long as Robert kept in touch with her, as long as she had his love to sustain her, she would never do anything she would be ashamed to tell him about. But one day, she might have to face a world in which he was no more than a memory. Unless she prepared for such a possibility now, the pain, if it did become a reality, would be beyond bearing.

She had already decided that tomorrow she would go back to the Erawan Shrine and talk to Buddha. It would do no harm, either, to go down to Patpong afterwards and make some enquiries. She might even talk to some of the girls around the bars. Maybe some bars were better than others.

Of course, she would never get involved in any of that sort of thing personally, but it would not do any harm to find out – just in case.

Part Two
Innocence In Retreat

Chapter Twenty-One

The accident had changed Doungjai's life dramatically in several ways, all of them for the worse. It had brought about a huge upheaval for her family, she had been forced to leave school early and find a full-time job and it had resulted in an abrupt end to her contact with Robert.

More than two years had passed since she and Robert lost touch. Until the accident they had communicated regularly by letter and tape. They had even spoken on the telephone several times. Then disaster had struck and since her return to Bangkok, she had lost count of all the jobs she had tried. Most of them had consisted of standing on a busy pavement selling from a makeshift table, or sometimes just a box. Clothes, bags, belts, lighters, even video films, she had tried them all.

In between, she had worked as a waitress in a restaurant, where the food was German and the atmosphere friendly, until the owner became a little too friendly. As a barmaid, in a small beer parlour in the Night Plaza beneath the expressway in Ploenchit Road, she had quickly discovered that some of the customers expected more of her than just a Singha, or Kloster and the bill. Although she had not suffered the same personal problems when she had turned her hand to retailing, filling shelves in a twenty-four hour supermarket, especially in the barren hours after midnight, carried little job satisfaction and soon she was almost wishing for a friendly grope to break the monotony.

Doungjai could have coped with any of these job limitations had the pay been adequate to cover her family's needs. As it was she was constantly on the move, continually on the lookout for a few extra bahts.

Now she was back selling again. This time it was watches, displayed on a square of board supported on spindly legs, on the crowded pavement of Silom Road.

While watches provided a better financial return than most of the other jobs she had tried, they also created more uncertainty. Competition was particularly fierce, but a greater threat was posed by faceless people from thousands of miles away. International copyright pressure on the Thai authorities was filtering down increasingly to street level, in the form of police interference. As a result, imitations of prestige makes like Rolex, Gucci, Cartier and Dior had to be displayed with ever more caution. Normally the grapevine warned when the police were out to enforce the embargo, thus enabling the trays to be cleared of the sensitive makes. Unfortunately, most tourists only wanted the name brands, so a way round the problem was quickly found. When danger threatened, small books with pictures of the banned watches replaced the real thing, which could be produced instantly on request from a hidden store. It was still a constraint on business though, for would-be buyers preferred examining the merchandise to making a selection from a book of pictures.

Some vendors took a chance and kept their wares

on display at all times, despite the considerable risk. If the police caught them and were feeling bloody-minded, they could impose a huge fine and confiscate the lot, thus crippling or even terminating the business at a stroke. To underline the official resolve and convince overseas critics, pictures of thousands of illegal watches being flattened under a road roller appeared occasionally on the television news channel. Yet on nights when they were not on the warpath, the police would walk past glittering arrays of expensive looking copies without a second glance. The whole situation was farcical.

With commission constantly uppermost in her mind, Doungjai had developed an analytical approach to potential customers, dividing those who stopped and showed any interest in her watches into three categories: there were those who clearly had no intention of buying and were merely window shopping; those who just might buy, given the right sales pitch; and those definitely on the lookout for a watch to take home.

Michael caught her attention not only because she had placed him in the second category and, therefore, needed some extra persuasion, but because he stood out from most of the other tourists. Tall and good looking, with an athletic build, his dress was unusually smart for an evening stroll along the narrow, pot-holed path between the stalls.

She was less sure about the air of self-confidence and authority, amounting almost to arrogance, that he exuded. But she immediately caught on to his dry sense of humour.

'Are you sure this Cartier was made in France?' he asked in a mid-Atlantic accent. Not a hint of a smile.

'Of course,' she assured him blandly, as if any other

possibility was unthinkable. 'Only arrived from Paris yesterday.'

'How much?' He held the watch towards her.

'Five hundred bahts.'

While he appeared to consider the price, his eyes never left her face. She was a little beauty, he decided.

She held his gaze and tried to move the bargaining on. 'All right, to you four fifty.'

She was not to know that at twenty five, Michael Paquet was the youngest board director in his company's history and was rarely bested in anything to do with money. He decided to complicate the game.

'How much for two of these and . . .' he leaned across and selected a Rolex Oyster. '. . . this one?'

'You buy all three?'

'If the price is right.'

Doungjai suspected he was stringing her along for his own amusement, but she could not afford to miss out on any sale, so she kept a straight face as she cautioned: 'That one is more expensive.'

'How expensive?'

'Eight hundred.'

'And if I buy it with the two Cartiers?'

'For three, I charge you . . .' She made a show of doing complicated sums in her head, although she already knew exactly what to quote and how far she would come down. '. . . for sixteen hundred.'

It was hot and humid, the passersby kept bumping against him and a cool Martini beckoned from his luxury hotel suite. Yet the thought of giving up and moving on never entered Michael's head. Bargaining with this little Thai sales girl was proving far too much fun. It presented other possibilities too.

'I think you must want me to walk back to my hotel

tonight.' He pretended to look hurt, but his affluent appearance hardly supported the plea of penury and left her unimpressed.

'A *tuk tuk* is very cheap,' she informed him, then switched back to serious business. 'So how much you give me?'

'How about twelve fifty?'

She ignored the offer as if it were too absurd even to acknowledge. 'Since you are nice man, you can have all three for fifteen hundred.'

She was persuasive as well as sharp, but he shook his head sadly. Reaching for the pocket calculator sitting on the tray, he punched in '1300' and presented it to her.

'You want my boss to kill me?' She pretended to look scared and placed a hand over her heart. Every word, every mannerism was irresistible.

'I certainly wouldn't want that. Look, make it thirteen fifty and you've got yourself a deal.'

Her face screwed up as if she were in pain. Then she sighed as though about to make the supreme sacrifice. 'OK. I give very special price for you – fourteen fifty for all three.'

'Done.' Michael raised both hands in a gesture of surrender while inwardly he was satisfied that he had struck a good bargain. He could have paid three or four times as much without giving it a second thought, but winning was what mattered. It made no difference whether he was negotiating a multi-million dollar contract, or buying a counterfeit watch in Bangkok's Silom Road.

He studied her as she carefully placed the three watches in individual plastic sleeves. Her expression was blank as she handed them over and took his money, giving no hint of whether or not she was satisfied with the deal. He found himself feeling a little sorry now. An extra fifty or a hundred bahts could have meant a lot to her, yet was peanuts to him. Even if she was used to bargaining every night for a few bahts either way, he wondered if he had played a little bit too rough.

'Do you work here regularly?' A tempting idea was forming in his mind.

'Every night, till one o'clock after midnight.' She was rearranging the watches as she replied, filling the gaps left by her latest transaction.

'Maybe I'll see you again?' he suggested.

'I hope so.' She looked up at him, and a big smile spread slowly across her face. It was like the sun emerging, warm and bright. 'Maybe you buy another watch?'

'It's possible.' He had run out of small talk and knew the book was closed, at least for this evening. 'Goodnight.'

'Goodnight.' Ten yards further on he risked a look back through the non-stop stream of bobbing heads. She was already trying to attract the attention of a middle aged couple. One transaction completed, on with the next . . .

Michael returned the following evening slightly earlier. Everything was exactly as it had been on his previous visit, except this time Doungjai greeted him like an old and valued customer. He produced the Rolex and asked if she could adjust the size of the metal bracelet. He could have done it for himself, but it presented a perfect excuse to resume their conversation.

As she checked the size of the strap round his wrist to determine if any links needed to be removed, he became aware of a man standing by his shoulder. He looked Thai, was dressed casually in a loose fitting sweater shirt, jeans and sneakers, and just stood there looking down at the watches without touching them, or even speaking. Eventually he moved on. Although they had not said a word to each other, Michael sensed that Doungjai knew the man.

'Who was that?' he asked.

'Police.'

'And he doesn't mind you selling all these makes?'

'Tonight police not come, so no problem.'

Michael did not pursue the point. While Doungjai fiddled with the watch strap, he moved quickly to more weighty matters.

A few direct questions elicited that she was seventeen years old, 'nearly eighteen', and had her own room in Bangkok, 'very small'. She had four brothers and two sisters and, most important of all had no boyfriend. Or at any rate, none that she was admitting to. Further questioning revealed that she had two days' holiday a month and spent these visiting her family, who lived about two hours by bus out of Bangkok.

It did not provide much of an opening for what he had in mind, for ever since the previous evening he had been unable to get this gorgeous little Thai miss out of his mind. In a roundabout way, he explained he worked in Bangkok but knew hardly anybody and would like to get someone to show him round the city.

A polite smile was the only response.

'I've been told I must try some Thai food while I'm here.' He shrugged and tried to look helpless. 'Only I wouldn't know where to go.'

'Plenty of Thai food restaurants in Bangkok.' Was

this her way of telling him to stop bothering her.

'But I wouldn't know what to order. I could use some help.' Was that a broad enough hint, he wondered.

Her silence suggested she did not see that as a major problem. If he was going to make any progress here, he was going to have be more direct, and risk an equally direct rebuff.

'How about joining me for a Thai meal?' He tried to make it a casual suggestion.

Having adjusted the strap, Doungjai handed the watch back to him without saying a word. Outwardly, it appeared she had not heard him; inwardly she was in a turmoil, unsure how to respond.

'Well?' he persisted, when she remained silent. 'Will you?'

'Sorry, I work every evening.'

He wondered if it was a genuine excuse or an easy way of refusing.

'Then how about during the day, before you go to work?'

'Why you ask *me*?'

'Because I'm on my own and would like some company.' They both knew there was more to it than that. 'OK,' he conceded, smiling weakly. 'Because I think you are very attractive and I would like to know you better.'

'There is nice Thai restaurant in Landmark Hotel,' she volunteered, tidying her display, eyes averted.

Was that her way of saying 'yes'?

'That's on . . .' He waved his hand vaguely.

'. . . Sukhumvit Road.'

'Will you have lunch with me there?'

She knew she should politely refuse and stop this now. Her only previous involvement with a *falang* had come to nothing but heartache. Robert had been her first and her only love and would always have a very special place in her memory. Only after long months of diminishing hope had she eventually accepted that she would never see him again. No one, except her mother, really knew how devastated she had been by that realisation and even now, nearly three years after those idyllic days together in Bangkok, it still hurt whenever she thought about him.

But she had to break free from the past eventually. She worked long hours and in her leisure time, to avoid spending money, rarely went out. Perhaps, just this once, she should relax her self-imposed exile.

'When?'

'How about tomorrow?'

'OK. What time?' One day was very much like another.

A relieved and delighted Michael quickly completed the arrangements.

'Till tomorrow then,' he concluded. 'Oh, I don't know your name.'

'Doungjai.' She was already wondering if she had been foolish in accepting his invitation.

'Doung-jai,' he repeated slowly. His pronunciation impressed her. 'I'm Michael.'

As he hailed a meter taxi, it never crossed his mind that his lunch date for tomorrow would have to stand in the sweltering heat, amongst jostling crowds, for several more hours yet. Nor that she would not be back in her room until well after he had put aside his bedside reading and turned out the light.

171

Chapter Twenty-Two

Michael stood on the steps of the Landmark Hotel, above ever bustling Sukhumvit Road, and scrutinised each approaching pedestrian and every disembarking taxi passenger. Yet he failed to recognise the shapely female bottom backing out of a *tuk tuk* at precisely 12.30. Only when its ravishing owner mounted the steps towards him, did he realise that it belonged to Doungjai. She looked fresh and lovely in a green cotton blouse and tight fawn skirt, drawn in at the waist by an ornately buckled, black leather belt. With just a hint of lipstick, a little make up to emphasise those large dark eyes, and hair cascading in thick swathes across her shoulders, she turned many a male head. Michael could only stare at this stunning, honey-skinned vision and marvel at the transformation from the perspiring little watch vendor of the previous evening.

'You sure know how to pick 'em, Paquet,' was the self-congratulatory thought uppermost in his mind.

The look on his face was sufficient proof of his approval and Doungjai was similarly pleased that her own initial assessment had not been deceived by the haphazard artificial lighting of Silom Road. Indeed, in daylight he was even more handsome. His lightly bronzed features were complemented by thick ash blond, carefully coiffured hair which he wore medium length.

'Hello.' His broad smile screened a sudden flash of doubt. Should he kiss her on the cheek or shake her hand?

'Hello, Michael.' She settled his uncertainty by offering her small hand.

'I . . . I hardly recognised you,' he confessed. 'You look wonderful.'

'Thank you.' She had been tense ever since she awoke that morning, reprimanding herself for having accepted this invitation. In the *tuk tuk*, her misgivings had multiplied and she almost told the driver to turn around and take her home. But surprisingly, now the moment had arrived, she felt calm and composed.

'I hope you're hungry, because I am,' he challenged cheerfully. 'I wanted to work up a good appetite for this meal so I only had a light breakfast.'

'I hungry also. Mama says I always hungry and have appetite like buffalo.'

Michael smiled politely and took her arm as they entered the hotel and rode the long escalator up to the Nipa Restaurant. He was immediately impressed by the light panelled Thai style decor and the elegant waitresses in their long, intricately patterned dresses. They were shown to a cosy alcove and the menus were presented. Although he had been in Bangkok some time and had encountered a few Thai menus, he was genuinely still unfamiliar with Thai dishes and was glad of any assistance.

He looked up and caught Doungjai watching him. 'This is where I need that help I was talking about,' he reminded her.

She dropped her eyes to the menu and, after

173

studying it for a few moments, spoke rapidly in Thai to the waitress who had been hovering beside them.

'What did you order?' Michael asked her when the waitress had retired with the order and a graceful bow.

'A selection,' she said mysteriously. 'I think you like.'

An hour later, Michael sipped contentedly at his coffee. A full social life and generous business expense account ensured that he usually dined well in top-rated establishments, with well connected company. Yet he could not remember when he had enjoyed a meal as much. The food had been a revelation to his taste buds and converted him instantly to Thai cuisine. But it was his lovely companion who had really made the experience special for him. And not only was she beautiful, but she was possessed of a lively personality, a sense of humour, and was capable of discoursing on a wide range of topics.

Doungjai was equally captivated by her host, and any earlier doubts were quickly forgotten. The time flew past and she was genuinely sorry when Michael at last called for the bill. It had been an occasion she would remember with pleasure.

'How about doing the same tomorrow?' he suggested, tucking the change into his hip pocket and placing a tip in the bill folder.

The possibility that he might want to meet again had never occurred to her. She hesitated.

'I not sure . . .'

'Don't be silly. You enjoyed yourself, I enjoyed myself, and we had a super meal.'

When put like that, it would indeed have been silly, even churlish to decline his offer.

'All right. Tomorrow same time.'

One date led to another, and they met every day during the next week to lunch in a different restaurant. Whatever his work schedule, Michael always found time to take her shopping afterwards and insisted on buying her a present before they parted. This was usually something to wear, and soon Doungjai had built up a whole new wardrobe.

It all seemed too good to be true and yet Michael's generosity left her a little uneasy. For him to spend more money in an hour on these excursions than she earned in a month seemed not quite right, albeit that she was the beneficiary. Such extravagance did not sit comfortably with the Spartan nature of her upbringing.

When she mentioned these reservations to her friends, she was told not to be silly and to make the most of it while it lasted. So although she always raised a demure objection to every gift as 'too much', her protestations were not as wholehearted as they might have been.

It was not until she had been seeing Michael for over a week that Doungjai's resistance to his financial blandishments was fully put to the test. On this particular day they had a buffet lunch at the Emerald Hotel, out on Ratchadapisek Road in the north east of the city. Michael explained that he had a business meeting nearby later in the afternoon, hence the choice of venue. For Doungjai, it brought back memories which she would rather have stayed dormant, for just before they reached the hotel they passed Tum Nak Thai Restaurant. She had dined there with Robert a few days before he had returned to England.

After the meal, Michael insisted on taking her to one of the many branches of Robinsons Department Store, situated between the Emerald and Tum Nak Thai. As soon as they entered the cool interior, it became obvious that he was looking for a particular department. He found it on the fourth floor, in the music and television section, where he bought her a 22" colour television set, paying for it in cash from the thick wad of notes he invariably carried.

In previous conversations she had mentioned, with no ulterior motive, that she did not own a television. She had not meant it to be a hint, but she wondered now if her wistful hopes had been too pointed. When she protested vigorously that she could not possibly accept it, he brushed her objections aside.

'Let's call it an early going away present.'

'You going away?' The disappointment in her voice underlined how attached to him she had become in the space of a few days.

'Maybe. I'm not sure yet. I'll have a better idea after my boss has visited Bangkok next week.' He placed a comforting arm round her shoulders, pleased at her reaction to the prospect of his departure. It would make his next move that much easier.

The television set was duly checked out, boxed and transported down to the street where a taxi was hailed and the large cardboard container deposited on the back seat. Although her instincts admonished her for accepting such an expensive present, especially from someone she had known for a matter of days, Doungjai had difficulty in concealing her excitement. If there was one thing she had always coveted but had not the slightest prospect of owning, it was a TV set.

It had all happened so quickly and unexpectedly, but if her feelings were mixed and already confused, that confusion was compounded when Michael took her arm, as she was about to get into the taxi, and drew her to one side.

'Would you do something for me, Doungjai?' he asked, his face unusually serious.

'Of course, Michael,' she agreed, although something in his voice caused her a twinge of unease.

'You told me that when you go home on your days off, you have a friend who looks after your watch stall.'

'Yes?' The unease took firmer root.

'Would you ask your friend if she will take over tomorrow night so that you can have dinner with me? Tell her you'll make it worth her while.'

She looked away, her mind racing. It was the crossroads in her relationship with Michael. The smooth talk, the meals, the clothes and now the TV set, they had all been leading up to this moment and she had not even seen it coming.

'I don't know, Michael.' She needed time to think. 'Maybe my friend have other plans for tomorrow night.'

'But will you ask her?' He drew her round to face him. 'It's been wonderful seeing you these last few days, but you always have to hurry off to get ready for work just when we start to enjoy ourselves. I would love to see you in the evening, maybe have a candlelit dinner and no need to hurry afterwards. You know what I mean?'

Doungjai had a pretty shrewd idea what he meant.

'You will try, won't you?' He pressed a five hundred baht note into her hand. 'This might help to persuade your friend.'

To Doungjai it felt more like payment for services to be rendered. However, she said nothing and stuffed the note in her purse.

The taxi's engine was ticking over, the TV set in its brand new box was nestling in the back seat and Michael was waiting anxiously for her reply. He was pressurising her, and she knew it. The big question was, did it really *really* matter?

She looked up at him, her face unsmiling. 'All right, Michael, I ask her.' She scrambled into the taxi anxious now to be away.

He leaned through the open door. 'Will you let me know?'

'I telephone your hotel tomorrow morning.'

Only when the door closed and the taxi pulled away did she realise she was trembling. There was not a lot of room in the back seat and she looped one arm protectively over her new possession as if to draw comfort from it. She could not help wondering how much Michael's generosity was going to cost her.

As Doungjai had suspected, for five hundred bahts her friend was only too pleased to look after her stall the following evening.

Doungjai was not sure whether she shared her friend's pleasure. However, as promised, she telephoned Michael the following morning with the 'good news'. There was no mistaking the satisfaction in his voice, and it came as no surprise when he suggested his own hotel as the venue for their dinner. By now she was too committed to dispute the point, and she agreed to meet him there at eight.

For her this was a giant step. Since Robert, she had shunned involvement with men, and especially *falangs*. Now here she was about to go down the same route as three years before, with the same probable outcome.

She must be mad, she decided.

Chapter Twenty-Three

Narrow, noisy and crowded, Soi 22 is no different from many of the other small side roads that feed into Sukhumvit, apart from the density of the traffic it carries. This is partly because it leads to Bangkok's largest hotel.

About three hundred yards from where the soi joins one of the city's busiest thoroughfares, the Imperial Queens Park Hotel, with its fourteen hundred bedrooms, suddenly rears up. One of Bangkok's newer hotels, it rises solidly to the ninth floor, much of which is taken up with the biggest of its two swimming pools. Two giant towers then reach a further twenty eight storeys above the Bangkok skyline.

Behind the hotel is Queens Park, or Benjasiri Park as it is also known. A lake occupies the centre of this green oasis in the heart of the city and the meticulously maintained lawns are dotted with sculptures in metal and stone. At night, the park is lit by lamps perched on black wrought-iron posts reminiscent of those that illuminated the London of Jack the Ripper.

In a city unequalled for its range of fine hotels, perhaps the most striking feature of the Imperial Queens Park is its reception area. Alleged to be the largest in Asia, it could accommodate a football pitch with something to spare.

Michael waited for Doungjai in the plushly

furnished Sundowners Lobby Bar facing the main entrance. From its dimly lit anonymity, he was able to take in most of the reception area and spotted her the moment she showed up. The large glass door was opened for her by a doorboy in traditional Thai costume. After a brief exchange he pointed in Michael's direction and Doungjai trekked across the acres of gleaming marble. She was wearing the outfit Michael had bought for her on their first visit to the shops – a dark red blouse with black stripes and slashed sleeves, jet black trousers, tight across the bottom and wide-legged. Both garments were of the finest Thai silk, made to measure on Michael's instructions and a perfect fit. The black leather shoes with large brass buckles lent her extra height and a gold chain, supporting a gold medallion with 'good luck' spelled out in Chinese, also a present from Michael, provided a glint of colour at her throat.

Unseen, but given just as much thought when she was preparing for the evening, were the miniscule powder blue briefs and matching bra, further presents from Michael. Until recently, her underwear had always been blandly coloured and covered all the right places more than adequately.

Although always reluctant to interfere, if Doungjai's mother had seen her, she would probably have suggested as diplomatically as possible that perhaps her daughter should tone down the outfits she had been wearing since she met Michael. She might have pointed out that dressing as a twenty-five year old could give the wrong signals, especially to someone who might not need a lot of encouragement anyway. Wishing only to impress her sophisticated new friend, such thoughts never entered Doungjai's head.

Michael took both her hands gently and told her how lovely she looked and asked what she would like to drink. Perched gingerly opposite him on the edge of the extravagantly cushioned settee, she asked for a fresh orange juice. Whatever the rest of the evening had in store, she was at least determined to have full control of all her faculties. Michael, having already consumed two doubles of his favourite Malt, ordered another and sipped it while he studied the huge glossy menu. Demonstrating his growing confidence, after a few questions of the waiter, he ordered for both of them.

The meal was excellent, but Doungjai tackled it with less than her usual enthusiasm. Neither was Michael his normal relaxed self. They retired to the lounge for coffee, but the tension remained. Michael fidgetted in his seat, stole repeated glances at his watch and kept looking around as if afraid that someone might be hovering nearby and trying to listen in. Doungjai caught his mood and their conversation, usually so spontaneous, became increasingly forced and intermittent. Several times Michael roused himself and leaned towards her, seemingly about to make some weighty observation, only to draw back and settle for a banal comment that hardly seemed worth the effort.

As the last dregs were squeezed from the coffee pot and their conversation, Michael knew he could delay no longer. He looked again at his watch, this time with a flourish.

'It's nearly 9.30.' He turned his wrist so that Doungjai could see the watch face, as if she might doubt him. 'Still quite early.'

After a slight pause, he leaned forward again and fixed her with his most persuasive smile. 'Would you like to come up to my room? It's much quieter there.'

It had been painfully slow going for someone who had never had the slightest problem or hesitation in charming the birds and pulling their feathers, but he was nearly there at last.

'Quieter for what?' she might have asked, or simply observed that the lounge where they were sitting was extremely quiet and peaceful. Doungjai knew it was her last chance to bail out, but she let it pass. An inescapable sense of obligation to Michael, coupled with an intense curiosity, kept her on a path that seemed inexorable.

'Up to you, Michael,' she heard herself saying.

The patent relief on his face made her glad she had not turned him down. Without further delay he waved to the waiter, signed the bill and steered her towards the lift. When it reached their level and the doors slid silently open, a friendly disembodied female voice announced, 'Thirty fifth floor, going down.'

The corridor was dimly lit and deserted and their tread was silent on soft carpeting. Michael inserted the piece of cutout plastic into a slot in the lock, turned the handle and the door swung open. Slipping the plastic into a slot beside the door activated all the lights, and Doungjai found herself in a huge, luxuriously furnished lounge. Cool coloured tiles and scatter rugs underfoot blended with the picture draped walls. There was a step up to the panoramic window, that dominated one end of the room. Michael drew the long, green velvet curtains, cutting out a superb view of the city by night.

'Very nice,' she murmured appreciatively.

'It's not bad, is it?' His nonchalant response concealed the satisfaction the look on her face had given him. 'The bedroom and bathroom are through there. Come and have a look.'

He ushered her round a white leather settee and opened a door beside an ornately carved writing desk. A similar display of luxury met Doungjai when she stepped into the thickly carpeted bedroom. Her gaze swept the room, from mirrored doors to built-in wardrobes, another gilt-framed mirror behind a glass topped dressing table, several matching chairs and small tables, but irresistibly it was drawn to the vast bed in the centre.

'Nice,' she repeated, trying to blot out the bed from her thoughts.

He came up close behind and turned her to face him. 'Thank you for having dinner with me tonight.'

'You always very kind to me, Michael.'

'These last few days have meant a great deal to me.' He put his arms round her and drew her close. It was the first intimate gesture he had shown. The subtle scent of her skin and hair and her very physical nearness made it the natural thing to do.

He placed one hand behind her head, drew it into his chest and nuzzled his face into her hair. 'Will you stay with me tonight,' he murmured in her ear. 'Sleep with me?'

She did not reply and they stood like that in silence for long moments.

'Doungjai?'

She pulled away and looked up into his face. 'You want to make love, Michael?'

'Very much.'

She seemed to weigh her next words carefully. 'I never make love before.'

'You've never slept with a man before?' The tone of his voice suggested incredulity.

'I sleep once,' she admitted. 'But we no make love. I still virgin.'

In all his planning towards this moment, it was the one contingency he had not even considered. His uncertainty was palpable, but Doungjai took his hand.

'Never mind, Michael, I sleep with you if you want.' She stood up on her toes and kissed him gently on the cheek.

He watched her, hypnotised, and she held his gaze as she slowly unbuttoned her blouse and shrugged it off her shoulders. The trousers followed. All that remained were the powder blue bra and panties that fitted her like a second skin. The bra accentuated the extravagant thrust of her breasts, without concealing the dark protruding nipples. The panties were little more than a G-string, a tiny V stretched taut over her female mound, emphasising her clearly defined love lips.

The spell was broken as Doungjai eased off her shoes and toed them aside. Michael took her by the shoulders, kissed her lightly on the lips and embraced her while his fingers dealt with the hook on her bra. He drew the straps away from her shoulders and her breasts were suddenly bare and free. He could not wait to test their fleshy firmness, nor to explore the rest of her generously curved body.

He moved her gently towards the bed and she fell back on it, arms above her head in casual surrender. He wanted to rip off her panties, but, exercising great restraint, he slid the elastic gently over her hips instead. Doungjai lifted her bottom to assist him and drew her knees up to her chin so that he could guide the panties up her thighs, round the angle of her knees and down over her feet. Even when the wispy garment had been cast aside, she held the pose briefly as if stating that now she had come this far she would withhold nothing.

Michael tore his eyes away just long enough to dispense with his own clothes. Feeling strangely relaxed, Doungjai watched him, although her admiration of his tanned muscular body became tempered with apprehension when his rampant penis sprang into view.

Michael's love making was usually inclined towards urgent self-fulfillment rather than a slow build-up. But as he drank in the nubile nudity stretched before him he felt compelled to make a closer, more intimate examination of Doungjai's firm young body before moving on to more serious action. He bent closer and the warmth of his breath and the caress of his fingers quickly dispelled Doungjai's affected detachment. Her own breathing quickened as he smothered the front of her body with light kisses; she sighed when his tongue lapped at her nipples and baby-tight vaginal lips; she gasped when it penetrated within them and titillated her clitoris.

As Doungjai's juices began to flow, she almost welcomed the moment when he coaxed her thighs apart. As he brushed his bone hard erection along the tight groove formed by her engorging lips, Doungjai knew a very special moment in her life had arrived.

Even so, she was not prepared for the stabbing pain when he penetrated her. As their sweat-slicked bodies locked together and he pistoned into her, the pain overshadowed any sensation of pleasure. But Michael was aware only of his own satisfaction and did not even seem to notice her small cries, or perhaps he took them as a sign of her rapture. He quickly reached his climax with a final deep thrust, accompanied by a drawn out groan. His body sagged onto hers and his breath rasped in her ear. Gradually these subsided into a rhythmic breathing, and he appeared to have fallen asleep.

In the ensuing calm, Doungjai's thoughts were still of that special moment that she would never know again. It had not been at all as she had imagined, especially the intensity of the pain, and yet she could not forget the exquisite sensations that had accompanied it. As she slowly slipped into sleep, her thoughts were still a mixture of doubt and satisfaction, guilt and achievement.

Some time in the night, Michael manoeuvred himself on top of her, eased her into a receptive position and again drove into her while she was still half asleep. The pain returned, though less intense this time, and her passion was still mounting when he climaxed again and fell away.

As the dawn light groped round the heavy velvet curtains, they again came together, only this time Doungjai took the initiative. She was a quick learner and scrambled on top of Michael. Brushing her sex lips against his penis until it returned to full erection, she teased the swollen head with gentle fingers before carefully guiding it into position and lowering herself slowly until his full length was inside her. Closing her thighs, so that he was tightly trapped, she moved up and down, gradually increasing the pace and penetration, but always controlling the action with her weight until she reached her first orgasm with a man. By then, Michael had been literally ridden to exhaustion.

During the next few days, Doungjai's association with Michael was dominated by sex. Having gained access to its naked secrets, his desire for her fabulous little body became an obsession. To be with her, he invented business meetings and cut real ones short, but no matter how many extra hours he managed to create, he was never able to get enough of the sight, the feel and the scent of her.

As for Doungjai, although she insisted on returning each day to her own small room, she spent her nights at the hotel. For a regular incentive, her friend was happy to take over near-permanent charge of the watch stall. Although at first Doungjai was not entirely comfortable with the arrangement, any residual feeling of guilt faded as her physical relationship with Michael developed.

Soon she was taking the initiative in their love-making as often as not, and her enjoyment of the peaks of pleasure was no less than Michael's. Told repeatedly how beautiful she was and how much he enjoyed looking at her, she was persuaded to strip for him as soon as she arrived each day at his suite, and would remain in a naked state the whole of the time. He even succeeded in cajoling her into shaving off her pubic hair.

As her inhibitions diminished, Doungjai came to revel in her nudity. It seemed to endow her with a strange power over Michael and soon she was adopting provocative poses for him on the huge bed. She found it deliciously exciting to flaunt her most intimate parts, especially since it hastened the moment when Michael's hands and tongue would be exploring every sensuous curve and every secret crevice.

It was all so new that Doungjai failed to notice the almost total absence of patience and tenderness in his love-making. With no experience of such matters, and mesmerised by the frantic pursuit of sensual pleasure, Doungjai had no yardstick to measure by, and remained in lovestruck oblivion of Michael's shortcomings.

She was to be made aware of them all too soon.

Chapter Twenty-Four

A week after Doungjai had surrendered her virginity, she met the President and CEO of New Age Computers, Michael's employers,

Jurgen Gross was the archetypal self-made man. Beginning his career as a computer systems analyst, his meteoric climb to top management had been achieved through a combination of natural ability, keeping in with the right people, and an uncanny sense of timing. Picking his moment to change companies with care and circumspection had ensured that each move lifted him a step up the executive ladder, increased his managerial skills and added lustre to his CV.

Within NAC his progress was utterly predictable, and for some time before he became Chief Executive, he had been widely recognised as the heir apparent to the founder of the company. Asked about the secret of his success in business, his reply never varied: pick a management team that will back you, never fudge tough decisions, and never allow personal considerations to influence those decisions. It was a formula that had kept him firmly in control of a successful international company, it had also made him a lot of personal enemies. This had never worried him, for his skin was as thick as his bankroll. When Gross wanted something, he went all out for it. Bruised feelings and trodden toes were the least of his concerns – as long as they were not his.

To a degree, Michael was Gross' protégé. He had spotted the young man's potential at the first interview and had backed his appointment to the board. With South East Asia the company's principal target for long term development, he saw Michael as the ideal person to spearhead the assault. The blend of a talented young man, a dynamic company, and the world's fastest developing region, seemed like a recipe for great expectations. Perhaps even more important, from Gross' point of view, was that Michael, while possessed of an air of authority and expertise, would ultimately do whatever he, Gross, told him to do, in the interests of holding onto a promising future.

Having booked Gross into the hotel's Penthouse Suite for his stay in Bangkok, Michael arranged to meet him for an early evening dinner. He wanted to bring his boss up-to-date with a preliminary review of the company's achievements in Bangkok. At the same time he guessed that, after a long flight, Gross would probably prefer an early night before embarking on a punishing succession of meetings over the next few days. During their long distance telephone conversation to finalise arrangements for the visit, Michael had let slip that he had met a 'new friend' in Bangkok.

'Bring her along, Mike,' Gross had insisted, guessing the sex of Michael's new friend. 'It'll be nice to unwind with a pretty face across the table. I take it she is pretty?'

'Very,' Michael confirmed, somewhat taken aback by Gross' response.

Doungjai was even more surprised when Michael

told her that she had been invited to dinner with his American boss.

'You sure you want me to come, Michael?' she queried anxiously.

'Quite sure.' He spoke with more conviction than he felt, for he was beginning to wish he had never mentioned Doungjai to Gross. It was well known at NAC that, socially, Gross could be as appreciative and charming with women as he could be domineering and obnoxious to his business colleagues. Without quite knowing why, Michael had a feeling that inviting Doungjai to join them for dinner was something he would come to regret.

They met in the Lobby Bar for a pre-dinner drink and Michael's doubts were quickly reinforced. Gross was obviously fascinated by Doungjai the moment he set eyes on her – and with good reason. Doungjai looked absolutely stunning in the new outfit Michael had bought her for the occasion. The short royal blue jacket with wide puffed shoulders was intricately interwoven with gold thread. The skilful cut artfully contrasted the fullness of her breasts with the slimness of her waist. Her skin tight cream skirt only retained its sheer unlined grip of her hips, thighs and bottom because she wore nothing underneath, and this was obvious to all discerning bottom-watchers. The skirt ended six inches above her knees, leaving bare much of her well-sculpted legs, which were further enhanced by matching stiletto-heeled sandals, in royal blue to match the jacket.

They ordered their meal at the bar from huge menus presented by the head waiter and, while they waited to be called, Gross' attention remained totally focused on Doungjai. More than once Michael tried to raise a business issue, but his boss's vague responses told him plainly that his thoughts were on other matters.

Gross sat opposite Doungjai at dinner and most of the conversation was between them. Michael, sitting beside his boss, felt like an uninvited guest. Gross was intrigued when Doungjai told him she sold watches for a living and questioned her intently about the commercial aspects of her business.

For Doungjai, it was a novel experience to meet the middle-aged, stocky American with his iron grey hair and craggy features and she was quick to spot the change in Michael's demeanour. Normally outgoing and confident, he had become edgy and deferential. She could not understand the reason, although she guessed it had to do with Gross' presence. Perhaps that explained why she felt uneasy towards Michael's boss, albeit that she was flattered by his attentions, and could not fault his behaviour towards her.

Near the end of the meal, having shown no sign of travel fatigue, Gross asked Doungjai with a hint of more than small talk: 'Tell me, Doungjai, are your sisters as beautiful as you?'

'Much more beautiful,' she affirmed without hesitation. 'Oiy, she very pretty and not so fat like me.'

'You're not fat,' Gross protested.

'Have fat ass,' Doungjai informed him solemnly. 'Grandpapa him always tell me. Other sister, Meng, she very beautiful and very clever.' She touched her head. 'She have good thinking brain.'

'Is that right?' Gross looked at Michael and said casually. 'Perhaps we could arrange a foursome while I'm here?' Then back to Doungjai. 'Does your sister have a boyfriend?'

Doungjai appeared to ponder this possibility before slowly shaking her head. 'I not think she have boyfriend.'

'How old is she?'

'She nine next birthday.'

Michael turned quickly away and coughed into his napkin. Gross appeared lost for words for the first time that evening. His already florid features deepened in hue, and he signalled for the wine waiter to refill his brandy glass.

From Michael's point of view, the evening had been an unexpected success. The fact that it had not been possible to talk business was more than off-set by Gross' excellent humour, which he put down to Doungjai's presence.

Doungjai excused herself and clip-clopped off to the Ladies. The two men watched her cross the dining room, tall on her stilettos, her tightly skirted bottom swaying like a catwalking fashion model's. As soon as she was out of earshot, Gross whistled.

'Jesus Christ, Mike, that is the most fuckable piece of ass I've ever set eyes on and I've eye-balled a few I can tell you. Where did you find her, you lucky bastard?'

Michael brushed off his 'luck' with a modest shrug. 'I ran into her the other day when I was shopping. I asked her where I could get a good Thai meal, we got talking and she agreed to show me a typical Thai restaurant. We've met a few times since, but she's just a friend.'

He did not know why he made so light of their relationship, but Gross seized on it at once.

'Just a friend, eh?'

'I've only known her a few days,' Michael stressed defensively, beginning to feel uneasy about his boss's excessive interest in Doungjai. But Gross said no more before she rejoined them.

After some more small-talk the party broke up. Gross exchanged a quick word with Michael about the following morning's arrangements, his eyes continually straying towards Doungjai. He was effusive in his appreciation of her presence, and when they politely shook hands he seemed to have difficulty letting go of hers.

Although Doungjai was unused to such attention, the evening had not been the ordeal she had feared. Gross had been the perfect gentleman throughout and yet . . . and yet . . . There was something about his manner, especially towards the end of the evening, that made her feel slightly uncomfortable. She was too innocent, too naïve to know how to recognise the signs of male lust.

Chapter Twenty-Five

Doungjai was back at Michael's hotel and in his arms in the late afternoon of the next day. Even as he held her to him, she sensed that something was not quite right. His usual welcoming smile seemed slightly strained and he did not ask if she had had a successful day as he always did.

He sat silently on the edge of the bed as she undressed. She was conscious of him watching her every move. When she returned from the bathroom, fresh and cool from her shower and totally at ease in her nakedness, he drew her towards him until she was standing between his legs. He ran his hands over her velvet smooth skin, down her back and over her hips before palming the firm cheeks of her bottom. His head was level with her breasts and he pressed his face into them, nuzzling her nipples with his nose and tongue.

Doungjai passively accepted this homage to her opulent nudity and wondered if her initial impression, when she arrived, had been mistaken. She squirmed when he stroked her taut belly, smooth hairless mound and vaginal lips. She raised her arms and stretched to her full height, luxuriating in this exquisite exploration of her intimate bodily treasures. The light perfume she had splashed on in the bathroom, mingling with the natural female scent of her young body, heightened Michael's own sexual arousal. She became aware of his erection against her thigh and felt so aroused now that she could hardly wait for him to strip off and satisfy her.

He eased her back onto the bed, allowing one hand to remain trapped beneath the weight of her buttocks while he brushed the length of her body with his other, carefully following every curve and hollow.

It wasn't like him to be so unhurried. Doungjai, accustomed to his fast and furious technique, wondered what he was waiting for. When a fingertip began to agitate the bud of her clitoris, she could bear it no longer.

'We make love now, Michael?' she begged.

'I have to go away tomorrow,' he blurted out.

Her body stiffened. 'Where you go?'

'Only on business,' he said, dodging the question. 'I'll be back in a few days.'

He forced a smile, but something in his expression warned her there was more to come. 'Er . . . Jurgen – you know, my boss – was speaking about you today. He was very . . . er, impressed by you and really enjoyed your company last night.'

Doungjai felt her arousal start to subside. Her instinct told her he was leading up to something. She said nothing.

'While I'm away, he'd like to have the pleasure of your company,' Michael spilled the words out and, with an awful certainty, Doungjai realised that all these sexual distractions were intended to soften her up. A cold shower could not have drowned her passion more effectively. She slithered away from him, towards the top of the bed.

'You mean he wants to go shopping and have dinner with me when you away?'

'I'm sure he would like that.'

Michael stood up and walked over to the window. The view over Bangkok was in a state of transformation: high rise buildings were mushrooming everywhere, many of them still festooned with scaffolding beneath towering cranes. None of this visual confirmation of Asian economic growth and prosperity registered with him. When he turned, his face was solemn and he avoided her eyes.

'Doungjai, please understand, Jurgen is an important man and you would be doing me a great favour if you help make his stay in Bangkok as pleasant as possible.'

'You mean you want me to make love with him!' she accused. How could he even think of such a thing?

'It would certainly be a great help to me . . . er . . . if he were to ask you. I know he would want to show his appreciation.'

'So you not mind, Michael?' Her eyes glistened with unshed tears. 'It OK for me to go to bed with your boss?'

'It would only be for a few nights and then I'll be back.'

'And where you going?'

'I've told you already,' he said, with a show of irritation. 'I have to go away on business.'

'Hah! You mean you go stay in another hotel in Bangkok, because you cannot stay in same hotel as your boss.'

He did not argue her reasoning. He came away from the window to sit beside her on the bed. Hoping that physical contact might soften her attitude, he tried to take her hand, but she rejected the gesture and drew away from him.

'You're making far too much of this, Doungjai.' His tone suggested she was being unreasonable. 'Jurgen is very good company and I'm sure you will have a great time with him. He's very rich. You got on well together last night, didn't you?'

Doungjai moved to the far side of the bed and sat on the edge with her back to him. 'When he tell you he wants me to go with him, what you say?'

'I said I would ask you.' Michael licked his lips, glad she wasn't facing him. 'Look, Doungjai, this is no big deal. We've had a good time since we met and there's no reason why we can't carry on as before after he's gone.'

'You think so, Michael?' Doungjai rose from the bed and started to dress.

'What are you doing?' he demanded, surprised and exasperated.

'I have to go back to my place.'

'Do you want me to come with you?'

She shook her head.

'You won't be long will you? I've planned for us to eat at a new restaurant tonight.'

She stepped into her shoes and looked up at him. Her face was calm, but there was a sadness in her eyes. He had never seen her look more serenely beautiful. 'I come back in about one hour, maybe little more.'

'Are you sure?'

'I promise.' She turned without another word and let herself out of the room, closing the door softly behind her.

After Doungjai had gone, Michael was restless and on edge. He tried to read some business reports, but quickly put them aside and paced the room feeling angry and confused. Normally so assured in both his work and social life, he suddenly found himself in a situation that was beyond his ability to handle. Trapped between the carnal desires of his influential boss and the ethics of a little Thai watch-seller, he was completely out of his depth.

Why the hell had he given Gross an opening in the first place, the randy bastard? Instead of the 'just good friends' routine, he should have emphasised his closeness to Doungjai and hinted at future permanent plans, rings on third fingers even. But even though he had caved in to Gross' request, he had been unprepared for the vehemence of Doungjai's response. She was obviously hurt by his proposition. The way he had leaked it out, under her interrogation, had made it seem all the more sordid and underhand.

He turned to the minibar, but two whisky miniatures failed either to sharpen his mind in search of solutions, or dull it into indifference. He jumped when the telephone on the desk suddenly shrilled for attention, fraying further his already shredded nerves. 'Hello?' he croaked, hardly recognising his own voice.

'Is that you, Mike? It's Jurgen.'

'Hello, Jurgen, what can I do for you?'

'Sorry if you're . . . er, busy, I'm leaving shortly and there are a couple of points I would like to check out with you before I meet this guy.'

'Of course, would you like me to come up?'

'No need. If it's all right with you, I'll pop by on my way out. It will only take a couple of minutes.'

'No problem, I'll be here.'

Michael rang off and had barely topped up his glass with another miniature before there came an imperious rat-a-tat at the door. Glass in hand, Michael went to answer it.

'Hi, Mike,' Gross said, as he swept into the room, briefcase at the ready.

He refused Michael's offer of a drink and slumped onto the settee.

'I wondered if you could tell me anything about Santini's private life,' he said, opening his brief case and rustling papers. Any particular likes or dislikes, hobbies, that kind of thing. You know him pretty well, so I figured you might be able to give me a few leads. A little personal rapport can often help break the ice.'

'Works all the time,' Michael agreed, suddenly struck by the thought that Doungjai might return while his boss was here. In view of her reaction to the prospect of Gross as a bedmate, it might be as well to keep them apart for now.

'The little lady not here yet?' Gross asked suddenly, as if reading his thoughts.

'Er . . . she should be along soon.' If he admitted she had been there already this afternoon, Gross might guess they were more than just friends after all. He became increasingly uneasy at the prospect of a confrontation between Doungjai and Gross.

'Do you think she'll come across?' Gross was not making it any easier. Why did he have to make it sound so sleazy?

Michael turned away without answering. He wished his boss would not stare at him like that. Surely he did not suspect?

'So what can I tell you about Santini?' He tried to sound casual, whilst secretly desperate to hasten Gross' departure. 'He's a keen golfer and pretty good by all accounts, plays to a genuine seven handicap and . . . '

There came a knock on the door and he paused and looked up sharply.

She was back. He even recognised her knock.

'You'd better answer it, Mike. It might be the little lady,' Gross suggested cheerfully.

Chapter Twenty-Six

Doungjai was as aware as any other streetwise Thai teenager that sex and money are potent factors and used constantly to gain friendships and favours. But surely special friendships, like that between her and Michael, were in an entirely different category?

Such illusions were irrevocably shattered as Michael had unveiled his proposition to loan her to Gross. The impact was as great as if he had struck her. In an instant, the sham of this comfortable new world that had gently embraced her these last few days, was exposed as shallow and duplicitous.

As the reality of her relationship with Michael sank in, she felt physically sick. She could not think straight. Her only priority was to get out of the hotel and away on her own. In this state of semi-shock, she stumbled down Soi 22, oblivious of the traffic noise, the heat and the other pedestrians, impatient to find a taxi and cocoon herself from the outside world.

In the taxi, some semblance of order returned to her troubled mind. Her outrage towards Michael was overtaken by anger and disgust towards herself. Ever since she returned to Bangkok to make money to maintain her family, she had steered clear of any relationship, although she had not lacked for opportunities. When finally she had been induced to give herself to a man, he had proved to be a selfish, unscrupulous opportunist.

What hurt most was the probability that Michael must have weighed her up immediately. He had calculated that she could be bought. From there it was a short step to being hired out for his advancement.

Her feeling of personal guilt intensified when she thought about her mother and brothers and sisters. What would they think of her if they knew? Of course, it was unlikely they ever would learn of her fall from grace, but nonetheless, she intended to atone for it if she could. From that moment in the hotel bedroom, when she realised what Michael was hinting at, her instincts had suggested only one course of action. By the time the taxi reached her apartment, she knew exactly what she had to do.

As Michael had expected, his visitor was Doungjai. She was wearing the same outfit he had seen her in that first night in Silom Road when he had stopped to look at her watches – the same baggy black trousers, the same loose fitting T-shirt and scuffed trainers. She wore no make-up and her hair was tied back in a ponytail. She could have passed for fourteen or fifteen. The usual wide smile was missing. Instead there was a strange, almost despairing, look in those lovely eyes that made him catch his breath.

'I promise I come back, Michael,' she said softly. Looking past him, she caught sight of Gross and added in an even lower voice so that only Michael could hear. 'I come say goodbye.'

'What are you talking about?' he protested in a loud whisper. 'Come in and . . .' as he opened the door wider, he saw that behind Doungjai was a heap of bulging plastic bags, most of them bearing the names and logos of Bangkok's premier department stores. 'What have you got there?'

'Thank you for all you give me, Michael,' she said, her voice low and subdued. 'You been very kind to me, but now I bring everything back you buy for me – clothes, jewellery, shoes, tape player – everything.'

'Come on, Doungjai, this really isn't necessary,' Michael pleaded, glancing warily over his shoulder, fearful of Gross overhearing.

She dragged the bags closer to the door. 'I hope clothes not creased too much.'

Michael stared helplessly at the mountain of multi-coloured plastic and was still searching for the right words when Doungjai produced her well-worn purse and extracted all the banknotes from one of the pockets. She slipped one back and placed the others in Michael's hand.

'This is all money I have left you give me, three hundred twenty bahts. I keep fifty bahts for *tuk tuk* to go work tonight.'

'Look, Doungjai, I don't know what this is all about, but if I've upset you I'm very sorry. Whatever I've done, I promise I'll make it up to you.' He tried to take her hand and draw her into the room, but she stepped back away from him.

'No, Michael.' She took a deep breath as though bracing herself to deliver a rehearsed speech. There was a slight tremor in her voice as she went on: 'I was wrong to take all these lovely presents you buy for me, but I like nice clothes too much. I never have like this before. You been very good to me, Michael, very kind and I don't mind when you fuck me. You been special to me, Michael, and I think I special to you and it OK to fuck if people like each other very much.'

'I do like you very much,' he insisted.

She ignored his protest. 'I not a whore, Michael. I not make love with anyone but you. I was virgin before I met you, but when you ask me to sleep with Mister Jurgen, I know you not respect me and it all my fault. When I go back to my place tonight, I think what to do. Now I know I am very bad girl, am too greedy. I take many things from you I not work for, but let you do everything to me instead. I let you think I cheap. I sorry.' She lowered her eyes, losing the battle against the tears that had started to well.

'I've never thought anything like that about you, Doungjai.' Shocked by her interpretation of his motives, Michael struggled to find the right words to placate and reassure her. 'It's not the way you think – give me a break will you? And anyway, I certainly don't want any of these things back. I bought them to make you happy.'

He could tell from her face that he was making no impression. With the plastic bags piled round the doorway, Doungjai standing tearful but unyielding out in the corridor, and Gross almost certainly an avid listener in the room behind him, reasoning with her was impossible.

'I send you back TV as well,' Doungjai said, clearly not moved by Michael's pleas.

'This is absolutely crazy, Doungjai . . .' he tried again, but she was not listening.

'Goodbye, Michael,' she spoke with quiet dignity. 'Thank you for everything and good luck to you.' Without another word, she turned and headed for the lift at the end of the corridor.

'Doungjai, please come back,' Michael called after her, but she did not break her step or turn her head.

He had never felt so helpless and the emptiness that engulfed him was all the greater because he knew it was due to his own bad faith.

He stared at the closing lift door, his last sight of her. Shaking his head in remorse and regret, he returned to his room to face his boss.

By the time the lift reached the lobby, tears were streaming down Doungjai's face. She weaved across the huge foyer, heedless of the stares she attracted. Out in the heavy heat and traffic noise, she waved down a *tuk tuk* and, with one last look up at the towering hotel building she had just left, climbed aboard.

During the ride she recovered some of her composure. She paid off the driver beside the Hongkong Bank in Silom Road. Her mind was still numb and her heart heavy, but her eyes were dry. Her friend was setting out the display of watches and tried to hide her disappointment when she saw Doungjai. She was a middle aged, bouncy woman who lived on her own in the same apartment block. They had become friends soon after Doungjai had moved in a few weeks earlier.

'Have a quarrel with your boyfriend?' she joked, not realising how close she was to the truth.

Doungjai tried to look unconcerned as she moved some of the watches around on the tray. 'I forgot he was going away today. I'm not sure when he'll be back.' She did not offer any further explanation.

Her friend gave her a long look, but did not probe. 'So you don't need me tonight after all?'

'I think I can manage.' Doungjai forced a smile. 'Thank you for helping me out these last few days.'

When her friend had departed, Doungjai took up

her vigil beside the tray of watches. It was a hot humid evening and she could already feel the beads of perspiration popping out on her face. She could have been freshly showered and all dressed up by now, ready to go out to dinner. She wondered where Michael had planned to take her tonight. He had promised somewhere new. Wherever it was, it would have been a top class restaurant. Michael always insisted on giving her the best.

She looked at her watch. It would be four hours before she packed up and returned to her small room, alone. Without all those lovely clothes, hanging in colourful splendour round the hardboard walls, and especially after she had returned the TV set she loved so much, it was going to seem very empty.

A few weeks after Doungjai had ended her relationship with Michael, an article appeared in one of the inside pages of the Business Section of the *Bangkok Post*. It referred to the international computer company, NAC, and the unexpected resignation of its Overseas Sales Director, Mr Michael Paquet.

The article concluded; 'Mr Paquet's sudden departure has surprised many in the industry. After his high profile appointment at such a young age, and his perceived success in the job, observers believed that he was destined for the very top echelons of the company. It was widely hinted that he may even succeed Mr Jurgen Gross as the next Chief Executive of NAC. No reason has been given for Mr Paquet's sudden resignation, but the parting is believed to have been amicable.'

The article made no mention of the deterioration in the personal friendship between Michael and his boss, Jurgen Gross, and its origins. Fortunately for the parties concerned, the press had not been privy to Michael's dalliance and Gross' pecadilloes.

Doungjai's reaction to Michael's clumsy attempt at procurement, had taught him a great deal about integrity. It had come as a considerable surprise to discover that not everyone has a price. As for Doungjai herself, she now knew that there is no such thing in life as a free lunch. Alone in her room, she reflected many times on those days and nights she had spent with Michael and one thought kept intruding: if only it had been Robert who had come along Silom Road that evening looking for a watch, everything would have been so different.

As she had so often wondered before, so she wondered again: would Robert ever return to Bangkok and, if he did, would he still want to know her?

Part Three
Return To Uncertainty

Chapter Twenty-Seven

What the hell was he doing here? Alone in his room Robert Stone sat on the edge of an unyielding mattress and looked about him. His surroundings were not prepossessing, to say the least. He derived little inspiration from the stained wallpaper, so faded its pattern was no longer apparent, even less in the threadbare beige carpet and the small fridge tucked into an alcove beneath the ancient TV set, and none at all in the view from his window across a narrow courtyard. Apart from the flat drone of the air-conditioning, the room was silent.

On that first visit to Bangkok with his parents, the company for whom Robert's father then worked had met all expenses. But there was no company to pay the bills this time. Recession followed by redundancy had wiped away twenty years of loyal service and with it the family's lovely house and second car. His father, like so many executives of his generation, was having to start again, and his mother had had to find a job to help make ends meet. He himself had been lucky to be taken on as a management trainee.

But the biggest blow to Robert amid all the family misfortunes had been the severance of his contact with Doungjai. A few months after he returned home, she had stopped writing to him, abruptly, without any hint of her intention to break off communications. Now three years later, having accumulated a bare minimum of funds plus a month's leave, he was back in Bangkok to try and rediscover his lost love.

Waves of fatigue swept over him as the effects of the flight and the whole uncertainty of his visit all hit him at once. He took a deep breath and stood up. This was not the moment to cave in. The bed was inviting, but if he succumbed to its soft invitation he would sleep round the clock and feel twice as bad when he awoke. No, he must stay on his feet and on the move, and try to stay awake at least until the evening.

His best chance of finding Doungjai was clearly to visit the house where she had lived three years before. Even if she was no longer there, someone should be able to tell him the family's new address. It was an obvious first step, but he was reluctant to take it today. If he drew a blank, he had little else to go on and his quest would be virtually over before it began. No, he would save that visit until tomorrow; today he would follow his second best lead – the shop where she had worked part-time.

He reached for his wallet and took out a photograph. It was the one he had taken on the bridge in the park the day of their first chance meeting. As he stared at it, a lump formed in his throat. God, she was beautiful. He never tired of looking at that photo, even though it filled him with regret for what might have been.

Whatever happened in the future, he knew he was unlikely ever to recapture the exhilaration of those first days they had spent walking the busy streets of Bangkok in each other's company. Their only enemy had been time. It had loomed over their every precious moment together, like a patient predator, watching, waiting, inevitable.

What had become of her after she left school? he wondered. Perhaps she had tired of keeping in touch at such long distance or met someone else, even another tourist on holiday, and re-enacted all those things they had done together. She might even be married by now, to a local Thai boy, or a foreigner who had taken her back to his own country. She may have a child of her own, or more than one. Such thoughts were torture to Robert. Maybe after all it would have been better never to know, to hold on instead to the memories which, left undisturbed, would be forever unspoiled.

That, of course, was the soft option. Robert had known he would regret it for the rest of his life if he did not make at least one effort to try and trace Doungjai, and resume their relationship if that were possible. Or accept that it was over for good.

After a shower and a change of clothes, he felt slightly better, though still not exactly bursting with energy or enthusiasm. He decided to unpack later and, at the Reception Desk, cashed some travellers cheques and placed his passport, flight ticket and extra cash in the hotel safe deposit. On his previous visit to Bangkok, the shop where Doungjai worked had been within walking distance of the hotel. This one was further away, so he waved down a *tuk tuk* and, too tired to bargain, accepted the fare quoted to him.

The *tuk tuk* made good progress in the morning traffic and the high pitched whine of the two-stroke engine, combining with the swirl of air around the open canopy, helped to lift Robert's flagging senses. They stopped at the end of Soi 3, just past the Grace

Hotel. He paid the fare and, yawning, trudged into Sukhumvit Road. Crossing Soi 5, he glanced up at the Amari Boulevard Hotel, a hundred yards along on the right. With its smoked glass windows, sloping front and white aerial mast, Robert thought how much it resembled a giant robot gazing west up Ploenchit and Rama 1.

He remembered her instructions quite clearly from his previous visit and paused as he neared Soi 7, there to receive his first shock. The shops were no more than open spaces, filled with goods right up to the entrance. He had forgotten how alike they looked. He had no idea which shop Doungjai had worked in. It could have been any one of the twenty or so that occupied the street between Sois 7 and 9. Her shop had sold mainly clothes, plus some leather goods hanging from the roof and across the entrance, but that didn't help him identify it, as most of the shops on this stretch offered a similar range.

Picking a stall at random, he found a girl who spoke passable English.

'I'm looking for a friend who used to work along here,' he told her, waving vaguely along the street in each direction. 'Her name is Doungjai.'

'You know which shop she work?' the girl asked.

'Well . . . er . . . that's the problem. I'm not exactly sure, but I do know it was one of these. How long have you worked here?'

'About one year.'

This was disappointing. Unless Doungjai had continued to work there for another two years after he had returned home, it was unlikely this girl would know her.

'Do you know if any girl called Doungjai works in

216

one of these shops? She would be about seventeen or eighteen years old now.'

The girl shook her head emphatically.

'Would you mind asking the other girls in the shop if they know anyone of that name?' The feeling of hopelessness was creeping back already, but an ember of hope was rekindled when he remembered the photo in his wallet. He took it out and showed it to the girl. 'This might help.'

There was no sign of recognition on the girl's face as she scrutinised the photo. 'I ask,' she promised and retreated into the shop.

Robert watched the girl speaking to her colleagues. They glanced over at him before clustering around the photograph. Their expressions and gestures did not look promising.

The girl returned and handed Robert the photo. 'Sorry, nobody know. How long you say she work here before?'

'I'm not sure, but I do know she was working in one of these shops when I came to Bangkok three years ago.'

'Three years?' the girl repeated incredulously.

'That's right.'

'Long time,' she said, with another doleful head-shake. Her tone suggested that she thought he was either mad or joking.

Robert tried to dispel her disbelief. 'That was when I last came to Bangkok, but she might have worked here for a long time after that.'

The girl tapped the photograph. 'When take this photograph?'

'Three years ago.' He was beginning to feel a little ridiculous about the time lapse.

Again the girl arched her thin eyebrows. 'Maybe

she look different now,' she suggested logically if not very helpfully. The thought had occurred to Robert all too frequently.

'I realise that, but it's the only photo I have of her.' Further exchanges seemed futile. 'Anyway, thank you for your help. I think I'll try further along.'

'You welcome.' The girl was heading back into the shop when he looked back. Robert could imagine her telling her friends about her conversation with this crazy young *falang* looking for a long-lost girl friend.

He stopped at all the shops between Sois 7 and 9 that carried a similar range of goods to the one where he remembered Doungjai had worked. The result was much the same. No one remembered her, no one recognised her from the photograph. It was barely lunchtime on his first morning back in Bangkok and one of his only two real leads had already proved to be worthless.

The portents were not favourable.

Chapter Twenty-Eight

Giving up all hope of finding Doungjai through her shop, Robert walked on down Sukhumvit Road. Although it was seven hours since he had picked at a mushroom omelette somewhere over the Bay of Bengal, he was not at all hungry, though he could have used a drink.

The self-serving City Food Centre at the Ambassador Hotel seemed his best bet. He and Doungjai had eaten there on occasions, but when he reached the entrance he saw that major changes had taken place in the intervening years. Parking was now restricted to the centre of the wide area leading up to the hotel. Down each side the cages of exotic birds and the old restaurant had been replaced by row upon row of small shop units, while the whole had been renamed 'Bangkapi Plaza'.

Although it looked much smarter than he remembered, Robert still found the changes depressing, especially the absence of the birds. He and Doungjai had strongly disapproved of all those lovely creatures being held within a few square yards of wire mesh and yet their disappearance represented another break with the past.

The self service restaurant had been re-located behind the row of shops on the right. Robert bought a supply of vouchers, exchanged some of them for a shell of ice cold coconut milk and took in the other changes. The new eating area boasted endless rows of bright yellow metal tables and chairs. Down one side several television sets, all blaring at full volume, had been installed.

When he had emptied the coconut shell, Robert checked in his unused vouchers and looked around uncertainly. He considered retracing his steps along Sukhumvit in the hope of happening on someone who remembered Doungjai. But he could not face more incredulous looks or shaking heads, so decided to return to the hotel.

He felt slightly more in control of events after he had unpacked. Stowing away the empty suitcase in the tiny wall cupboard seemed finally to mark the end of that interminable journey from England. He lacked the energy to go out again and decided that a couple of hours by the swimming pool would be as good a way as any of whiling away the afternoon.

The hotel pool proved to be a very poor relation of the one he and his parents had swum in with Doungjai. It was about a quarter the size and tucked away on the third floor, as if to discourage guests from using it. The hotel walls loomed over three sides restricting direct sunlight to a few short hours each afternoon.

To begin with, Robert had the pool to himself. He flopped wearily onto a sunbed and nodded off almost at once, only to jerk back to wakefulness when a loud voice spoke in his ear.

'How's it going, pal?'

The tone was deep, thick and Scottish; it's owner turned out to be a stockily built man of about thirty.

'OK,' Robert responded warily, unsure whether to encourage further conversation.

The decision was taken out of his hands when the man dropped onto the next sunbed and pulled his Lacoste sweat shirt over his head.

'On holiday?' he enquired.

'Sort of,' Robert said, suppressing a yawn. Then feeling he should elaborate: 'I just arrived this morning, so I'm feeling a bit whacked.'

'I know what you mean. I enjoy coming here, but I hate that bloody journey. By the way I'm George, but everyone calls me Cully.' He stuck out a hand as big as a baseball glove and Robert's was completely swallowed by it.

Cully had a large, slightly pudgy face, with clear blue eyes. His dark brown hair was long and unkempt and he had the pasty complexion of high northern latitudes. A raised white scar scythed angrily from beneath his left ear, following his jawline and petering out an inch from his chin. It was not the kind of scratch acquired while shaving.

The Scotsman's physique was impressive to say the least. He was perhaps a couple of stone overweight, but his barrel chest, barn door shoulders and massive biceps should have carried a health warning for anyone foolish enough to bear him aggressive intent.

'I'm Robert, hello.' The teenager was relieved when his hand was returned intact.

'Sort of on holiday, what does that mean?' Cully probed.

'Yes . . . well I'm here to try and find someone I've lost touch with.'

'So you've been here before?'

'Three years ago, I . . . I . . .' Why not talk about it? He had nothing to hide and it might help to lighten his gloom. 'I met this girl and we got on great together. We wrote to each other when I went home and then . . .' This was the hard part. 'She stopped writing.' To cover up the surge of emotion he reached for his wallet and produced Doungjai's photograph.

'Very nice,' Cully approved after a long appraisal. 'When were you last in touch with her?'

'About two and a half years ago.' Robert shrugged defensively. 'I can't understand it. I would have come back sooner, but other things at home got in the way.' He felt that hopeless feeling creeping back. Perhaps it had not been such a smart idea to open up to a stranger.

Cully handed the photo back and nodded sympathetically. 'I know, these Thai birds do get under your skin. The first time I came here, I got involved with this wee thing. Her name was Tan and she came from Lumpoon. That's up near Chiang Mai where they say the most beautiful Thai girls come from. As well as their full name, which is usually unpronounceable, they have short nicknames, like Kai, Ging, Wan, Bee and Nok. I can never remember them, except this particular one, perhaps that's because she was the first.' The Scotsman's mouth twitched into a little smile as his thoughts reached back. 'When we first met, I played it pretty cool. You know, keep them at arm's length, don't get involved, nothing heavy. But when she came to see me off at the end of the holiday, I cried like a bairn. Did you ever hear anything so bloody daft?'

Robert nodded gratefully. If this shaggy powerhouse, who looked as if he could walk through a brick wall without noticing it was affected to such an extent, perhaps he was not such a softy after all.

'I suppose you'll try her old address first?' Cully said, turning the spotlight back onto Robert's problems.

'Yes, I'm going there tomorrow, although I don't expect she'll still be at the same place. I sent several letters there after she stopped writing and I can't believe she would have ignored all of them. Anyway, if she has moved, I'm hoping someone there can tell me where she's gone.'

'You might have difficulty with the language,' Cully warned. 'Once you get away from the hotels and the shops, English speakers are a bit thin on the ground.' He pronounced it 'groond'.

Robert had not thought of that. 'Do you speak any Thai?' he asked.

Cully shook his head. 'How much?', 'thank you', and 'you're welcome' is about my limit. I'd like to be able to speak more, but it's very difficult to learn unless you live here. It's not just knowing the right words, nor even how to pronounce them, you need to have the right pitch in your voice as well. I can count in Thai.' Cully claimed, as an afterthought. 'Take a tip from me, whenever you go to a foreign country, even if you can't speak a word of the language, at least learn to count. It can be very useful when you're shopping, especially if you want to bargain. It also helps sometimes with taxis, paying bills, telling the time and so on. And it impresses the locals.'

'I'll remember that.' Robert was beginning to enjoy the conversation. It was far better than keeping everything bottled up and spinning the doubts and misgivings around in his head. Besides, for all his rugged appearance, the Scotsman had a friendly personality and seemed to talk a lot of sense. Robert found he was warming to him.

'Are you here on holiday . . . er . . . Cully?'

'Aye, I'm here for a month. I try to get over once or

twice a year for a break. It makes a nice change from Glasgow.'

'Is that where your home is?'

'Just outside, in Clydebank, but I work in the city. I'm a doorman at a night club,' he grinned. 'A bouncer if you like.'

That was not surprising. 'How did you get into a job like that?'

'Just fell into it. I was out of work and a friend told me about a club who were looking for someone, so I applied. I've always been able to look after myself, which helps.'

'I wouldn't imagine it's the most restful of jobs,'

'Och, you get the occasional episode, but no often. If a customer looks like getting a wee bit out of hand, a few discreet words usually settles things down.' Cully made a bouncer's job sound about as exciting as helping an old lady across the road. Then he fingered the scar beneath his ear.

'This is the only decoration I have to show from my stint in clubland. I was still fairly new at the job when I got it, and didn't know that rule number one is never take any situation casually.

'Anyway, this guy was getting a bit over excited, effing and blinding about the beer and the company. I went over to tell him to cool the language and he seemed to calm down and turned away. Then the next thing I knew, he swung back at my face with a knife. I think he was after my ear for a trophy and nearly got the jugular instead.'

'What happened then?' Robert's exposure to such events was confined to a few lurid inches of copy in the tabloids.

'I hit him.'

'And then?'

'He went down like a sack of bricks.' Cully stared into the pool as he recounted the episode. There was no element of bravado or intent to impress. It was as if he were describing an event that had happened to somebody else.

Almost self-consciously, he looked up and grinned at Robert. 'What I couldn't understand as I looked down at him was the fact that he was covered in blood. It turned out to be all mine. So they carted me off to the hospital, pumped in a few pints of the red stuff, stitched me up and I was right as rain in a few days. It taught me a lesson, I can tell you.'

'What happened to the bloke with the knife?'

'Needless to say, he was on drugs. If it's no drugs it's drink. He had the usual sob story about a broken marriage and no job. Apparently he spent the night in clink, was released on bail and ended up doing a wee stretch of community service.' Cully shook his head disgustedly. 'The way the judicial system works back home these days, it's a bloody wonder they didn't pin a medal on him and lock *me* up for assault.' He glanced around. 'Och, but that's in the past. This is much more my scene – peace and quiet.'

'Do you know many people here in Thailand?' Robert asked.

'Some of the girls on the stalls and a few who work in the bars. As a matter of fact, I met a nice wee thing the last time I was here. She's just gone home to see her family, somewhere out near the Cambodian border. When she comes back, I'm hoping to take her down to Koh Samui for a few days. Have you been there?'

'No, last time I was here I was with my parents. Apart from a few days up in Chiang Mai, we spent all our time in Bangkok.'

'If you catch up with this girl of yours, take her to Koh Samui. It's well worth a visit,' Cully advised. 'Bangkok is OK, as long as you don't need to go anywhere in a hurry, but the traffic is a bastard and seems to get worse every time I come. Now they've started on this overhead rail project and about bloody time too. Trouble is, while they're building it, the congestion will be even worse.'

They continued to chat until the sun eased behind the hotel building and the pool was thrown into deep shadow.

'That looks like our ration of sunshine for the day,' Cully observed, pulling on his shirt. 'I was going to have a swim, but don't think I'll bother.' He stood up. 'It's been good talking to you.'

'I've enjoyed it too,' Robert acknowledged and he meant it. He had even shed several layers of tiredness.

'If you feel like a jar before turning in any night, I'm usually in the bar later on.'

'Thanks, I'll remember that, though I don't think it'll be tonight. I'm just hanging on till this evening and then I'll crash out for twelve hours.'

'Well good luck tomorrow. I hope you find her.'

As the bulky figure disappeared into the hotel, Robert gathered his things and followed. Somehow he didn't even feel quite so lonely now.

Chapter Twenty-Nine

Robert still had the piece of paper that Doungjai had given him three years ago. It was creased, torn and dog-eared, but her address was still legible. She had written it in Thai so there would be no misunder-standing when he showed it to the taxi driver. The driver looked long and hard at it with a dubious expression before finally nodding. Robert wondered why, and would have asked had he known how to speak the language.

Doungjai's house was in the Ding Daeng area of the city. Robert remembered nothing of the route until the last half mile when they turned off the main thoroughfare and down a narrow *soi*, which carried two-way traffic where there was scarcely room for one-way. As he peered out expectantly, when the taxi reached the end of the *soi*, he could not believe his eyes. The well-remembered square of open ground was still there but instead of the single-storey wooden structures that surrounded it, were lines of identical off-white buildings five or six storeys high. Clearly the taxi driver had made a mistake.

Robert waved his piece of paper in front of the driver. 'This isn't right,' he insisted loudly, but the driver was adamant, pointing at the unintelligible Thai script and indicating the buildings around them. When he saw that Robert was not convinced, he called to a man who was passing and spoke to him in animated fashion. The man listened attentively, read the address and nodded in confirmation.

'But that's impossible,' Robert protested desperately, knowing he was fighting a losing battle.

A young woman came by at that moment and stopped when she heard the disagreement. She was well dressed in a light grey suit, tightly upswept hair and high heels.

'Can I help?' she asked. Robert was never so relieved to hear someone speak English.

She went through the same ritual again, hearing what the taxi driver had to say, looking at the piece of paper and listening to Robert's protests.

'This is the address on the paper,' she confirmed at last. 'I live here so I should know. The only difference is the name. Now they are called "New Sithavee Apartments". I believe the name changed when they re-developed the area.'

'Do you know how long ago that was?'

The woman shook her head slowly. 'I'm not sure, I think about one year, maybe two. I've only lived here for six months.'

Robert thanked the woman and prevailed on her to ask his driver to wait a few minutes. At least he wanted to try and identify the spot where Doungjai's home had once stood.

The task proved to be beyond him. None of the paths she had guided him along existed any longer. The whole complex had been completely gutted and re-designed and he had no idea where to go.

The sinking feeling returned as Robert realised he was no nearer finding Doungjai and his best prospect had just evaporated. A redevelopment on this scale would not have happened overnight. Doungjai was bound to have known beforehand, and if they were to be re-housed in one of the new apartments, or had moved to somewhere else, she would have had plenty of time to let him know. It was beginning to look increasingly as if she had just decided to stop writing.

After a final lingering look in the general direction where he thought Doungjai once lived, he returned to the taxi and asked the driver to return him to the hotel.

What now? A telephone call to the airline to book an early flight back to the UK figured prominently in his thoughts, but to give up so soon after two set-backs, however severe, seemed rather premature. Bereft of leads he may be, but he still had a couple of wild cards to play: he and Doungjai had spent a lot of time together in the various McDonalds establishments dispersed around the city, and the chances were she still frequented one or more of them. He would trek round them all, armed with Doungjai's photo. If she was a regular customer, a member of the staff might well recognise her.

Perhaps he should try and recruit a Thai person with a decent command of English. With an interpreter to pose his questions and field the answers, he might even make another stab at the shops in Suk-humvit Road. By the time the taxi drew up outside his hotel, he had resolved to adopt a more systematic approach. What he needed was someone who knew his way around Bangkok to bounce a few ideas off.

He collected his key at Reception and swung round, to collide with another man who had just arrived at the desk.

'Sorry!' he exclaimed, then, recognising the other party: 'Oh, hello . . . er, Cully.'

'Hello, pal.' The Scotsman's grin gave Robert a much needed lift. He dropped his key into the box on the desk and they walked across the lobby together. 'Any luck this morning?'

Robert shook his head. 'It was worse than I feared. Where my friend used to live has been pulled down and re-developed. It was unrecognisable.'

'That's bad luck,' Cully sympathised. 'So what now?'

Robert shrugged in resignation. 'I'm nearly out of ideas. I just don't have anything else to go on.'

They stopped at the door to go their separate ways.

'Tell you what,' Cully suggested. 'Why not join us for a meal this evening? My girl friend, Nang, is back and she'll be over in a couple of hours. We're off to Koh Samui tomorrow afternoon and I'm just going down to the travel agents to pick up the tickets.'

Robert hesitated. 'Thanks, but I'm not sure I'd be very good company tonight.'

'Come on – it'll do you good and Nang may have some ideas you hadn't thought of.'

Robert gave in. After the morning's fiasco, he was not looking forward to spending the evening alone, brooding over his second failure in two days.

'All right, thanks, I'd like that,' he said gratefully.

'Terrific, let's meet down here about 7.30.' Robert's knees buckled as Cully clapped him on the shoulder, but already he felt more cheerful.

He even smiled as he watched the Scotsman stride off down the road, declining successive offers of a *tuk tuk*, a watch and a massage, before he was absorbed in the crowd.

Chapter Thirty

Cully and his girl friend, Nang, were waiting for Robert when he descended to the lobby just before 7.30. She gave him a polite smile and a murmured greeting in English, when they were introduced.

She was a pretty girl with elfin features that were nicely complemented by her hairstyle – straight fringe at the front and cut short and thick round the nape of her neck, so that it resembled a black helmet. Her make-up was a little overdone by Robert's standards, otherwise he could see why Cully was attracted to her, notwithstanding that her slim elegance was at odds with the Scotman's shambling bulk. A computer dating agency would never have matched them. But if they were physical opposites, their temperaments seemed well suited.

They took a taxi to the Narai Hotel, near Silom Village. Leaving behind the pounding traffic in Silom Road at the swing doors and, passing between the coffee and pizzeria pasta shops, they mounted a wide staircase to the restaurant on the first floor. Their table by the metal railings overlooked the spacious reception area below, like the balcony of a theatre. Behind them, a four-piece band played country and western music fronted by a young man and woman in stetsons, chanting Tennessee lyrics with a Thai accent.

The whole place had a bustling, cheerful atmosphere and without consulting the menu, Cully recommended the king size prawns.

'They serve the best in the world after the Mandarin Hotel in Hongkong,' he claimed expansively. 'And they're a lot cheaper here.'

Robert accepted his recommendation, but Nang opted for a Thai dish with the obligatory rice base. At first, conversation was rather strained and Robert felt very much the odd one out. Cully made a point of drawing him into the conversation, and he soon began to relax. Nang told him about the variety of jobs she had done, including waitress, shop assistant and receptionist, all of which had helped her improve her English. Eventually, the money had led to her present job in a massage parlour, which was where she met Cully. She was taking a holiday to be with him in Bangkok, but would be returning to the massage parlour when he returned to England.

'I don't like her working there,' Cully frowned, then philosophically: 'But then if she didn't, I would never have met her.' More pragmatically, he admitted: 'And she does give a bloody good massage.'

'I always give special for him.' Nang said with a shy smile, placing her small hands over Cully's huge paw, leaving Robert to imagine how special was special.

'Do you like working there?' Robert asked her, genuinely curious.

She shook her head emphatically. 'No like, but need the money. I want to start my own business, selling clothes, so need to save. Also send money home to my family.'

'Do your family know where you work?' It was really none of his business, but he was intrigued.

'No.' Nang shook her head furiously. 'If they know I work in massage . . .' She clenched her hand into a small fist and punched the air, indicating dire consequences.

Then she gave a little shrug of resignation. 'I tell them I work in department store.'

'Well, it's Koh Samui tomorrow,' Cully reminded her cheerfully. 'Did you get the tickets this afternoon, Nang?'

She frowned. 'Tickets?'

'The air tickets. I said I would organise the hotel if you took care of the flight.'

She began to look worried and then, seeing Cully give Robert a quick wink, realised he was teasing her. Her face lit up with relief and she slapped his arm playfully. 'I tell you before, you terrible man, always you worry me.'

Cully chuckled heartily, but Robert's smile was tinged with sad reminiscence. It was another reminder of how he and Doungjai used to kid each other.

'What do you think of her?' Cully asked when Nang had gone to the Ladies. Just as Robert had quickly developed a liking for Cully, in return it seemed he had genuinely taken to the teenager and even valued his opinion.

'I think she's very nice. Good company, very attractive, and she's obviously mad about you.'

'Aye, I believe she is. She can be a bit bloody jealous and possessive at times, but I suppose that might be regarded as some sort of compliment.' Cully eyed his near empty glass reflectively. 'She wears a wee bitty too much make-up but she says it's because she wants to look her best for me all the time, so I can't say too much.' He looked up with that knowing grin. 'And she's fantastic in bed, so how can I complain?'

233

'Is it serious? Your relationship, I mean.'

His mood became sombre. 'I suppose I could do worse than settle down with someone like her. I'll be thirty-two next birthday. It's about time I stopped chasing around on my own and started to think about the future.'

Robert could not remember anyone opening up their innermost thoughts to him like this before. It surprised him, especially coming from an ex-bouncer. It made him realise that everybody, even people as outwardly self-assured and worldly as the big Scotsman, had private doubts.

When Nang reappeared Cully greeted her boisterously. 'Here she is, looking more like a movie star than ever.'

Though she swatted him playfully, her face showed pleasure at the compliment.

It was not until the coffee arrived that Cully raised the subject that had been on Robert's mind all evening. 'I told Nang you were looking for your girl friend in Bangkok. I've also been doing a wee bit of thinking myself.'

Robert waited while Cully took a slow deliberate sip of his coffee, clearly pleased with what he had come up with and enjoying the expectations he had raised.

'You said you've been to all the places where you think she might be,' Cully went on. 'Or where someone might know her, like her old home and where she used to work.'

'It seemed the obvious starting point.'

'I agree, but there's another angle you might consider as well.'

'What's that?'

'Have you thought about it from her point of view?'

Robert stared at him blankly.

'Look, what if she lost your address? She wouldn't be able to write to you.'

'But that's impossible,' Robert protested. 'I wrote to her for months after I went home, dozens of letters, and I put my address on every one of them. Even if she did lose her address book, or whatever she used, she only had to wait for my next one.'

Cully pursed his lips. 'OK, but what if they had a fire or something and your letters were destroyed? The family might have had to move out and maybe no one forwarded your subsequent letters, because they didn't know where she'd gone?' He grimaced at the doubt on Robert's face. 'I know it's unlikely, but it's possible.'

'Even if that did happen, I don't see how it'll help me to find her.' Robert shook his head.

'At least it would explain why she didn't write, and that it wasn't because she couldn't be bothered any longer.' Cully warmed to his theme. 'That would put her in a worse situation than you are. However much she wanted to keep in touch, if she had no address she would have no hope of finding the fare to come looking for you.'

This was just speculation. Robert decided to play along anyway. Cully meant well.

'So what might she do?' he asked.

Cully turned to Nang. 'What would you do in that situation, Nang?'

She had listened closely to their conversation, Cully having explained Robert's problem earlier. 'If I want to find my boyfriend but no have his address?'

'That's right, pretend that you're Robert's girlfriend.'

'You no have any friends in Bangkok where I can go and ask about you?'

Robert shook his head. 'Afraid not.'

'Maybe I ask at the hotel where you stay last time.'

Robert and Cully exchanged glances which said simultaneously. 'Why didn't we think of that?'

'Of course.' Cully clamped an arm enthusiastically round Nang. 'Did anyone ever tell you that you're absolutely brilliant as well as beautiful?'

From the look on her face, Nang was not even sure what he meant, only that she had said something that pleased them.

'Wait a minute,' Robert cautioned. 'I'm still not clear what you're suggesting. Even if she did go to the hotel where I stayed last time, where would that get her?'

'When you check in, you have to fill in a card that includes your name and home address,' Cully reminded him.

Robert was still not convinced 'But how long do they keep records like that? And if they did still have them, are they likely to hand such information over to anyone who comes in and asks?'

'There's one sure way of finding out,' said Cully. 'Tell you what, we don't leave for Samui till tomorrow afternoon. Would you like us to come to the hotel with you in the morning? I know they speak English there, but Nang may be able to explain better in Thai what we're after.'

It was unlikely to take him any further, but the way Robert felt, even a bit of moral support would be welcome. He nodded gratefully. 'Thanks, I'd appreciate that if you don't mind, Nang?'

She nodded. 'Of course, no problem.'

If no startlingly original ideas had arisen during the evening to help him find Doungjai, Robert had enjoyed the company. It was also comforting to know that he was no longer completely alone in Bangkok.

Chapter Thirty-One

The memories came crowding back as soon as Robert, with Cully and Nang close on his heels, walked into the hotel where he and his parents had stayed three years before. 'This is very posh,' Cully approved. 'Makes ours look a bit basic.'

'My father's company were footing the bill,' Robert explained.

'Aye, it's a lot easier to live in style if you don't have to pay for it out of your own pocket'.

It might have been only yesterday. Here at least it all looked exactly the same and even the faces of some of the staff on duty behind the long Reception Desk were familiar. It was amusing to see the looks of half recognition on their faces as he approached. He was inches taller, much broader, three years older, yet . . . ?

He greeted them as if it were only last week. After a brief exchange of pleasantries, he handed over to Nang who carried on the conversation in Thai. Cully stood back and admired the shining marble floors, huge gleaming chandeliers and heavily brocaded armchairs and settees, while Robert fretted and wondered what was being said on his behalf.

He was not too surprised when Nang informed him that the hotel staff were not aware of anyone coming to the hotel to enquire after him. Neither did they know of any telephone calls or messages being left.

'They say, if you like, they ask other people who work here on different shifts,' Nang said, following another burst of conversation. 'I ask how long they keep records of hotel guests, but they not sure. Need to ask manager.'

It was pretty much as Robert had expected. He shrugged stoically. 'Well it was worth a try. Thank you both anyway for coming with me.' He had reached the stage where any setback now was more expectation than disappointment.

As he looked around uncertainly, his eye fell on the battery of small safe deposit boxes, through a window, behind the Cashier's desk.

He turned to Nang. 'I don't suppose it will do any good, but would you mind asking how long they keep records of guests who leave their valuables in the hotel safe deposit?' His memory was of a large ledger and of his father scrawling his signature just before their departure, when they were reclaiming their valuables for the last time. He had no idea what details were entered. In any case, he was reaching an awfully long way into Doungjai's thought processes.

Nang again explained their quest to the girl at the Cashier's desk. Fortunately for Robert, the hotel was relatively quiet at this time of day and they had her undivided attention. After a searching look at Robert and Cully, the girl produced the same large ledger he remembered and turned to the first page.

As he twisted his head to read the information written there, it looked to Robert as if he had drawn another blank. The information was extensive, but seemed to offer little hope. He scanned the headings

– Date, Time, Guest's Name, Room Number, Box Number, Deposit, Clerk on Duty and then last on the right hand side, Date, Time and Signature of the departing guest, acknowledging the final closing of the safe deposit box. Interesting but academic as the date of the first entry was only six months ago.

'Do you keep the earlier books?' he asked, still not sure what he expected to learn, but driven by dogged persistence to pursue every lead until it produced results or proved to be a blind alley. The girl peered beneath the counter and produced two similar ledgers.

She opened one of them. 'When you say?'

'Three years ago in July.'

The girl tried the other ledger, skipping through the pages.

'Name?' She was certainly doing her best.

'Stone.'

She located the correct month and ran her finger down each page. 'Mister Brian Stone?' she queried and looked pleased when Robert confirmed that it was. 'Room 504?'

Robert leaned further across and saw the page was neatly completed with all the details on each line – except at the end of the line, where his father's familiar signature had been entered, there was another number. It was seven digits, written in a different pen and colour of ink and stood out because it spoilt the symmetry of the page.

The girl's finger paused beneath the number. 'I no understand this number,' she confessed.

Robert did not comment. He was busy copying the number onto a scrap of paper.

'Thank you very much,' he said, as he finished writing. 'You've been very helpful.' He turned to

Cully and looked at his watch. 'What time do you need to be at the airport?'

'We have to check in by two. The flight leaves at 2.45.'

'I've no idea if this means anything,' Robert confessed, holding out the piece of paper on which he had written the number. 'But just in case it's a telephone number, would you mind trying it, Nang? If someone answers, they're bound to speak Thai'

'Of course.' Nang took the paper and they stood close beside her while she dialed the number in one of the public telephones behind the Reception Desk.

Several tense seconds before she began to speak. At least it was a telephone number. Robert heard his name and 'Doungjai' mentioned in the conversation and looked expectantly at Nang when she replaced the receiver.

'I speak to man,' she explained. 'He say he not live there. Just staying for few days with girl friend, but she not there today. I ask if he know Doungjai, but he don't know. I ask him to tell his friend when she come back that you like to speak Doungjai.'

'When is he expecting his girl?' Robert asked.

'He not sure. Maybe tomorrow, maybe two or three days.'

It all sounded pretty vague and scarcely enough to warrant a celebration.

Cully noted the look of disappointment on Robert's face. 'So let's hope his girl will know something when she comes back.'

'I ask him to tell his friend to call you. Give your name and say where you stay,' Nang added.

'Thank you, Nang.' Robert forced a smile.

She and Cully had been great: supportive and

helpful. He would miss them when they flew off to Samui. There was nothing left for him to do now but sit around and wait and hope for a telephone call that might never come.

Chapter Thirty-Two

The next few days dragged by with painful slowness. With Cully and Nang away in Koh Samui, Robert was at a loose end, especially now that he had exhausted every lead for finding Doungjai. He spent many hours pursuing other lines of enquiry: questioned other members of the staff at the hotel where he had stayed with his parents, took another crack at the shops on Sukhumvit, and touted her picture around their previous haunts. All to no avail.

The one slender hope remaining was that mysterious telephone number and the remote chance that word might somehow filter through to Doungjai that he was back in Bangkok. The possibility of missing a call made him reluctant to leave his hotel. When he did venture out, he asked the operator to be sure to take any messages. Several times he tried the number that Nang had followed up for him, but it was always answered by a man who spoke only Thai.

Eventually, even this faint hope dwindled to nothing. It was time to admit defeat and return to England. He telephoned the airline and booked a seat on the flight out the following night. Although the overall disappointment and sense of failure nagged like an old toothache, once he had made the decision, he felt relieved. He would be sorry not to see Cully and Nang before he left. They were due back in

Bangkok in a couple of days. On the other hand, seeing them so obviously enjoying each other's company had only heightened his own feeling of isolation. No, better to go home and write the experience off to . . . well, experience. At least he had tried.

On Sunday evening, Robert organised his clothes for packing. He cleared out the bills, tickets, receipts, plastic bags, brochures and all the other oddments one gathers on holiday. As he sorted through these, tossing them one by one into the waste bin, he came across the piece of paper on which he had scribbled the number obtained from the hotel safe deposit ledger. A fat lot of good that had been.

He screwed it up and tossed it in the rapidly filling trash bin – and missed. He picked it up off the floor to place it where it belonged, then paused. With no particular aim in mind he slowly opened up the tiny ball of paper and stared at the number. There was really no point, but what had he to lose? Totally devoid of any expectation, he smoothed out the paper beside the telephone, picked up the receiver, pressed 'O' for a city line and dialled the number. The ringing tone was a series of long low bleeps. On the third bleep a male voice answered in Thai, confirming the futility of the exercise.

Robert spoke slowly and precisely. 'Hello, could I please speak to Doungjai?'

Silence, apart from the faint sound of other voices in the background.

He repeated his request, expecting the man at the other end to replace the receiver at any moment. Instead, he muttered some unintelligible words in Thai, and Robert heard the clunk of the receiver being put down, followed by louder background voices. Whatever was happening the line was still open.

The distant Thai chatter seemed to go on interminably. He began to wonder if they had forgotten him. The voices faded. Another minute ticked by. He was about to hang up when he heard the receiver at the other end being picked up again.

'Could I please speak to Doungjai?' he tried desperately, raising his voice the way the English do when confronted with a foreign language.

Another silence, complete this time because the background voices had been silenced. Then a voice spoke, soft and uncertain, but crystal clear.

'Lobut?'

Just his name, but it could not have created a greater impact if it had come from the grave. His heart missed a beat.

'Doungjai,' he said, or at least tried to say; it came out as a hoarse whisper.

'Lobut?' the voice repeated. 'Is that you, Lobut?'

'Doungjai!' His voice strengthened. 'Yes, it's me.'

'Where you speak from?' Incredulous now, excited. 'Are you in England?'

'No,' he said, laughing and trembling with joy. 'I . . . I'm here – in Bangkok. I'm staying at the Sun Hotel off Surawong Road.'

'Oh, Lobut, it not true. You really in Bangkok?' She too was laughing now.

He nodded, as if she could see him. 'I've been here over a week, I came to find you. Are you staying at that telephone number?' Although his thoughts were in turmoil, his first priority was to secure a line of communication.

'No, my friend live here.' A slight hesitation. 'I live alone in other apartment.'

'Doungjai?'

'Yes, Lobut?'

'Can I see you tonight?'

'No can tonight, Lobut.' Another awkward pause. 'I working.'

'But it's after seven o'clock.'

'I work late every evening. Tonight I late already.'

There was a hint of unease in her voice which Robert did not notice until later when he began to analyse their conversation.

He felt a pang of disappointment. After all the anxiety and trouble he had been through, she seemed more concerned about being late for her work than seeing him.

As if reading his thoughts, she tried to explain. 'I very sorry, Lobut, but my boss him angry if I late. Can we meet tomorrow?'

Upset by what he interpreted as her brush off, his response was uncharacteristically brusque. 'Of course. Where and what time?'

'You remember Ambassador Hotel?'

'Yes, what time?'

'Ten thirty, by entrance?'

'All right by me.' It couldn't be too soon for him.

'Lobut?'

'Yes?'

'I very happy you come back to Bangkok. I sorry I have to work tonight, but my boss . . .' she trailed off either reluctant or unable to explain. 'We talk tomorrow.'

'Of course, I can't wait.' His natural warmth was already reasserting itself. 'We've got lots to talk about.'

'I see you tomorrow, Lobut. 10.30 at Ambassador Hotel. Sorry, I must go now.'

'Tomorrow then,' Robert repeated, unwilling to end the conversation. 'You will come?'

'Of course I come. Goodnight, Lobut.'

'Goodnight, Doungjai.'

The line went dead.

His mind was showered with a cascade of questions as soon as he replaced the receiver, but uppermost was a feeling of emptiness. Against all the odds he had found her, but was she the same Doungjai he had known? She had certainly sounded the same, and yet he had sensed a certain reluctance, evasiveness even, in her voice. Perhaps it was only his imagination. Perhaps he expected too much from this first contact. He should have been more coherent, more assertive. Yet he could not help feeling she was not entirely enthusiastic to hear from him. Maybe she had another boy friend. The prospect turned him cold. He tried to get a grip on his emotions. After all the disappointments, he had finally found her and surely that was enough for now.

Chapter Thirty-Three

Feelings of euphoria, impatience, anticipation, even apprehension were a few of the reasons why Robert slept only in brief snatches that night. A dozen times he checked the alarm clock by his bed. It seemed as if time was slowing down.

He had showered, dressed and was down in the coffee shop by 7.30, only to find he could not face the usual splendid buffet breakfast. He managed a grapefruit juice before strolling across the lobby to inform Reception he had changed his mind about leaving. He then walked to the airline office in the Charn Issara Building on Rama 4 to cancel his evening flight. With no idea what the next few days had in store, he re-booked ten days ahead with the assurance of the girl at the desk that, if his circumstances altered yet again, he would be able to postpone it further.

With over an hour still in hand, he returned to his hotel and changed. He discarded his short sleeved casual shirt, shorts and sneakers in favour of something a little more formal: a white shirt, with blue-grey edging at the collar, cuffs and breast pocket, and royal blue cotton trousers were the most formal items in his limited wardrobe. The new Hi-tec trainers he had bought just before leaving England were not as comfortable as the well worn Reeboks, that had pounded the pavements of Bangkok since he arrived, but today appearance took priority over comfort.

He thrust an aerosol can of deodorant inside his shirt and sprayed liberally around, then applied some Dior after-shave, a Christmas present from a favourite aunt. A last look in the mirror. Yes that was about right, discreetly casual. A final check that the Buddha figure on its gold chain, Doungjai's farewell gift, was safely in place round his neck and he was ready. He left the hotel, still with over an hour to spare.

As the taxi moved through the morning traffic, Robert rehearsed his forthcoming meeting with Doungjai. Three whole years. So much had happened and yet such is the mastery of memory over time that it seemed like only yesterday that he had been fussing and fuming about Doungjai's first meeting with his parents. It was the same all over again, except now, where should have been euphoria was only uncertainty. After turning off Petchburi Road and winding through a series of narrow *sois*, the taxi dropped him at one of the Ambassador Hotel's side entrances. Standing under the huge crystal chandelier in the centre of the ground floor, he again checked his watch. It was only 9.50, still forty minutes to go.

He turned to his right and exited the hotel again on the Sukhumvit side. He entered the new Bangkapi Plaza and wandered between the rows of tiny shop units. Eventually he came to the self service restaurant and slumped down in one of the yellow metal chairs. The place was virtually empty at this time of the morning, but all the television sets were on blasting out several different Thai programmes.

None of this registered, for Robert's thoughts were exclusively of his long awaited meeting with

Doungjai, now only minutes away. Would she look the same? What would she think of *him*? What would they talk about, and would the same spark still be there? Most worrying of all, nagging at the back of his mind, was whether she would turn up at all.

He looked again at his watch. Another ten minutes and he would have the answers to these questions and others. He returned to the main building and again checked his appearance in the Gent's toilet, before going to wait on the steps of the hotel entrance facing Sukhumvit Road.

At 10.26 precisely, a small, definitely female, figure appeared at the entrance to the car park some two hundred yards away. From this distance her features were still indistinct, yet somehow he was certain it was her. His mouth had suddenly gone dry and he struggled to control his already stretched nerves.

The moment had arrived.

The figure approached along the pavement in front of the glass fronted shops, where the bird cages used to be. Robert took a deep breath and, descending the hotel steps with exaggerated care, headed diagonally across to the footpath.

There was no one else around, just the two of them. Robert broke into a trot and the girl's features came into focus. It was his Doungjai all right, three years older and even more lovely than he remembered.

She was wearing a black, broad cotton dress with large gold buttons all the way down the front and divided by a wide white belt. The shaped bodice, though discreetly cut, could not conceal the ample thrust of her breasts. The skirt of the dress was flared, the hemline just below knee length. She had put on a couple of inches in height, but looked even taller because of the high-heel shoes.

She was smiling – that smile he remembered so well. Three years ago he had left behind a schoolgirl, now he had returned to a grown up young lady and it showed in her face, her figure and her clothes.

'Lobut!' she cried, as they came together, almost a collision.

Then they were in each other's arms. She felt full and firm and so very feminine, the jet black tresses against his face intoxicatingly fresh and fragrant.

'You're lovelier than ever,' Robert murmured in her ear, his voice husky with emotion.

'You always say nice things,' she said, laughing and crying at the same time.

He held her at arms length and drank his fill of her with his eyes. Her face was thinner than he remembered, the schoolgirl plumpness in her cheeks having assumed a more mature heart shape. Her full mouth still had that natural sensuous pout that she exaggerated when trying to get her own way.

But most striking by far were those huge dark eyes. He had no defence against them.

'You grow more tall,' she remarked, using the heel of her hand to smear away a wandering tear.

'You've grown too,' he grinned. 'All over.'

For a long moment they stood and looked at each other, savouring the occasion, words unnecessary. Then they both laughed, self conscious now and slightly nervous.

'Such a long time, Lobut, I not know what to say first.'

'I know, me too,' he agreed. 'Silly isn't it? I've waited so long for this moment and now . . .' He shook his head helplessly.

There was so much to say and a lot of explaining to

do, and maybe he would hear things he would prefer to stay ignorant of.

'How about a cup of coffee?' he suggested, waving towards the hotel. 'This might take some time . . .'

Chapter Thirty-Four

They sat in a corner of the near empty lobby lounge beside the black grand piano that stood silent at this hour of the day. A formidable set of buffalo horns loomed over them from the marble wall.

After a few tentative forays, the trickle of conversation gathered pace until, by the time the coffee was served, it was flowing almost as freely as it used to.

'Why did you stop writing to me?' Robert could not hold back the crucial question any longer and could think of no less direct way of putting it.

'I very sorry.' She didn't flinch from his questioning gaze. 'You remember where we live? Behind where you never see was factory where they put gas in containers. One day, something go wrong. There is big accident and everything explode.' She gestured graphically.

'I was at home with Mama and small brother and sister. We hear big bang and everything crash and go on fire. My mama take my sister and I carry my brother and we run and run away. People in other houses run also and then I fall and something hit me on head and I remember nothing till later.'

Robert listened with growing concern, which turned to horror when Doungjai turned her head and held up her hair to show him an ugly, crescent shaped scar just above the hairline.

Coincidentally, Cully had touched on the possibility of a fire to explain why Doungjai had stopped writing.

'What about your mother and brother and sister?' Robert was almost afraid to ask.

'My brother and sister OK, only very frightened, but Mama she get fire on her arms and legs and have to go to hospital.' Tears gathered anew in her eyes. 'Lobut, we lose everything. You remember our nice home where you visit and meet Grandpapa?'

Robert had never forgotten that afternoon. He had often replayed it in his memory.

'It all gone in fire, everything, your photo, tape player, all your letters, nothing left.'

Now the tears were running in glistening trails down her cheeks. As he stretched out a comforting hand, Robert had the same helpless feeling as on the night she broke the news to him of her grandfather's death. He did not even mention insurance, assuming the family finances had never run to such luxuries.

She sniffed and dabbed her face with a handkerchief. 'I sorry, Lobut. This happened long time before, but I feel sad when I talk about it.'

'I had no idea. I'm sorry too.' He squeezed her hand. 'But why didn't you let me know?'

'No can,' she cried. 'Everything destroyed. No have your address any more.'

'But I wrote to you every week for ages after you stopped writing. My address was on all the letters.' He knew this was not the right moment to press for an explanation, but he had to know.

Doungjai shook her head. 'Your letters not come. After the fire, we move out of Bangkok, back to Petchaburi where we lived when I was baby. It not very nice house, but we have nowhere else to go. No

254

have money to stay in Bangkok.' She paused as if expecting Robert to protest further but he remained silent.

'When I come back Bangkok later to find work, everything is changed. They pull down houses and make space where we lived and build new apartments. I ask about letters from you, but no one know anything. Post Office say they no keep information on letters they not deliver.'

'Did you put that number in the book in our hotel?'

Her quick smile was an answer on its own. 'I think long time, Lobut, maybe one day you come back. I go your hotel and ask lady to put my friend's telephone number next to your papa's name in the book. I think . . .' she hesitated. 'It difficult to explain in English . . .'

'You thought I might go back to the hotel to see if you had been there and left a message?'

Doungjai nodded. 'I hope you think same like me.'

'Well it worked, but only just. I asked a Thai girl to telephone the number, but the person who answered didn't know you.'

'You telephone my friend's apartment. I know her long time, but she was away when you telephone and her friend don't know me. My friend come back yesterday and last night I go see her when you telephone. Lucky for me.'

'Lucky for us,' Robert corrected mechanically, remembering how close he had come to throwing the number away.

More details of the destruction of Doungjai's home and the aftermath emerged as Robert probed deeper. He established that while her mother still suffered from her injuries incurred in the explosion, her younger brothers and sisters were safe and well, while the two older brothers were now married and already starting families of their own. With four younger children all at school and her mother unable to work, it was apparent that the responsibility for keeping the family together now rested with Doungjai.

She asked after his parents; he told her they were well and sent their love. He omitted to mention his parents' financial difficulties. Compared with the problems endured by Doungjai and her family, they were trivial.

'Where are you working now?'

'In hotel reception,' she told him.

'What time do you finish?'

'Not till two o'clock.' She avoided his gaze.

'In the *morning*?' he demanded incredulously.

'Someone must be there all night. I work late to make more money.'

'What about days off?'

'Have two days' holiday every month.'

'One day every two weeks?' Robert protested. 'I hope you'll be able to get more than that while I'm here.'

'Maybe, Lobut, but very difficult to find good job. I work hard to keep this one and help Mama. If I take more holiday, my boss him tell me he get someone else who no want so much holiday.'

Robert kept his annoyance in check. This was not the moment to debate her working conditions.

'How long you stay Bangkok, Lobut?' she asked.

Robert shrugged. 'I'm not sure. I've been here a week already and I had planned to go home tonight, but I changed my return flight after last night's telephone call.' He held her gaze. 'It's up to you, Doungjai. Do you want me to stay?'

'Of course I want!' Her tone was indignant and yet

256

with an undertone of something he could not define.

'Will you try to get more time off work?'

'I try. Tomorrow I must go home to see my family. I arrange before I know you come Bangkok, and they expect me. You wait till I come back?'

The frustration returned; two steps forward, one back.

'How long will you be gone?' he asked tetchily.

'Two days. I go work tonight, then catch first bus to my home tomorrow morning. I stay home tomorrow night, come back Bangkok Wednesday afternoon. It only one day holiday.'

She could see he was not liking this news. 'Lobut, I sorry. I want to ask you to come with me, but we have very small house, with no bathroom, and there is no hotel where my family live. I speak to Mama, perhaps we arrange something and you come with me next time. You understand?' Her eyes were pleading.

'Of course I understand.' Robert said gruffly. He couldn't conceal his disappointment, though he realised it was making her uncomfortable. It wasn't her imminent absence that bothered him so much as the feeling she was holding something back.

'This afternoon I go shopping to buy things to take home. You come with me?' Doungjai lowered her eyes before fixing him with that familiar shy smile. 'I go to Pratunam. You remember last time we go shopping in Pratunam?'

Robert remembered only too well. He smiled at the recollection and his suspicions subsided.

'Not buying dress this time,' she assured him and they both laughed, a glimmer of their old rapport.

Robert paid the bill and, hand in hand, they left the hotel. Crossing the car park with Doungjai beside him, he felt really alive and at peace for the first time since his return to Thailand. If some surprises still remained to be sprung, they would have to wait their turn. For now, he would settle for Doungjai at his side and the rest of the world could look after itself.

Chapter Thirty-Five

Their taxi eased into the Sukhumvit Road traffic and, passing under the expressway, continued up Ploenchit. As they neared the Meridien President Hotel, Doungjai spoke briefly to the driver and, instead of turning right into Rajdamri Road and on to Pratunam, they pulled in outside the Sogo Department Store.

'We stop here for few minutes?' Doungjai suggested.

Since he had last been in Bangkok, all the taxis had converted to meters so, apart from the occasional cowboy who liked to try his luck with a *falang*, bargaining was no longer a feature of the trade. Robert looked over the driver's shoulder, mentally rounded up to the next five bahts and paid him off.

Only when they were walking towards the corner with Rajdamri Road did he realise where Doungjai was heading. He followed her through the iron gates into the Erawan Shrine which as usual was thronged with people.

'You wait for me, Lobut?' Doungjai pointed towards the seats ranged along the iron rails that ran parallel with the road.

Robert obligingly threaded his way through the crowds who had come to pray, or merely to look, and sat while Doungjai went across to the stall at the far side. Since he was last here, it had been moved from just inside the gate. He watched her light the candle and joss sticks from a small pilot light and approach the golden Brahma image. She set down the small wooden elephants she had purchased on a table in front of the surrounding iron fence, placed the lighted candle and smoking joss sticks among the many others in a bed of sand, and knelt to pray.

When she rejoined him she looked more relaxed and her eyes gleamed with the old sparkle and certainty.

'You remember we come here before, Lobut? Then I give elephants to Buddha to thank him for letting me meet you. I promise him if he keep you safe and bring you back one day I give him more. Lobut, I very very happy you come back to Bangkok. It difficult to say how much happy I am to see you again.'

If any doubts still remained, they were dispelled by those magic eyes gazing into his, glowing and joyful.

'I'm very happy too,' he responded lamely, and they sat for several minutes in reflection, holding hands. They went on to Pratunam by *tuk tuk* and Doungjai worked her way through a formidable list that consisted mainly of food and children's clothes. Robert dutifully offered to carry most of the shopping and by the time Doungjai had made her last purchase he was laden with plastic bags. He wondered how she would have managed on her own.

They reached the Arnoma Swissotel, opposite the World Trade Centre, just in time to take advantage of the lunchtime buffet in the hotel's Buttercup Restaurant. Flopping exhausted into a seat, Robert would have gladly traded his coveted Chelsea season ticket for the cool fresh orange juice which quickly arrived and was even more speedily despatched.

In contrast, Doungjai showed no sign of fatigue; on the contrary, the shopping expedition seemed to have acted as a pick-me-up. Between visits to replenish her plate at the buffet, she extracted a succession of articles from the bags and held them up for his approval.

'For Mama,' she proclaimed, producing a couple of audio tapes. 'Bing Crosby. She like Bing Crosby. Granpapa, him also liked Bing Crosby.' Then more solemnly. 'Still miss Granpapa.' Her last words were accompanied by a sad little smile and the flicker in her eyes of distant memories, briefly recalled.

She leaned towards him and placed her small hand over his. 'I never forget what you told me, Lobut. You said, remember good times and happy memories. We have many happy memories, you and me.'

'And we'll have many more,' he assured her.

'I hope,' she said simply and replaced the Bing Crosby cassettes in their bag.

'Would you like me to help you back to your room and then to the bus tomorrow morning?' Robert volunteered as they came to the end of their meal.

She shook her head. 'Thank you, Lobut, I manage OK.' Then to soften her refusal. 'Maybe you like to visit my room when I come back. First I want make it look nice for you.'

'I don't mind how it looks as long as you're in it.'

'It important for me,' she insisted, and he did not press the point.

'Before you go, you must let me have your address.' Apart from the telephone number of her friend, he still had no way of reaching her.

She produced an old receipt and pen and wrote slowly and deliberately. As he read it to make sure he understood, he saw she had written the address in English as well as Thai.

Doungjai read his thoughts and explained with a note of pride. 'I learn to write English little bit,'

'That's great; your English beats my Thai,' he responded enthusiastically.

She pointed to the words in Thai. 'Show driver when you come.'

'Do you have a telephone number?'

'No have telephone in my room.' She took back the pen and paper and added a number. 'This in corridor. If you telephone, ask for room 276.'

'*Sawng, jet, hok,*' Robert said.

'You learn to speak Thai also,' she cried, patently impressed.

'Only a few words, mainly numbers.' Cully's advice was paying dividends already.

Doungjai looked at her watch. 'Must go now or I be late for my work. I go home first, do some washing and change clothes.'

'When will I see you again?'

She pondered. 'Today Monday, I stay at my home tomorrow night, Tuesday, and come back to Bangkok Wednesday afternoon, have shower and go to work. Thursday about two o'clock? I come to your hotel?'

'I'll be waiting,' he said with resignation, grudging the period of separation and wondering how he would spend the next two days.

Outside the hotel they stood uncertainly. He did not want to let her go, but knew he must. He insisted she take a taxi. When one pulled in, he helped her load her shopping inside and thrust some baht notes into her hand for the fare. Her departure was imminent, and still the most crucial question of all remained unanswered.

'When you come back it will be like it was before, won't it?' he said anxiously, still ducking the issue.

She took one of his hands in both of hers and looked up at him, her face solemn. 'You still my very best friend in world, Lobut, never forget.'

'But will you come and stay with me at my hotel?' Finally it was out in the open.

Doungjai paused for a moment, remembering an occasion only a few months before when a similar question had been put to her, by another *falang*.

'I not finish work until two o'clock in the morning,' she reminded him. 'You be asleep then.'

'I don't mind,' he assured her.

She gave vent to a small sigh. 'We talk about it on Thursday.'

'OK.' Robert held the taxi door for her with a sense of relief. At least the subject had been broached.

He stood on the pavement until the taxi was out of sight, experiencing that deep sense of loss that arose at every parting, so well remembered from the past. It proved that his feelings for her were unchanged. If possible, they were even stronger now after the years of waiting and hoping. Yet he still could not dispel those doubts which had persisted ever since their first exchange of words on the telephone, less than twenty-four hours ago.

Although he had recovered his energy and enthusiasm while he was with her, Robert now felt mentally jaded and lonelier than ever on the way back to his hotel. Visions of Doungjai's warm, shapely body climbing into his bed at three o'clock in the morning, swirled around in his mind's eye. It was true she hadn't said 'yes', but she hadn't said 'no' either.

Chapter Thirty-Six

After another restless, dream-plagued night, Robert rose early. He ate a full breakfast in the coffee shop and wandered out to the pool to try and lose himself in the paperback he had bought at the airport on the way out. It was tough going, for his mind kept darting off in other directions. And one direction in particular.

Doungjai would be home by now and he tried to imagine what it was like there, with just her mother and four young children. It made his own existence seem selfish, having only himself to look after. He was annoyed with himself for not thinking to buy a gift for Doungjai to take to her mother.

But these were minor concerns. For the first time since he arrived in Bangkok, Robert felt a sense of achievement. No longer was he weighed down by that awful feeling of hopelessness, and the certainty that he was playing out a pointless charade which would only end when he boarded the plane for London.

As his memory continued to sift through past events, he smiled at the lighter moments. Shopping in Bangkok was always an adventure. Only yesterday, with Doungjai, he had encountered for the first time displays of 'Jumping Jolly Peckers' and 'Clockwork Boobs' on one of the stalls in the market.

And what about that girl in the Pata Department Store in Pratunam? She was diminutive, under five feet and could have passed for ten or eleven, although she was probably nearer thirteen. She was dressed, like so many girls of her age in Bangkok, in a short black skirt and Doc Martin-type boots that would not have been out of place on a parade ground. But it was the wording on her black T-shirt that had caught Robert's attention as he trailed along behind Doungjai: *'Never Mind The Bollocks Here's The Sex Kitten'*, it proclaimed.

He had yet to unravel the slogan. He was smiling at the memory when a familiar Scottish voice range out across the pool. 'I wonder what the wee Sassenach's smiling about?'

Robert had forgotten that Cully and Nang were due back from Koh Samui today. He waved to them, and they came around the pool towards him, hand in hand. Cully was grinning broadly.

'So you're still here?' he greeted, seizing Robert's hand and pumping it vigorously.

'Hello, Robert.' Nang's greeting was no less enthusiastic if less physical.

'Hello, Cully, hello, Nang. Yes, still here. Did you have a good trip?'

'Bloody great.' Cully drew up another sunbed and he and Nang perched on the edge, facing Robert.

Cully had a perpetual air of enthusiasm, but to Robert he seemed particularly elated, and Nang was equally bubbly. As they told him about their trip, they were laughing, interrupting and pawing each other like courting teenagers.

Eventually Cully said: 'Will you tell him or will I?'

'You.' Nang suddenly looked coy.

'Tell me what?'

'We're going to bloody get married!' Cully shouted the words 'And you're the first to know.'

'Look, look.' Nang thrust her left hand under Robert's nose. On the third finger a precious stone sparkled.

'That's wonderful – congratulations.' Robert was genuinely pleased for them. He leapt to his feet and grabbed Cully's hand again. 'Am I allowed to kiss the bride?'

'You no have to ask him,' Nang cried, pulling Robert towards her.

'I'm very happy for you, Nang,' Robert said sincerely and gave her a hug followed by a big kiss full on the lips.

'Hey, are you marrying him or me?' Cully demanded in mock protest.

They parted laughing, and Robert placed an arm round each of them.

'Now I can sleep with her and it won't matter if her mother finds out,' Cully grinned.

Nang shook her head. 'Now we engaged, everything change.' She tried to look serious. 'Till we marry we must sleep in separate rooms.'

'The woman's a total sadist,' Cully groaned. 'All right, if that's the way it's to be, we'll forget about this marriage business and carry on as we were.' He pretended to remove Nang's ring and she pulled away giggling.

'You terrible man,' she giggled.

It was a magic moment, one of great happiness and yet tinged with a certain poignancy. Here was Cully, the bouncer from Glasgow, who had seen more than his share of the heavy side of life in his thirty odd years and taken a few knocks in the process. And there was Nang, who in her short life had been round a few blocks as well. Two people from backgrounds a million miles apart, for whom a massage parlour had been the scene of their first encounter, had fallen in love. If not the stuff of childhood dreams and fairy tales, it was every bit as romantic and deserving of a bright future.

'Hey, wait a minute.' Cully stopped the congratulations in full flow. 'We've been so full of our own good news, we didn't ask how you got on, Robert. Have you had any luck?'

It was Robert's turn to look smug.

'As a matter of fact I met Doungjai yesterday.'

'Well, that's bloody marvellous.' Cully slapped him on the back. 'He's found her,' he said to Nang, who nodded eagerly. 'So why isn't she here, sitting on your lap?'

'She's gone to see her family,' Robert explained, a shade uncomfortably. He felt Doungjai should be here too. 'They live some way out of town. It's something she arranged before she knew I was here.' Robert went on to regale them with the story of his fortuitous telephone call and how the accident to Doungjai's home had caused them to lose contact.

'That's tough.' Cully shook his head sympathetically, but quickly saw the positive side. 'Never mind, you'll have plenty of chance to make up for lost time when she gets back, will you no?'

'There is another problem – she works evenings in a hotel and doesn't finish until two a.m.'

'That's a bit of a bugger,' Cully conceded. 'I know they work some funny bloody hours over here, but not finishing till two doesn't leave much time for romantic dinners. Surely when they know the circumstances, they'll give her some extra time off. Anyway, we've both got something to celebrate.'

Cully refused to be negative for long. 'When did you say she'll be back?'

'Tomorrow afternoon, but she has to go straight to work so I won't see her again until Thursday.'

'In that case, how about you and me having a few beers tomorrow night?'

'Won't you want to be with Nang?'

'She's already arranged to go and see some friends to share the good news so I've still got a few nights of freedom left. You're no going to let me spend them on my own, are you?'

Robert grinned. 'Since you put it that way, how can I refuse?'

Chapter Thirty-Seven

Doungjai caught the first bus of the day from the Southern Bus Station. It was full, but Doungjai's ticket guaranteed her a seat. She reclined it and stretched out to doze. It was a long-standing routine and she was usually drifting into a light sleep before the bus had backed out of its bay and manoeuvred clear of the crowded terminal. Today, though, her mind was hyperactive and throughout the journey, her thoughts combed the problems at home and at work – and the reappearance in her life of Robert Stone.

When they reached the bus terminal in Petchaburi, Doungjai would have normally hired a motor cyclist to take her the last few miles out to her home, this being the cheapest form of transport. But today she was so laden with shopping that she had to pay extra to be driven in a small pick-up. Sitting up front, surrounded by her plastic bags, she suffered the jolting rock'n'roll of the vehicle as it negotiated the potholes in the narrow country road.

When at last her home came into view, she underwent her customary sinking feeling. It was so primitive – just a framework of thick bamboo uprights supporting the roof, with a row of thinner canes providing token walls. The roof was a thin thatch of reeds and straw and, although it kept the sun and the birds out, it leaked like a strainer in the rainy season.

Doungjai paid off the pick-up and struggled through a narrow gap in the ragged hedge which served as a nominal boundary between the dusty lane and their "garden." A Spirit House was perched just inside the gap and created the only bright splash of colour against an otherwise colourless and dusty backcloth.

Her mother was standing in the doorway under the roof overhang that served as a porch, looking out for her. As soon as she spotted Doungjai, she hobbled over to meet her. The burns on her legs had never really healed and walking caused her severe pain. Only a major operation would restore full mobility, and the kind of money that would take was way beyond Doungjai's reach.

As soon as she saw her mother's face, Doungjai knew she was going through one of her more painful periods. But she had learnt to conceal her feelings and gave a cry of delight as they embraced, parcels and all.

'You look great, Mama,' she lied.

'I'm fine,' her mother lied back. 'A few twinges occasionally, it must be old age catching up on me.'

They both laughed.

'You've been spending too much money again, Doungjai,' her mother scolded as she helped her daughter with the packages. 'You must keep more for yourself. You never know when you're going to need it in Bangkok.'

It was a familiar piece of parental advice, which Doungjai never heeded. The pleasure she derived from the looks on the faces of her mother and family, as they delved into the parcels, was beyond any monetary consideration.

'Mama, I've got wonderful news.' Doungjai blurted, unable to contain herself any longer.

'Oh? What's that?' Her mother did not necessarily see eye to eye with her eldest daughter on what constituted "good" news.

'Robert is back in Bangkok,' Doungjai said gleefully. 'I saw him yesterday.'

'If you're happy, dear, then so am I,' her mother replied cautiously. She had nothing against Robert personally, but she was not convinced that it would be in Doungjai's best interests to get involved with him again.

The destruction of their home had been devastating for the whole family, but particularly for Doungjai, as it had also destroyed her link with Robert. Many months had passed before she came to terms with the probability that she had lost him for good, and the wound had never completely healed. Was it now to be reopened? Doungjai's mother knew she could do little to influence the situation, except to give Doungjai all her support – and hope for the best.

'How is your job?' she said, to change the subject. 'Are you still enjoying it?'

'It's going very well, Mama,' Doungjai did not mention that she was thinking of taking a day job as well. Her mother would only worry that she was working too long hours and, in any case, Robert's arrival meant she would have to wait a while.

Doungjai kicked off her shoes at the doorway and slumped in despair when she looked around the gloomy interior of their home. It consisted of a single large room, and a good half of this was taken up by a raised wooden platform. Everyone in the family slept on it, and the space beneath was used for storage. It was clammily hot for, although a power line was fed in from somewhere, they could not afford to run the old fan non-stop.

'Would you like a drink?' her mother offered.

'I'll get it,' Doungjai insisted.

Leaving the house, she walked down a well trodden path to the stream that crept slowly past, fifty yards away. Bending down, she pulled a bottle from the water, one of several that were kept there. When she returned, her mother had two glasses out and, while they sipped their lemonade, they chatted about what had been happening since Doungjai's last visit a fortnight ago. Doungjai worked discreetly round to the state of her mother's health. It only upset her mother if she thought Doungjai was worrying about her.

'What did the doctor say about your legs?'

'The usual – they won't get better until I've had an operation. So keep taking the pills.' Her mother thus disposed of the endless pain, and poured out more lemonade. 'But tell me about your big news, young lady. How did you meet Robert?'

Doungjai explained the circumstances that had brought them together again. 'He looks very well, Mama – much taller and very handsome.'

'And how do you feel about seeing him again after all this time?'

Doungjai skirted round her mother's question. 'It was a big surprise obviously. I thought I would never see him again. Of course I'm happy, only I'm not quite sure what he's expecting. We're both three years older and . . . ' She gazed into the distance, 'it's been such a long time.'

'Doungjai . . .' Her mother had no wish to interfere, yet her sense of parental obligation was strong. 'Remember how upset you were when Robert went

272

home the last time? It would not be good to build your hopes too high only to have them knocked down again.'

'I know, Mama, I know,' Doungjai soothed. She was not only thinking of the potential complications arising from Robert's return, but of other aspects of her life of which her mother was wholly ignorant. Keeping the truth from Robert might prove more difficult.

When her brothers and sisters returned from school, dropped off at the end of the lane by the elderly school bus, Doungjai strolled up the dusty track to meet them. Their joy at seeing her alleviated some of her worries. Their pleasure was always heightened by expectation, for whatever the budgetary constraints of the moment, she never failed to bring a personal gift for each of them.

The ritual opening of their parcels was always like a mini *Song Khan*, the Thai New Year. When all was revealed, she duly received a hug and a kiss from each brother and sister. They sat in a circle on the floor, and she faced a ceaseless barrage of stories and questions, each of them eager to relay his or her particular experiences first. She loved every minute of this family ritual.

The juiciest scandal was exposed by Chut, the older brother. To the others' high pitched giggles, he announced that their sister, Oiy, had a boyfriend. Oiy, who was nearly thirteen, exhuberant and extremely self-assured, categorically denied the allegation at first and then retaliated by reminding everyone of Chut's own amorous attachment. He was a whole year older and, as Doungjai reflected wryly, not much younger than she and Robert had been when they first met.

Doungjai's younger sister, Meng, now nearly nine, was quieter and more introspective than the others. She looked very much like Doungjai had done at her age, with big soulful eyes and a slightly woebegone expression. She tended to mother the youngest member of the family, her small brother, Chai, and the two of them were inseparable. Later in the day, while Doungjai was setting up more bottles in the stream, Meng came to join her, taking her hand.

'Doungjai, there is something I want to tell you.'

'Yes, Meng?'

'I think Mama's legs are getting worse. She doesn't say anything, but in the last week I've heard her get up during the night to sit in her chair. I know she has a lot of pain and you can see for yourself she walks more slowly than she used to.'

This merely confirmed what Doungjai had feared the moment she saw her mother that morning.

'I'm glad you told me, Meng, but you mustn't worry.' Doungjai tried to appear unworried. 'The pain comes and goes. It will pass, and Mama will be fine again. You'll see.'

'Are you sure, Doungjai?' The innocent eyes looked up at her anxiously, seeking reassurance.

'I'm sure.' Wishing she really was, Doungjai crouched down and stroked her little sister's hair back from her face. 'Don't forget you and the others can do a lot to help Mama by seeing she rests her legs as often as possible. I'm relying on all of you to take care of her when I'm not here.'

The little girl nodded solemnly and threw her arms round Doungjai's neck. 'We miss you when you are in Bangkok,' she murmured in her ear. 'I wish we could be together all the time.'

'I wish it too, Meng, but we need the money.' As

Doungjai held the little girl close, she looked over her shoulder at the humble dwelling where the family lived, with its scarcely private outdoor shower and toilet and the dried-up trees and shrubs that seemed to draw just enough moisture to keep them standing. She turned her head to take in the sluggish stream, which served as both chiller and washing machine.

Their straitened circumstances would have crushed the most optimistic spirit, but Doungjai rose above her despondency with the single thought that always sustained her at such moments: one day, one day . . .

She held Meng by the shoulders and studied her troubled face. 'Meng, I want you to promise me one more thing.'

'Yes, Doungjai?'

'Promise me that if you ever hear anything bad about me, you will speak to me about it first.'

The little girl frowned. 'I don't understand, Doungjai. Have you done something wrong?'

Doungjai laughed dismissively. 'Of course not. I just wouldn't want you ever to think bad things about me before we had a chance to talk. And I want you to promise me you won't talk to anyone about our little chat.'

'Not even Mama?'

'Not even Mama. It will be our secret. All right?'

'All right,' Meng said, puzzled, but unquestioningly loyal. 'If you say so.'

By the light of the pale flickering oil lamp, the family talked and played games until late into the evening. No one wanted to go to bed, and calm only settled over the little house when natural fatigue took over.

Doungjai was exhausted. Apart from dozing in the bus on the journey from Bangkok that morning, she had not slept for two nights. Even so, she was the first to waken in the morning, perhaps because of the unaccustomed stillness. The soft dawn light soaked slowly through the walls and roof, picking out the shapes of her family around her.

Preparing breakfast and getting the children ready for school was a big enough job, even with Doungjai's help. Not for the first time, Doungjai wondered how her mother coped alone with her disability. Before the children departed for school, she spoke privately to Chut telling him to let her know immediately if their mother got any worse.

The morning passed all too quickly after the children had departed. Doungjai had arranged for the pick-up to call at one o'clock and she had the usual difficulty in suppressing her emotions when it came to the hardest part of her short stay.

Her mother put a similarly brave face on their fare-wells.

'Take care of yourself, Doungjai. I don't have to tell you how important you are to the family and to me. I worry about you in Bangkok on your own and work-ing so late at night. I wish you could find something different.'

Doungjai hoped she didn't suspect anything.

'It's difficult to find a job that pays so well, Mama,' Doungjai reminded her, as always. 'You look after yourself, that's the main thing.'

They embraced and separated reluctantly.

'I'll see you in two weeks, and maybe I'll bring Robert with me next time,' she called out of the window. 'Goodbye, Mama,'

Through the pick-up's rear window she watched her mother's frail figure standing by the gap in the fence until it was obscured by the dust cloud churned

276

up by their bouncing wheels. As she turned away to stare through the window at the straight, featureless road ahead, determination fought to overcome sadness and despair.

In a few minutes she would be at the terminal and aboard the bus to start that familiar journey back to Bangkok, where Robert awaited her.

Chapter Thirty-Eight

'Which bar do you want to try first?' Cully asked, as he and Robert stood on the corner of the short link road between Patpong One and Two.

'I'm in your hands.' Robert shrugged. He was not sure he wanted to try any of them.

When Cully had suggested a celebratory drink the previous evening, Robert did not appreciate what he was letting himself in for. Now the moment had arrived he was even more uncertain although, walking between the stalls and the girlie bars, it was difficult not to be caught up in the unique atmosphere of Patpong.

They had already eaten in Bobby's Arms, where three years earlier Robert had initiated Doungjai into the game of darts. Now they were being subjected to the wiles of the bar touts to draw them inside their establishments.

There was no lack of inducement and the barrage of exhortations were supported by small hand cards and larger posters. These suggested that visual goodies with a high degree of inventiveness awaited the bold, the broad-minded and the curious. From SMOKE CIGARETTE SHOW through DRAW PICTURE SHOW, BURST BALLOON SHOW, EXCITING FIRE SHOW, to PAINTING ON SEXY GIRLS BODY SHOW. For the benefit of those with little imagination, or others who may have felt that Bangkok was a long way to come just to watch cigarette smoking, drawing pictures, and bursting balloons, other messages appealed to feline lovers, with PUSSY AND PING PONG BALL, PUSSY BLOW OUT CANDLES, and PUSSY SHOOTING BANANA.

Ignoring these exhortations, Cully moved towards a group of yelling youths, uniformly dressed in white shirts, black ties, baggy dark trousers and heavy soled shoes. With welcoming sweeps of their arms, they ushered him and Robert through a curtained doorway.

Once inside, they stood still and waited for their vision to adjust to the subdued lighting. On the stage, in the centre, half a dozen girls in bikinis and leotards were gathered, doing what appeared to be a slow motion dance, while peering out for prospective clients. A youth sidled up and ushered Robert and Cully to table against the wall. They sank tentatively onto a long padded bench. Cully ordered two beers but even before the drinks arrived they were joined by two pretty girls. They volunteered their names and snuggled up to Robert and Cully, firing questions in competition with the music blasting from the speakers above their heads.

While Cully slipped one arm round the girl next to him and used the other hand to hold his cigarette, take an occasional swig of beer and generally gesticulate, Robert tried to remain politely aloof from the girl who had attached herself to him. When she failed to draw him into conversation, she began to massage his neck and shoulders. It felt good, but he couldn't help thinking about Doungjai. Letting a bar girl seduce him would be a fine way to revive their relationship.

It seemed Cully had no such qualms. His hand had wriggled under his girl's loose fitting costume and was doing some massage of its own on a malleable Thai breast. He caught Robert's glance and winked cheerfully.

'Buy Coke for me?' Robert's girl whispered in his ear, as she rubbed his neck.

Another dilemma. Ever present thoughts of Doungjai did not help his decision, so he delegated it by leaning over to Cully and shouting in his ear. 'She wants me to buy her a Coke, what shall I do?'

Cully shrugged and roared back. 'It's only seventy bahts and she's a nice wee thing, but it's up to you. I'm getting one for mine, then we'll move on.'

'OK.' A relieved Robert nodded to his girl, his conscience appeased.

The girl placed her hands together and bowed in a gesture of thanks, checked the number on the small beaker-like container on the table that already held Robert's beer bill, and departed to get her drink. She returned with a small glass of Coke and ice and insisted on clinking glasses before taking a sip.

Cully was right, she was a nice wee thing and would have accompanied Robert back to his hotel in an instant. At a price. But he and Cully were not in the market for that kind of activity. Ten minutes later they moved on, abandoning two disappointed bar girls.

Reunited with the colour and clamour of Patpong, Robert looked questioningly at Cully. He was ready to call it a night, but the Scotsman had other ideas.

'Let's take a look at one of the places where they advertise those acts,' he suggested. 'I was in one the other night and there was a girl doing a sensational dance with fire sticks. She was stark naked and brushing these flames all over her body. She had the most gorgeous arse you've ever set eyes on, a figure that defies description, and she was a real beauty as well – not that many people were looking at her face.'

'All right, why not?' Just looking wouldn't do any harm, Robert thought.

'It was somewhere around here . . . now what was the name?' Cully glanced from side to side uncertainly. 'Something like "The Dark Pussy . . ." ' He scanned the array of coloured neon signs projecting from the buildings all the way up the street. 'No, there it is, look – "The Black Pussy". Come on, let's see if she's there again tonight.'

Intrigued, in spite of his reservations and sense of disloyalty, Robert trailed after Cully.

He tried a last weak protest.

'Won't Nang wonder where you've got to?'

'She'll no be back from seeing her friends.' Cully fell into step and gave Robert an evil leer. 'But if she wants to know where I've been, I'll tell her you dragged me into all these awful places.'

When he saw Robert was not laughing, he threw an arm round him. 'I'm only joking. I told Nang where we were going. She's broad minded. She'll no be expecting us back yet.'

Robert followed Cully up a narrow stairway to the Black Pussy. The interior was bigger than the previous bar, the stage in the centre more brightly lit and customers were thicker on the ground. But instead of a group of scantily clad dancing girls on the stage, a solitary girl was lying on her back projecting darts from a blowpipe which protruded from between her legs. Around the stage customers were obligingly holding up balloons as targets and a rapid series of 'pops' gave ample testimony to the girl's accuracy.

'Mind you don't get in the line of fire,' Cully warned in Robert's ear as they blundered to their table. 'I was in a bar one night and a girl sitting next to me got a stray dart right between the eyes.' He whistled at the recollection. 'Not funny.'

Once seated, they were invited to order a drink and two girls descended on them, armed with a repertoire of ploys to exploit certain male weaknesses. The girl on Robert's side, while looping one arm round his neck, placed the other on the inside of his thigh and wasted no time in moving it upwards with obvious intent. Robert kept his eyes straight ahead and his mind on higher things. His stance of non-cooperation began to falter when fingers unzipped his fly and grasp his bunched male flesh, which promptly stiffened up.

'Feel good?' the girl murmured in his ear while she took a firmer and more possessive grip on the growing member.

He moistened his lips and said nothing.

'Big boy,' the girl whispered approvingly.

Robert stole a quick glance towards Cully and was relieved his face was turned away, his attention wholly on the other girl. On stage the dart act had been succeeded by two naked girls displaying considerable expertise in an uninhibited lesbian act. From the way they squeezed and sucked, they appeared to have forgotten they were only putting on an act. Or were they?

Robert's irrepressible companion was bringing him to the point of no return, but he lacked the willpower to pull away. He gave a long shudder.

'How about a drink,' he croaked in desperation.

The massaging ceased, but a gentle grip was maintained as the hand appeared to ponder this unexpected offer.

'You buy me Coke?' its owner queried.

'Yes . . . yes, Coke, anything.'

The hand deserted his erection and was placed palm to palm with the other in a *wei* gesture of thanks. With very mixed feelings, Robert watched her drift away into the gloom in search of her drink and only just remembered to zip up his trousers.

A temporary cessation in the music at that moment heralded the end of the lesbian performance and the two smiling participants bowed their way off the stage to polite applause. The sanctuary of relative silence was short lived; a bare three seconds later a new fanfare of sound signalled the start of the next act.

Another girl appeared, carrying two flaming sticks high above her head. Robert and Cully were seated well to the side and towards the rear of the stage, which jutted out into the bar like a well lit causeway, so their first view of the girl was from behind. From this disadvantageous position, they could see that her long hair was drawn back and tied high on her head well out of the way. She was stark naked.

Eyes fixed on some invisible point above the heads of the audience, she advanced with slow spring-heeled steps to the end of the walkway. The firesticks were now held straight out from her body at shoulder length and the random play of shadow on her smooth, dark skin added an element of stealth to her progress.

Cully leaned towards Robert and indicated the stage. 'This is the girl I was telling you about,' he yelled. 'She's really special. Let's see if we can get a closer look.'

Robert followed him between stools and tables across to the front end of the stage. Although other customers were already there, a gap seemed to open up and they found themselves within touching distance of the stage and only an arm's length from the girl, who gyrated directly above them, naked and gorgeous.

The girl's large luminous eyes sparkled in a beautiful face and she displayed her astonishingly lovely body with a natural grace and absolute lack of inhibition. Her large, pointed breasts, tipped by black daubed nipples, had that special bouncy firmness of a fully-developed teenager. She had a jutting backside, and her lower body – slim waisted, wide hipped and taut bellied – was the stuff of erotic dreams. The absence of body hair emphasised the perfection of the girl's plump labia, and the sensual effect was heightened by her well-oiled skin.

And when she knelt, spread her thighs and arched upwards with that generously contoured bottom, her sex pouches and the tight O of her anus were displayed for all to see.

To the appropriate strains of 'Take My Breath Away', the girl stretched, swayed and postured above her admiring audience while, like an ardent lover, the flames licked every sumptuous curve, every hidden hollow and each secret orifice.

For a finale, she first extinguished the flame from one stick by throwing back her head and thrusting it into her mouth. Then, after taking a sip from a glass, she placed the rekindled torch to her lips and exhaled a great gust of flame. It was a sensational act, guaranteed to excite every penis in the place, and enthusiastic applause followed the girl all the way off the stage.

'What a performance,' Cully shouted in Robert's ear, as they stumbled back to their table. 'That girl's bloody fantastic. And what an arse.'

Robert was even more overwhelmed and sank into his seat, speechless and disbelieving. She was everything Cully had described, but to him she was much much more than a spectacular stage show. For the girl they had just been watching was his Doungjai!

Chapter Thirty-Nine

The girls were still seated at the table waiting for Robert and Cully. Robert's girl was clutching her Coke and, as he slumped onto the bench, she insisted on clinking glasses with him. He scarcely noticed, but sat frozen with shock.

'What wrong?' the girl said.

Forcing rational thought into his stunned brain, he shouted in her ear: 'That girl with the fire act – how long has she been working here?'

His companion looked thoughtful before calling to her friend, who continued to snuggle up to Cully as they considered Robert's question.

The girl turned back to Robert. 'We think she start few months ago.'

It was suddenly important to know whether she confined her blatant behaviour to her stage act, or whether she performed other services for customers who could afford it.

'Does she mix with the customers and let them buy her drinks?' he said, making it sound as if he were interested in her.

'Of course, we all do. You like to speak with her?'

'N . . . no, I was just . . . wondering.'

'You like another beer?' She held up his empty bottle. Talking about another girl in the bar didn't help to pay her rent.

'Er . . . perhaps in a minute. Is there a toilet through there?'

'Along passage.' She pointed to a door behind the stage on the far side of the room.

Robert rose again from the table and shouldered his way across the room. Doungjai must have gone through that same door at the conclusion of her act, as it was the only exit from the stage.

On the other side of the door was a well-lit passage, with several doors leading off on either side. The contrast of the bright lighting overhead made him blink and he hesitated while several girls squeezed past him in various stages of undress, chattering like sparrows.

Then Doungjai suddenly emerged from the last doorway on the left side of the corridor. Robert ducked back into the bar, holding the door ajar to watch. Doungjai had been followed by three men and was now arguing furiously with the smallest of them. The other two stood impassively, one on either side of the small man, who appeared to be their leader. The music in the bar drowned what was being said, but if it was in Thai, as seemed probable, Robert wouldn't have understood anyway.

Doungjai was wearing a loose fitting dark cotton jacket that came to mid thigh, held closed by a sash. She stood in profile to Robert, but was clearly distraught, flapping her arms as she spoke. The small man was middle-aged and more Chinese than Thai in appearance. While his impassive Oriental features registered no emotion, his body language shouted displeasure. His small deep set eyes were cold and menacing, and whenever he spoke he emphasised his words by thrusting a finger aggressively into Doungjai's face.

Far from being cowed, she stamped her foot and appeared to be more than holding her own. The argument came to an abrupt end when the man pushed the palms of his hands at Doungjai as if fending her off and, to a final flurry of words from Doungjai, he turned and stalked along the passage towards Robert. The other two men followed him.

Robert let the door swing shut and retreated into a corner of the bar. The trio passed within touching distance, but did not spare him a glance. The middle-aged man paused for a brief word with the barman, then they were gone.

After a moment's hesitation, Robert approached the barman. 'Who was that man you were talking to?'

The barman looked at him in silence with an expression which seemed to say, 'what business is it of yours?'

'I'm sure I met him last time I was in Bangkok.' Robert hastened to justify his interest. 'If he's who I think he is, I have some business I would like to discuss.'

The barman pulled a glass from the sink of running water and placed it beside a row of others on the draining board. 'That Mister Brown,' he informed Robert finally.

'Mister Brown? Is that his real name?'

The barman grunted, which could have meant anything.

'Does he often come in here?' Robert tried to sound casual.

'Most days. Many business in Patpong.'

Robert nodded his thanks at the barman who seemed relieved that his interrogation was over and scuttled off on an imaginary errand.

It was not hard to guess that Doungjai was in some

288

kind of mess, and Robert was determined to find out more. Not here though, not tonight. He would have to wait until tomorrow, when they were alone.

He looked across to his table and could just make out the figures of Cully and the two girls. He decided that, until he had straightened matters out with Doungjai, he would not involve Cully. And maybe not even then.

It occurred to him that Doungjai might well circulate in the bar between acts. If so, chances were she would spot him. With a nervous glance over his shoulder, he hurried across to Cully, who was clearly revelling in the girls' attentions.

'What's up, chum?' the Scotsman asked.

'Sorry, Cully,' Robert said. 'I've got to go. I'll explain later.'

'Wait for me then.' Cully patted his girl's bottom. 'Sorry, lassies, it's past our bedtime. So if you don't mind, we'll pay up and be on our way.'

Chapter Forty

Doungjai knocked on Robert's hotel door at two minutes to two in the afternoon. She looked fresh and lovely in a knitted pink sweater and tight fitting, grey skirt. They accentuated her curves, but did nothing for his resolve to get at the truth.

If his greeting seemed on the cool side, Doungjai did not appear to notice. She looked round the room with an air of confidence that contrasted sharply with the last time she and Robert had stood alone in a hotel bedroom. Then, they were gauche fourteen-years olds, keyed up and quaking. The knowledge that Robert's parents were asleep only feet away on the other side of the wall had not helped.

'I'm afraid it's not exactly the Savoy,' he admitted, reading her thoughts.

She had never heard of the Savoy, but understood the inference. 'It is enough just to see you, Lobut.' Her smile only stirred up his inner torment.

'The view is a bit limited.' He pointed out of the window at the wall opposite, stalling for the right opening to say his piece. 'How's your mother and your family?'

Doungjai perched on the edge of the bed. 'Mama is not very well, but everyone else is fine.' She looked at him, frowning. 'Lobut, is anything wrong?'

So she had noticed his lack of ardour. He sat down

opposite her on a high backed chair. He had spent most of the night wondering how to broach the subject and decided that a head-on approach was as good as any.

'I went with a friend to the Black Pussy bar in Patpong last night,'

Doungjai's face was expressionless and, far from turning away to avoid his gaze, she looked straight at him. 'Did you see me?' she asked softly.

'I saw a lot of you. In fact, I saw all of you – the same as everyone else who was there.'

Doungjai's gaze dropped. Her face still showed no emotion, but inside she was in turmoil.

'Don't you think you owe me an explanation?' Robert pressed when she remained silent.

'I sorry, Lobut,' she said miserably. 'I should have told you where I working, but I think you be angry.'

'You're dead right I'm angry, especially since you lied to me.' Her deceit troubled him at least as much as her job. 'I thought we had no secrets from each other. It seems I was wrong.'

When she remained silent, offering no defence, his anger got the better of him.

'What was wrong with the shop, or some other job? Do you enjoy going off with men to some seedy hotel and . . . and . . . ?' He couldn't bear to say the words, to envisage what happened between her and her "clients." 'If I'd known, I don't think I would have come back. I even wonder if you went to see your family the other night, or whether you were . . .'

A sharp rap on the bedroom door stilled his accusations. He turned. Standing on the threshold were Cully and Nang.

'The door was ajar,' Cully's tone lacked its usual warmth.

'Come in,' Robert smiled weakly. 'Cully, Nang, you haven't met . . .'

'I know who she is,' Cully cut in. Pointedly ignoring Robert, he went across, tugging Nang along with him, and shook Doungjai's hand with exaggerated care. 'I'm very happy to meet you, Doungjai. I saw you at the Black Pussy last night and I thought you were terrific. Congratulations. This is my girl friend, Nang.'

The two girls greeted each other with a mutual *wei*, but the interruption had come too late to staunch the tears that were sliding down Doungjai's cheeks.

'I very happy to meet you' She dabbed her eyes. 'Excuse me.'

Robert could only look on feeling rather foolish. Already he was sorry for his outburst.

Cully had instantly summed up the situation. 'Look, why don't you girls go down to my room, have a drink and get to know each other? I want to have a word with Robert, we'll join you in a couple of minutes. Men's talk, you know,' he added, as an afterthought.

Doungjai looked gratefully towards the big, rugged *falang*, who spoke a strange form of English, which she could barely follow.

Nang spoke rapidly to Doungjai in Thai and, placing a sisterly arm round her shoulders, escorted her from the room.

There was a tense pause lasting several seconds after the girls' departure, then Robert asked tentatively: 'Did you overhear what we were talking about just now?'

'Enough.' Cully's voice had a harsh edge. He was a different person from the knockabout, gentle giant

Robert had become so attached to in the last few days.

'Do you think I was a bit hard on her?'

'Let's say you'd have been a helluva lot kinder if you'd put on some hob-nailed boots and kicked her arse round the room a few times,' Cully replied graphically.

'Did it really sound as bad as that?'

'Worse.' Cully sat down, not wishing to intimidate his young friend. 'For goodness sake, Robert, use your head a bit and come down off that bloody pedestal you seem to view the world from.'

'But you saw her last night,' Robert protested. "How would you feel if you had come halfway round the world to discover your girl friend's the star turn in Bangkok's redlight district.'

Cully snorted. 'Don't you think you should hear her side of the story before you jump to too many conclusions?'

'Come on, Cully, you saw her last night.' Robert was not mollified. 'She looked as if she was trying to seduce every man in the place the way she moved and showed off everything. And when I asked one of the girls afterwards, she told me that they all mix with the customers when they're not dancing. Do you need to have it spelled out any clearer than that?'

He was more confused than ever. It was true he had not heard her side of the story. Not that he expected it to mellow his perception. Performing naked on stage was bad enough; what she did afterwards was unthinkable and unforgivable.

'There's something else,' Robert said. 'You may remember I went off to the Gents directly afterwards. I was actually looking for her. Anyway, I was about to go through to the back of the bar when I saw her in the corridor arguing with some bloke I didn't much like the look of.'

'I take it she didn't see you?'

'No. I did think of tackling her straight away, but then I felt it probably wasn't the right time or place. You see, there were two other men besides the one she was arguing with – typical heavies like you see in gangster films. Doungjai was going at this bloke hammer and tongs and he looked really mad. After he'd gone, I asked the barman about him. Apparently, he's some kind of local businessman. He looked more like a thug to me.'

Cully looked thoughtful. 'Have you told Doungjai yet that you saw her arguing with this guy?'

'No, you arrived before I got round to it.'

'Well, we weren't eavesdropping, pal,' Cully said with a crooked grin. 'Your door was half-open, and we couldn't help but hear. It was a good job we arrived when we did, or you'd be looking for a new girl friend.'

Cully's voice had softened somewhat. Now he patted Robert's shoulder. 'Come on, don't look so pissed off. You don't know how bloody lucky you are to have a girl with the looks and a body like hers.'

'But I don't want to share them with every tourist in Patpong,' Robert protested.

'There you go again, jumping to conclusions,' Cully admonished. 'One thing's for sure – she's more likely to spill the beans to Nang than to you, the mood you're in. Let's go down and see if we can salvage this relationship. If you've blown it, you've only yourself to blame.'

When they descended to Cully's room to rejoin the girls, they were surprised to learn they were planning an excursion. Doungjai greeted Robert with a nervous smile. He tried to make his reciprocal smile friendly and encouraging, but it still felt more like a grimace.

Nang explained that they were off to view her apartment, which she would be vacating after her marriage to Cully. She was paying a monthly rent of five hundred bahts less than Doungjai for a bigger room with better amenities.

'Doungjai think maybe she like to take over my place,' Nang went on.

'We'll come with you, if you like,' Cully proposed.

Nang's rebuff was tempered with a teasing smile. '*We* want to make *ladies'* talk, Cully. It better that way.'

Robert wasn't sure he agreed. He was anxious to restore his credit with Doungjai.

'Are you all right?' he asked. He was reluctant to touch her, fearing rejection.

'Yes, thank you.' Always courteous and correct, her formal response only made him feel worse. At least her smile seemed a little warmer, or was that just wishful thinking?

'How long will you be?' Cully asked, as the girls were departing.

'Two or three hours.' Nang looked unsmiling towards Robert. 'If we meet two nice men we be longer, maybe we no come back.' Then they were gone.

'Well that puts us firmly in our place.' Cully grinned ruefully. 'Women have a knack of doing that when they think we're getting above ourselves. I tell you, Robert, they might seem soft, vulnerable creatures, but when they get together with a common aim, they can be as tough as old boots.' He walked across to the refrigerator. 'Since we're in the doghouse, how about a beer?' He peered in. 'Bugger it – there's none left.'

Chapter Forty-One

Sprawled in the only half comfortable chair, with a newly opened bottle of beer clasped in his ham fist, Cully was feeling sorry for his young - and as he saw it, misguided – friend.

'You're still worrying about it, aren't you?' he said.

'Yes,' a chastened Robert admitted. 'Of all the jobs to choose, why did she have to go and work in a Patpong bar and take the easy way out to make money?'

'So that's what you're thinking?' Cully placed the bottle slowly and deliberately on the table. 'You really believe that being a bar girl in Bangkok is the easy way out?'

'Well, isn't it?' Robert protested defensively. 'Asking men to buy you drinks, sleeping with anyone willing to pay . . .'

'Let me give you a few facts about this soft life in the bars,' Cully said with some heat. 'I've known quite a few of these girls. As a matter of fact, Nang was a bar girl once and I can tell you she was bloody glad to swap it for a job in a massage parlour.' The big Scotsman clamped his massive paw around the bottle, heaved himself to his feet and started to pace up and down. 'Trouble is, most people think all the girls are cheap whores who can be bought by any fella who fancies a quick screw. They forget that these are real people and like everyone else they have feelings and hopes and fears. They're somebody's daughter and sister and mother and they've got boyfriends and husbands. Most of them are really decent kids. Like your Doungjai, for instance.'

Cully took a healthy swig from the bottle. 'Get one thing straight, young Robert – it's about the hardest bloody way in the world to make a living. When they're no buggering about on the stage, their job is to try and get friendly with complete strangers. They don't try to get the customer to buy them a drink because they *like* the bloody stuff, but because for every drink bought, they get fifty pence for themselves. Their glasses are only about a quarter full of Coke and ice because they're doing this all night long. If they drank more, they'd never be out of the loo, and if they drank alcohol they'd be pissed out of their minds.

'But that's the *easy* part. Suppose they do get someone interested enough to take them away to a hotel for the night? They've no idea who they're going with, or if the guy's got a disease, or whether they're violent. They don't even know for sure if they'll get paid afterwards.

'Remember, they always have to be well groomed, they have all the usual worries about late periods – often with good reason – not to mention the risk of catching V D, or worse still AIDS.'

Cully took a final swallow before crashing down the empty bottle on the table. 'Are you beginning to get the picture? And all this goes on six or seven hours every night, with those lights flashing and that deafening racket they call music going non-stop.'

Robert looked uncomfortable. Cully was exposing a side of life as a bar girl that had never crossed his mind. 'But if it's as bad as you say, why do they work there?'

For an answer, Cully dipped into his pocket and held out a few crumpled banknotes. 'Because they don't know where else they can earn the same money, not that they make much by our standards.' He glared challengingly at Robert. 'How much *do* you think they earn?'

Robert shook his head.

'The equivalent of about seventy or eighty pounds a month basic,' Cully stated flatly. 'Oh, yeah, sometimes they can make a bit more with a speciality act, like those lesbians, or that girl with the blowpipe, or something like Doungjai's fire act. But the only way they can really increase their earning power depends on how many customers they can get to pay the bar.'

'Pay the bar?'

'If a guy wants a girl for the night, he has to pay the bar about eight to ten pounds to compensate the owner for taking her off the premises. How much he gives the girl after that is between the two of them.'

Cully resumed his pacing. There was little doubt he felt strongly about the subject.

'Don't get me wrong, I'm no condemning the system here, I'm just spelling it out. In lots of ways it's a bloody sight better than anything we've got back home. You don't see women walking the streets touting for business in Bangkok, and there's no kerb crawling or sex shops. And violence and drunken brawls, that kind of thing, is almost non-existent. People know how to behave themselves. 'As for the bar girls, quite likely most of them would prefer to earn their money some other way, though they seem resigned to their lot. It's also a fact that quite a few permanent relationships do develop between the girls and customers.'

Cully paused, but his sermon was not over. 'I'll tell you, Robert, what makes me really mad is the bloody moralists who sit on their fat arses shaking their heads and tut-tutting about the system. If a girl loses her job, she can't fall back on the State to bail her out. There's no Social Security to run to. So if anyone ever mentions morality to you, just remember to tell them it's bloody easy to be moral when you don't have to bother about a roof over your head, or wonder where the next meal is coming from.'

Cully slumped into the chair, seemingly depressed by his own commentary. 'It's no as if they stash their money away and then, when they've saved enough, get out. Whatever their own circumstances, they all send money home to help the family who often live in semi-poverty in the back of beyond. How many youngsters back home do that?'

He fixed his young friend with a disconcerting stare. 'Now do you still think it's the easy option, Robert?' he demanded.

'I had no idea,' Robert admitted, abashed. Was this really the life Doungjai had taken up?

'You're no the only one,' Cully grunted, then as if reading his young friend's thoughts: 'But you're going to have to make your mind up. You seemed so keen on this girl before, and couldn't wait to find her. If your feelings for her have changed that much just because you don't like the job she's doing . . .' He shrugged, leaving his opinion unsaid.

Put like that, Robert realised it made his notion of a special relationship seem pretty superficial. It was not quite as easy as that though. He now wondered if circumstances, fate, bad luck, growing up – whatever

– had changed both of them so much that they would no longer be able to love each other.

'She and I are going to have to talk some more.' Robert found he could no longer look Cully in the eye. 'There's still a plenty of unanswered questions.'

'Well, don't insist on too many answers,' Cully cautioned. 'Even in the closest relationships, it's better for some things not to be spelt out.'

'What about the bloke she was arguing with last night?' Robert said, in an attempt to shift the spotlight off his moral judgements.

'Aye, you should find out more about them,' Cully agreed. 'It may be something she doesn't want to discuss, but she may be in some kind of trouble.'

Chapter Forty-Two

It was early evening when Nang returned – alone. As she called a greeting and closed the door, Robert leapt from his chair.

'Isn't Doungjai with you?' he demanded, almost rudely.

'No. She want to be on her own for a little while.' She fixed him with a stern look. 'To think about things you say to her.'

Cully's 'Hah!' was a clear substitute for 'I told you so.'

A dejected Robert flopped back onto his chair and took consolation in gulping down the last dregs of his bottle of beer.

Unseen by him, Nang signalled Cully with her eyes.

He nodded and winked knowingly. 'I think I'll trot over to the tailors and pick up those shirts and trousers I ordered,' he announced.

'I stay and have coffee with Robert,' Nang declared. 'You no mind?'

'Of course not.' Cully boomed. He was already on his feet. 'I won't be long.'

After Cully had gone Nang sat down facing Robert. Her expression was not the sunny one he was used to seeing.

'Doungjai tell me everything, Robert.'

'Oh?'

'She say you very angry because she work in bar.'

Robert frowned. 'I'm sorry I spoke to her the way I did, but I still don't understand why she has to do that kind of work.'

'Did you know she have to take care of her family, and pay doctor many bahts for her mama who get hurt in accident?'

'She told me about that.'

'So. Her mama is ill for long time and Doungjai borrow money to pay for operation in hospital. Now Doungjai have big problem. She have to pay back money she borrow and she still not have enough for hospital. She tell me she owe same money she borrow, even when she pay back one thousand five hundred bahts every month.'

'That's crazy!' Robert exclaimed. 'How much did she borrow?'

'Ten thousand bahts,' Nang said.

Robert did some mental arithmetic: that was around two hundred pounds. Not a huge sum, but if Doungjai was paying an exorbitant rate of interest, the monthly repayments might well not be sufficient to make inroads into the original loan.

'That is why she take job in Black Pussy and do fire dance,' Nang continued. 'She make more money than other jobs. But, Robert, she tell her boss she not want to go with men to hotel. She only talk to them in bar, have drink and dance. Because she does very sexy dance and bring in customers, her boss say OK.'

Robert snatched at this straw of hope. 'Do you . . . do you mean she *doesn't* go off with men and sleep with them?'

'That what she tell me,' Nang nodded. 'And I believe her. Only . . .' She hesitated.

'Go on.'

'She say man she borrow money from, he want her to pay him more quickly. He tell her she must go sleep with men and make more money, or else . . .' Nang made a chopping motion.

Robert gulped. 'This man, the one she borrowed money from, do you know who he is or anything about him?'

'Everybody know Mister Brown. Him come from China and he very bad man. Nobody like him but he have plenty money, have big business in Bangkok, so everybody speak nice to him. If somebody make him angry, his men hurt them.' Nang punched a small fist into the palm of the other hand, to emphasise her point.

Robert drew a deep breath of mixed relief and anger. All was horribly clear now. Ever since he had witnessed that scene at the back of the Black Pussy, he had suspected Doungjai was under pressure of some sort, but he never suspected she might be in debt. His anger intensified as he recalled Brown's menacing behaviour towards Doungjai and her spirited response.

'The bastard,' he growled. 'How did Doungjai get mixed up with a bloke like that in the first place?' he demanded, almost as if it were Nang's fault.

'She need money to help her mama,' Nang repeated patiently. 'I already explain. No one else can give for her and then someone tell her maybe she can borrow from Mister Brown.' She shrugged. 'I think she not know him bad man till after she borrow money.'

Nang leaned across and put her hand on Robert's. 'I sorry, Robert. Doungjai say I must not tell you

303

about this. She not want to worry you, but I think you should know.'

Robert placed his free hand on top of hers. 'I'm very glad you did, Nang – thank you. I'm sorry about the way I behaved. Will you tell Cully?'

She shook her head. 'I tell no one, only you. Doungjai say she only speak me because she want to talk to someone, but no have friend she can tell. She very good girl, Robert. I like to help, but no have money.'

'You're a good girl too, Nang, and a good friend.' Robert gripped her hand. 'But now it's my problem.'

'What you mean, Robert?'

'I mean I'm going to have the whole thing out with this Brown character and the sooner the better.' He stood up so abruptly his chair fell over. His voice was unusually harsh as he went on: 'Just who does he think he is?'

'I don't think that is good idea.' Nang looked up at him anxiously. 'I hear bad things happen to people who speak to Mister Brown and he no like it. Him asshole.'

'I'm not scared of him.' Was this the normally quiet spoken, easy going Robert Stone he had been living with for seventeen years? He hardly recognised himself. 'He might frighten the local people, but he'd better not try anything with me.' He glanced at his watch. 'If I go down to Patpong now, I might catch up with him before the evening crowds build up. With any luck, by the time Doungjai gets to the club to-night, I'll have sorted him out.'

'Please, Robert,' Nang pleaded. 'Better you not go alone.'

Robert was adamant. 'Don't you see, Nang, I owe it to Doungjai to help her, especially after all the things

I said to her.' His anger was directed as much against himself as against Brown. 'I owe it to her,' he said, his voice subdued.

'Better you wait till Cully comes back,' Nang reasoned, now seriously worried. 'Talk to him first. If anything bad happen because I tell you, it be my fault.'

'Nothing bad is going to happen, Nang.' On an impulse, he bent and touched his lips to her cheek. 'Thanks for your concern, but Doungjai is my girl.' He managed a bleak smile. 'Come down to the bar later with Cully and we'll celebrate over a meal together?'

'Up to you, Robert.' She nodded reluctantly, still concerned. 'But take care.'

'I will. See you later, Nang.' Still fuelled by his anger, Robert stalked from the room. His mind was no longer clouded by suspicion and doubt: he was going to help Doungjai and atone for his own intolerance. At last he had a purpose.

Nang had no such fanciful thoughts as she watched his slim figure disappear. She was wondering what her good intentions had set in motion.

Chapter Forty-Three

The daily transformation of Patpong was complete when Robert dismounted from the *tuk tuk*. The non-descript, near deserted thoroughfare of the daytime was now crammed with stalls, touts and tourists at the start of another busy evening of bargaining and boozing and behaving badly.

During the short ride, Robert had time to reflect on his chosen course of action and Nang's warning. He wondered fleetingly if it was a little reckless of him to tackled Brown alone. But no, he decided, this was *his* problem because it was Doungjai's. It was a chance for him to atone for his behaviour towards her.

He meandered his tortuous way through the early evening crowds, smiling and shaking his head in response to the cries of the stall vendors. His mind was elsewhere, pondering his approach to 'Mister Brown'. Funny name for a Chinese, he mused. Perhaps his father was English, which would give them something in common – a sense of fair play, for instance. He could always hope.

He stopped at the entrance to the Black Pussy, still undecided whether to heed Nang's advice. How easy it would be to walk on by. Doungjai would never know; Nang would most likely be relieved for his sake. But he, Robert Stone, would know. And that was what really mattered.

He climbed the stairs slowly. As he reached the top, the door ahead of him was opened by a man seated on a stool just inside the bar. The darkness and the blast of music hit him simultaneously.

'Good evening, sir,' the doorman greeted him equably and shone a torch at the floor to indicate a step-up which had ambushed countless customers in the past.

Robert stood for a moment as the door closed behind him, while his eyes grappled with the near non-existent lighting. Up on the walkway behind the bar were two naked girls, looking bored and moving their weight from foot to foot. Just enough to prove they were living beings.

As his eyes became acclimatised to the gloom, Robert was relieved to see that Brown was not among the barflies. An attractive woman in a smart tailored suit and high heeled shoes led him to a stool. She looked like a secretary.

He asked her for a Kloster and caught the woman's arm as she was about to walk away.

'I'm looking for a man who comes in here sometimes – Mister Brown,' he shouted in her ear. 'Do you know him?'

The woman gave him a blank look. Perhaps she didn't understand English.

'Mister Brown?' he repeated.

She shook her head vaguely and turned away to order his beer. As she left, two girls predictably arrived to keep Robert company. They perched on the stools on either side, displaying lots of flesh, and began the familiar question and answer game: 'What your name? Where you come from . . . ?'

His beer arrived and, to his surprise, as she stuck the flimsy bill into the top of the receptacle on the bar beside him, the smartly dressed woman said: 'Barman says Mister Brown often come in here about this time. Maybe he come soon.'

Robert thanked her and immediately became aware of a cooling of the other girls' attention.

'You know Mister Brown?' one of them asked, with a nervous glance at her companion.

Robert had the impression that any friend of Mister Brown's was not someone to cuddle up to. So maybe here was a way to get these two out of his hair.

'Yes, he's a good friend of mine.' He gushed. 'Do you know him?'

'Know him, yes,' the same girl said with feeling. She exchanged a few terse words with her colleague, and as one they promptly hopped down from their stools and dissolved into the gloom.

Well pleased with the result of his subterfuge, Robert quaffed his beer and peered up at the stage. Two different girls had taken over, though they were no livelier than their predecessors.

An hour and several beers passed. Girls came and went on the stage. Customers came and went at the bar. Still no Mister Brown. As he drained his glass, he decided Brown wasn't going to show. At least he could honestly say he had tried. Maybe he would give it another shot tomorrow. He would go back to the hotel and track down Cully and Nang, then try and meet up with Doungjai when her stint was over.

As he swivelled round on his stool three men entered the bar. Although their features were indistinct, Robert was sure this was Brown and Co. Suddenly, he wanted to run, but some instinct warned him against it.

The barman made some sort of gesture to the trio, and they approached the bar. As the lighting fell on their faces, Robert's hopes and fears were confirmed: it was Brown and his heavies right enough, and they exuded no more bonhomie than they had the previous night.

Now the barman was pointing him out to Brown. Three inscrutable faces turned in his direction, then came round the bar towards him. Brown placed a slim leather-covered briefcase on the bar top and rested his backside on the nearest stool.

'The barman says you're looking for me.' There was an edge to his high-pitched voice. His English was fluent, with almost an upper class accent. 'What do you want?'

Plunge in or back off now, these were the choices facing Robert. He was tempted to plead mistaken identity, but thoughts of Doungjai's predicament, steeled his resolve. If she could stand up to Brown's threats and harassment, he certainly could.

'If you're Mr Brown, I want to speak to you about a friend of mine.' He tried to keep trepidation from his voice. It wasn't easy.

'Is this connected with business?'

'Yes, it is.'

'Then I suggest we talk through there, where it's not so noisy.' Brown indicated the door behind the bar, leading to the dressing rooms, and moved off. His two henchmen stood impassively waiting for Robert to follow.

Suppressing a gulp, Robert got down from his stool, and took off after Brown, the henchmen dogging his heels. He wondered vaguely if it were prudent to be leaving the public eye. Then they were passing through the doorway, into the corridor at the back of the bar. There, Brown turned to confront Robert.

'Now, what do you want to talk to me about?' His voice was neutral, perhaps expecting to hear a business proposition.

Robert sucked in air in the hope that it would boost his courage. 'It concerns a friend of mine who borrowed money from you. I understand you've been pressing her for bigger repayments than she can afford.'

Brown's expression hardened.

'What's your friend's name?'

'Doungjai Tilawan. She's my girl friend and works here at the bar.' When Brown made no comment, Robert added quickly: 'You were talking to her here only last night.'

'Ah, yes.' Recognition dawned on Brown's face. 'The fire girl.' His lips twitched into an appreciative smile, and he rapped a quick aside to the other two men who sniggered knowingly. 'So exactly what is bothering you?'

'She's been paying you one thousand five hundred bahts a month, but apparently still owes you as much now as she borrowed in the first place.'

'Interest payments. Surely you've heard of interest, Mr . . .'

'Stone.' So far he was pleasantly surprised by the man's conciliatory manner.

'Correct me if I'm wrong, Mr Stone, but in your country don't you also pay interest if you borrow money?'

'Not at the rate you're charging.' Robert felt his confidence increasing and he was further encouraged by the steady movement of people along the corridor on their way to and from the bar. Surely they wouldn't try anything here . . .

'As far as I can recall, nobody else would lend her

any money.' Brown sounded almost reasonable now. 'There was no security and her income is low. I was the only one prepared to help her and she knew my terms when she borrowed the money.'

Robert disagreed. 'I doubt if she fully appreciated what she was letting herself in for. Anyway, this can't go on. I would like to know exactly how much she still owes and I will help her settle it in one payment.'

Brown put a hand to his mouth and looked at the floor, apparently considering Robert's suggestion. 'We might work something out,' he admitted slowly. 'But we can't discuss it out here in the corridor. Let us go where we won't be disturbed.'

Again without waiting for a reply, he led the way along the corridor, and Robert found himself eased along with him in some subtle fashion. The door was unmarked and when they entered, he was startled to find himself in the men's lavatory. His earlier unease was rekindled when the door closed behind them and Brown turned to face him. The smile was gone.

So, it quickly transpired, was the reasonableness.

Chapter Forty-Four

It was a big room for a toilet and typically spartan. In the far corner were two stalls, doors ajar, with urinals to the right and wash basins near the entrance. Brown stood in the centre and slowly and deliberately took out a gold cigarette case, extracted a tipped cigarette and lit it. Every movement was precise, as if it had been carefully rehearsed. He flicked a speck of ash from his immaculately-tailored tan suit and blew a cloud of smoke at the harsh strip lighting that cast a cold glow over the stark setting.

'So you want to pay off your friend's debts,' he said, speculatively, as if he were thinking aloud.

'Yes. You've been telling her to make more money by sleeping with the customers who come into the bar. Well, you can forget about that.' He put his fists on his hips. 'We're going to be married.'

'Oh, indeed? Married, eh?' Brown took another slow draw on his cigarette. His eyes never left the young man's face, probing for the smallest sign of weakness or fear.

'Now listen to me, *Mister* Stone. If there is one thing that makes me annoyed, it is outsiders interfering in my affairs, and trying to make trouble between me and my clients.' He pursed his thin lips. 'Did you wonder how a Chinaman came to be called Brown?'

Robert made a dismissive motion with his hand.

'No?' said Brown. 'Well, I'll tell you, because it might help you to understand who you're dealing with. I spent many years in England and learned a lot about how to succeed in business, except none of it seemed to work for me. Then one day I heard a song by Frank Sinatra called "Leroy Brown", perhaps you know it? According to the words, he was the baddest man in town and it gave me an idea.'

Robert was not impressed by Brown's reminiscences, but opted to play along.

'I came to the conclusion that the best way to get out front in business,' Brown went on, 'was to build a tough reputation so that people know you mean business. So the first thing I did was hire a couple of good boys to help put some urgency into my negotiations, if you get my meaning?'

Robert understood perfectly. 'You mean to scare people.'

'Scare, persuade, call it what you will. Getting the right result is what matters. I also changed my name from Chang to Brown, after the song. I felt it was symbolic somehow, but the main thing is that it worked and I've never looked back since.' With the cigarette poised delicately between his fingers, Brown jabbed at Robert to punctuate his words. 'You talk to anyone who knows Mr Brown and they'll tell you it is not a good idea to cross him.'

Robert remembered Nang's warning. Maybe he should have taken her more seriously.

'Why are you telling me all this?' Robert said, staying outwardly composed. He had a feeling that to show fear would make Brown all the more likely to resort to his traditional methods of 'negotiation.'

'So that you understand what you've got yourself

313

into, and as a polite warning to mind your own business before you get in any deeper.'

'Do you really think I'm going to walk away and let you carry on bullying my girl friend?' Robert felt his anger building again, getting the better of his discretion. He knew it wasn't smart, but he couldn't help it.

'Hah, your girl friend!' Brown spat, his lip curling. 'That little bitch has been more trouble to me since I lent her money than a dozen other clients. Always moaning about how much she's already paid me. I've told her she should be like the other girls, get some pussy time in and make real money. Instead, she's come up with every excuse in the book and a few even I've never heard before.' Brown proceeded to enumerate her failings by counting them off on his fingers. 'First it was her three kids. She said she had to go home at night to look after them. Three kids! I'll bet she's still a bloody virgin. The next excuse was her mother who was supposed to be ill, so she had to look after her and . . .'

'Her mother is ill,' Robert jumped in. He hoped the bit about three kids was invented.

'Then her sister was ill, then her brother, then her other sister. I've never known such an unhealthy family.'

'Perhaps they all caught the same virus,' Robert suggested facetiously. 'Are you saying she was lying?'

Brown glared at him. 'Lying? That girl is the biggest bloody little liar I've ever met and I've known a few. And then, of course, after she ran out of relatives with one foot in the grave, she resorted to the oldest excuse in the book – her periods.'

'Didn't it occur to you that she simply doesn't want to sleep with customers?' Robert said mildly.

Brown took a step forward, his mouth working. 'Of

course. Do you think I'm stupid? I don't *care* what she wants or doesn't want. She has to make more money if she's going to pay off her debt to me. If the other girls can do it, so can she.'

'Not if she doesn't want to,' Robert rapped back, greatly daring, his voice reverberating round the bare walls. 'And what's more, you're going to leave her alone. I want to know exactly how much Doungjai owes you and we'll settle with you once and for all.'

'I've told you already I don't like people interfering in my business.' Brown said silkily. 'The current arrangement suits me very well and it's completely legal. He indicated his briefcase. 'As it happens, all the papers are here spelling out my terms with her signature agreeing to them.'

'So you would rather she keeps paying you every month while you screw her for more and more.'

Brown sneered. 'Mr Stone, I will leave the screwing to you. I am a respectable businessman . . .'

'You're nothing but a cheap crook,' Robert yelled, his self-control finally deserting him.

A hard shove from behind propelled him violently against the wall. Before he could even turn to defend himself, his arms were pinned from behind by powerful hands and he was swung round to face Brown.

'I do not like to be insulted, Mr Stone,' the Chinaman informed him. 'The trouble with you *falangs* is that you think you know everything.' He took out another cigarette, lit it carefully and propelled a cloud of smoke at Robert's face. Robert struggled to break free of his captor's hold, but could make no impression.

'I think you need convincing that I am a serious businessman. My two associates here are most efficient at reinforcing my warnings when they are not heeded. As you are about to discover, their message can be very emphatic without leaving any marks or bruises.'

Robert was still slightly dazed from his collision with the wall. He felt moisture trickling down his temple, but only discovered later that it was blood from a gash caused when he was thrown against the wall. He still could not grasp that this was happening to him.

His eyes shifted from Brown's leering face to the other man standing beside him. There was not much compassion in the flat features and the eyes that looked like slashes.

'Just remember, Mr Stone,' Brown warned, 'in case you should consider going to the police afterwards, my colleagues would be only too pleased to visit your girl friend for a . . . how do you English call it . . . a cosy chat?'

He nodded almost imperceptibly to the man beside him who stepped forward and drove his fist into Robert's solar plexus. Only the armlock of the second thug behind him, kept him from falling. Yet even as the pain spread through his body, his mind was crystal clear. He was in a mess, and he was going to get badly beaten. Unless he did something to prevent it.

Brown was intoning more homilies, but they were no more than a drone. Robert's attention was on the man beside him, now shaping to deliver another blow. With an instinct and timing that had brought him a string of goals for his school, Robert measured his distance and let fly with his foot.

His toe caught his attacker squarely between the legs. The man staggered back with a grunt, hands going to his groin, as if pulled by strings. Even as the kick landed, Robert threw his head back sharply, striking the man behind him squarely on the nose. The grip on his arms slackened, and he pulled free, half turning to face his adversary, who was clutching his nose. There seemed to be a lot of blood.

The unexpectedness of Robert's resistance had served him well, but his triumph was short-lived. The men were professionals and used to absorbing punishment. They recovered fast. Acting in concert, they stepped between Robert and the door, cutting off his obvious line of escape.

He knew they would not underestimate him again. He had had his moment of glory and now he must pay for it.

Brown had retreated to watch the scene unfold from one of the stall doors, an expression of anticipation lighting up his moonlike face. It was not often his two henchmen got personally involved with one of his victims. This was going to be interesting.

'Mr Stone, I'm very sorry for you,' he hissed, as Robert backed slowly and fearfully towards the wall behind him. 'Now you're really in trouble.'

Chapter Forty-Five

Cully knew something was wrong as soon as he passed through the automatic sliding doors of the hotel lobby. Instead of waiting for him up in their room, Nang was sitting on a settee by the reception desk. She rushed to meet him.

'Where you *been*?' she demanded, grasping his hand.

'Sorry it took me so long, but the trousers needed a wee bit shortening, so I decided to wait. Is anything the matter?'

'Robert!' Nang gasped. 'I think he may be in trouble.'

Cully stifled a groan. 'What kind of trouble?'

In her anxiety, Nang lapsed into Thai. Cully made soothing motions and escorted her back to the settee.

'Now start again, in English.'

She swallowed hard, and speaking slowly and deliberately, related to Cully the gist of her conversation with Robert.

'So he's gone to have a word with this loan shark,' Cully summed up. He could see no cause for so much alarm.

'But Mister Brown, him very big asshole, Cully,' Nang protested. 'He have two . . . I not know how you say . . . two . . .' she waved her arms frantically. '. . . two shit men.'

'Shit men?' Cully's mouth twitched.

Nang simulated fisticuffs. 'You know, men who do bad things to other people.'

'You mean *hit* men.'

She nodded furiously. 'Yes, hit men.'

'Come to think of it, Robert did mention Brown had a couple of mean looking characters in tow.' Cully scratched his head. 'But I doubt if they're hit men, Nang. In any case, they surely wouldn't do anything to a tourist?'

'For sure they try,' Nang responded vigorously. 'If anyone he not like, Mister Brown give big trouble – Thai, *falang*, all same.'

'Did you warn Robert about him?'

'I tell him, but he want to help Doungjai alone. I say wait for you, but he want to go by himself. He very st ... st ...' She gave up with a little cry of frustration.

'Stubborn's the word, my lovely. Anyway, there'd be no harm done if we go down to the bar just to make sure the silly wee bugger doesn't get into any bother. How long's he been gone?'

'About one hour.' Nang was already on her feet. 'I come with you.'

'OK, but I'm sure we're wasting our time. Even if this Brown guy is a mean git, I can't believe he would try anything with people around. In any case, it's unlikely that Robert will even find him.' In spite of his outward lack of concern, Cully had no illusion about the risk Robert was running in stirring up a local thug.

Still clutching his newly purchased trousers, he followed Nang from the hotel. 'Tell him to get moving,' Cully instructed her, as they climbed into a taxi.

Nang stared at him, then rattled off a stream of Thai to the driver as he thumbed the thirty five bahts basic charge into the meter.

Requesting a Bangkok taxi driver to hustle, is largely a pointless exercise. No matter how hard the driver tries, or how many back doubles he knows, his is but one of thousands of other vehicles, all similarly motivated.

Fortunately the Black Pussy was not far and, with the driver driving like a madman in the late rush hour traffic, they were pulling into the kerb in front of the Montien Hotel in a matter of minutes. Cully thrust the fare and a lavish tip into his hand and they crossed into Patpong One. The driver was still gushing thanks long after they were out of earshot.

'Doungjai may be at the bar now,' Nang reminded him as they weaved through the early evening crowds of browsers and buyers.

Cully hoped not. If there was going to be any rough stuff, it was better she stayed far away from it.

Through a gap in the throng, they glimpsed the doorway to the Black Pussy. Cully, panting now, urged Nang forward. Up the stairs they clattered, and by coincidence, at the top of the stairs they came up behind Doungjai. She turned in surprise when Nang called her name, but the pleasure of seeing them soon gave way to a look of fright when Nang explained in a flood of Thai why she and Cully were there.

'Shouldn't we go in and see if he's actually here,' Cully suggested edgily. 'If he isn't, we can stop worrying. But if he is. . .'

Doungjai's hand went to her mouth and she was the first inside, despite Cully's efforts to hold her back

The same strident music assaulted their eardrums. Immediately, Doungjai demonstrated the amazing ability of all bar girls to carry on a normal conversation amidst a noise level that made the floor tremble, not to mention enjoying perfect vision in virtually zero visibility. The man at the door professed not to have seen any young *falangs* so far this evening. Doungjai moved on to accost the barman. The exchange that ensued was short. Doungjai, looking alarmed, spoke quickly to Nang and then, remembering that Cully could not understand Thai, repeated her words in English.

'He say Lobut come here and Mr Brown also.' She gesticulated towards the door behind the bar. 'They go to back rooms.'

'What for?' Cully shouted.

She shrugged. 'He say to talk.'

'If that's all, they shouldn't object if we join the conversation.' Cully was already lumbering off towards the door with Doungjai and Nang at his heels.

The well-lit passage was empty, and when the door swung shut behind them, Cully looked questioningly at Doungjai.

After a moment's hesitation, she pointed to a door further along the passage. 'Maybe they in men's toilet.'

'Right!' Jawjutting, fists clenched, Cully strode to the door indicated by Doungjai and flung it open.

Chapter Forty-Six

Robert retreated step by step. He was no match for either of Brown's minders on their own, never mind together. He had also – foolishly – antagonised them by hitting back. Yet strangely, as they closed in on him, hands weaving in the best kung fu tradition, light on their toes their eyes fixed unblinkingly on his, he felt detached and resigned.

Surprisingly, the beating he was about to receive was not uppermost in his thoughts, which were of Doungjai. He had treated her badly: his suspicions, his questions and his anger had been misplaced. He had been wrong at every step and seen ill where there were only good intentions. All that was left was the hope that she would recognise that he had tried to make amends, and come in time to forgive him.

As if waking from a dream, Robert felt the wall at his back. There was nowhere else to go. Brown snapped encouragement to his men but even as the words left his mouth, the door flew open, crashing back against the wall.

Now Robert was sure he was dreaming, for filling the doorway with his bulk was the most welcome sight he could ever imagine.

'Cully!' he gasped.

Cully read the scene at a glance and the sight of

blood on Robert's face brought him to instant boiling point. Doungjai and Nang were crowding up behind him; Doungjai's scream of 'Lobut!' seemed to act as a spur and he launched himself into the washroom with a roar of anger.

The two thugs were unprepared for Cully's ferocity, and he swept through the first man's attempt to fend him off. His momentum smashed the man into the wall with a bone-juddering impact that made the room shudder. As he rebounded off the wall, Cully seized his arm and swung him in an arc, as effortlessly as if he weighed no more than a bag of shopping. The second man was dodged out of the way as his partner hurtled past him across the room to smash into the opposite wall. From that point on, he was a non-participant.

Without giving his dazed victim a second glance, Cully turned to deal with the other man, who realized that this intruder was a more worthy adversary. Even so, he was not alarmed. The element of surprise was now gone. Without it, this fat *falang* would soon regret his interference.

As Cully moved in closer a fierce kick, Thai boxing-style, caught him high on the head. Cully blinked and stopped in his tracks. Another kick crashed squarely against his jaw. Now he rocked on his heels. Back in Glasgow, he was used to deflecting fists, feet, bottles, knives and other assorted weapons, but he had never come across anyone who could kick so hard and so high.

Similarly, his opponent, having got home two of his best kicks right on target, had not expected the recipient to be still standing. What he did not know was that in Cully's line of business, you only survived if you could take it as well as dish it out.

With Brown screaming threats and advice from a safe distance, his man unleashed another ferocious kick, only this time Cully was ready for him. Reacting with a speed at odds with his bulk, he deflected the foot with an elbow. In the same movement, he swung a vicious, scything punch that caught the lighter man flush in the face. It was like being hit with a battering ram. The thug hurtled back through one of the stall doors and collapsed onto the toilet seat. He struggled like a stranded fish to rise, but Cully was out for blood.

'So you like using your feet, you fucking wee prick,' he snarled in his best Glaswegian. 'Well, how do you like this?'

He delivered a mighty kick to the ribs of his cringing opponent, who screamed and curled into the foetal position. Further kicks to various parts of his abdomen produced more howls and writhing. It was typically brutal bar room stuff, and Cully only desisted when the other man ceased to react. He hauled him to his feet like a sack of coal, pulled him out of the stall, and hurled him across the room into his partner who was levering himself painfully to his knees. They crumpled to the floor together, limbs intertwined, like weary lovers.

Brown had watched the destruction of his men with incredulity, which turned to fright when Cully's attention turned to him.

'Are you all right, Robert?' Cully asked, glancing towards his young friend, who was still backed up against the wall, stunned by the speed of events.

'I'm OK,' Robert managed to gasp. Never would he have suspected that the lumbering, amiable Scotsman could become a raging bull, capable of disabling two kung fu experts in about a minute flat.

Doungjai judged it safe to rush to her man's side, with Nang in close attendance.

'Lobut, you bleeding!' she cried, dabbing at his brow with a handkerchief.

He dredged up a grin. 'I'm all right. Don't fuss.' Then, as she threw her arms around him: 'Oh, go on then – fuss.'

'It's just as well for you my friend isn't hurt,' Cully said grimly, advancing on Brown.

'Don't touch me, don't touch me!' Brown squealed as the Scotsman lifted him clear of the floor by the lapels of his expensively-cut silk suit.

'I take it this is Mister bloody Brown?' he said mildly, to no one in particular.

'That's him,' Robert confirmed, over Doungjai's head. 'He's been giving Doungjai a hard time.'

'I heard all about it from Nang.' Cully peered into Brown's terrified face from no more than six inches.

'He said if I went to the police, he and his pals would know how to deal with her.' The threat to Doungjai had sickened Robert above all others.

'Oh he did, did he?' Cully feigned surprise. His grip on Brown's jacket tightened and the look he directed at the Chinaman was not pretty. 'So you and your fucking monkeys fight young girls, do you? You're a real hero and no mistake' He drew back a huge ham of a fist and held it cocked while he pinned Brown to the wall with his other hand.

'I was joking,' Brown gabbled, the cold sweat of fear oozing from his pores. 'I'm a businessman – I never hurt anyone.'

'I'll bet you don't. Scum like you never do your own dirty work. And I suppose that blood on my friend's face was just a joke too.' Cully roared the words into Brown's face, while the fist remained menacingly poised. Panic rendered Brown inarticulate. He could only make mewling sounds, trying ineffectually to ward the Scotsman off with his small, slender hands.

Cully altered his stance and eased back, dropping his fist but still keeping Brown jammed against the wall. 'I hear that my friend's girl borrowed money from you,' he observed almost conversationally.

'Yes, yes, I helped her.' Brown clutched at this thread of hope. If only he could convince this brute of his basic good nature and altruistic tendencies.

'Don't listen to him,' Robert said, crossing the room to stand by Cully. 'Doungjai's already paid him back what she borrowed, but he says she still owes as much as when she started.'

'Is this true?' Cully demanded.

'Interest,' Brown pleaded. 'Everybody pays interest when they borrow money.'

It was the wrong answer and Cully seemed to swell in size. The fist came up again, looking bigger than ever to Brown's terrified eyes. 'Pal, I don't think you've been paying attention,' he stated calmly. 'I'll ask you just once: how much does she still owe you?'

'Nothing, she doesn't owe me anything,' Brown burbled.

'You mean she's repaid you all the money she borrowed?' Cully insisted.

'Yes, yes, everything,' Brown agreed frantically. Perhaps he would be allowed to keep his head on his shoulders after all.

'He's got the papers in that brief case,' said Robert, suddenly remembering.

'Since the loan is repaid, you'll want to make it official.' Cully's grip on Brown's jacket remained in place, though the threatening fist was again lowered.

'I will give your friend a receipt,' Brown agreed eagerly.

'Not in here.' Cully looked round and suddenly realised that quite a crowd had gathered at the door, mostly curious bargirls. 'Doungjai, is there somewhere we can do some business with this gentleman.

'Yes. I show you.'

The spectators unjammed the doorway and Doungjai led the little group along the corridor to another door, leading to the girls' dressing room. It was brightly lit and one wall was an expanse of mirror with a narrow ledge at waist level. Before it, a row of stools were occupied by girls in their skimpy stage outfits, applying make-up and generally checking their appearance. At the far end, the noises of Patpong filtered through a half-open window.

As Cully marched Brown across the room and thrust him down onto a vacant stool, the girls looked on open-mouthed, make-up forgotten.

'Now, my wee man,' Cully said, snapping his fingers. 'Let's be seeing these papers, shall we?'

With hands that shook like bunting in a breeze, Brown opened his briefcase, while Robert watched with satisfaction. After some exaggerated shuffling of papers, Brown selected a garish pink folder and reluctantly handed it to Cully. It meant nothing to him or to Robert, who passed it on to a mystified Doungjai.

'Is this the paper you signed when you borrowed money from him?' Robert asked her.

Doungjai studied the single document it contained and nodded. 'Yes, but . . .'

'Your loan is paid in full,' Cully informed her and passed the document back to Brown. 'Write 'paid in full' and sign it.'

After the briefest hesitation, Brown took out a gold Mont Blanc fountain pen and scrawled across the paper. Cully relieved him of the pen and printed "Signature witnessed by George McCallum," then added his signature and the date. Just to be sure, he asked Doungjai to check what had been written, then consigned the receipted agreement into her keeping. The girls who had followed events in silence until now, suddenly broke into excited chatter.

'Nice pen,' he remarked, restoring Brown's property to its owner, who seemed not at all appreciative. 'There's one more thing you ought to know. I've got two brothers who live in Bangkok. They're both twice my size and they don't have my delightful personality. In fact they can get really unpleasant with anyone who upsets their wee brother. Now if I hear that this young lady ever as much as gets her nail polish chipped, I'm going to be very upset and my brothers will come looking for you and your two . . . er . . . shit men.' He looked meaningfully at Nang. 'And next time they won't walk away afterwards. In fact, they won't even *crawl* away. Do you understand what I'm saying, you dirty wee toe rag?'

'Yes sir, yes, I understand, thank you.' Brown clutched his brief case and edged nervously towards the door.

'Then beat it.'

Brown made good his escape and in his haste he even forgot to check if his unfortunate henchmen required any first aid.

Chapter Forty-Seven

Since he first watched her act at the Black Pussy, he had returned every night. He always sat inconspicuously in a corner, just inside the door, hunched over a Singha Gold bottle from which he took an occasional sip. Whenever one of the girls tried to engage him in conversation he would brush her off with a few terse words, and she would slip away to seek a more accommodating prospect.

He appeared to be uninterested in everything that went on around him, until she began her act. Then he came alive and alert and his eyes never left the stage until her act was over, when he would slip away, unnoticed and unmissed.

Soon after Doungjai walked out on him, Michael Paquet's circumstances had changed dramatically. He still wasn't sure what lay behind it, but he became aware of a growing hostility in Jurgen Gross' attitude towards him. He was no longer the boss's blue eyed boy.

It was a gradual process, but there seemed little doubt that Gross was intent on making his position untenable. He would set impossible targets, then openly criticise him for falling short. Cutting cost budgets to unrealistic levels was another ploy, designed to tie his hands. Worst of all was the undermining of his authority and belittling him in front of other members of staff.

The crunch came at a meeting of the company's directors back in the States. In a well rehearsed diatribe, Gross gave a totally one-sided report on the 'disappointing results' of the company's South East Asia branch, pointing the finger at imaginary short-falls in Michael's performance. Finally Michael lost his temper. In front of the whole Board, he told Gross where to put his job and his company before stomp-ing out.

Gross, while putting on a display of outrage, was well pleased with the outcome of his machinations. By forcing Michael to resign instead of firing him, he had saved the company a large sum in compensation. He even handled the public relations impeccably, announcing Michael's departure 'with regret', adding that the parting had been 'amicable.' He had won every trick, and when Michael returned to Thailand to put his affairs in order, he was jobless. The status, the income and the perks were no more and his future prospects were not propitious.

One residual benefit from his spell at NAC was the useful contacts he had built up. He was able to call in a few favours by being invited to undertake con-sultancy work. Keeping an income rolling in was crucial for, while at NAC, he had always spent lavishly and saved little. Even so, he was forced to downscale his lifestyle beyond recognition: the five-star hotel accommodation became a modest single room in an apartment block, in a less fashionable part of the city. No longer did his new clothes – such as they were – sport the Armani, Cerruti and Klein labels, and the days when his palate was titillated by a Chateau Petrus '79 or, now and again, a Mouton

Rothschild '82 were over. From being a very occasional beer drinker, Singha and Kloster became an integral part of his alcoholic intake.

At least his work permit had some months to run and, after much deliberation, he decided to stay on in Thailand until it expired. He knew of no country that provided better value for money in terms of food, travel and accommodation. He had also come to like the people. And one Thai person in particular.

As Michael settled to his reduced circumstances, his thoughts turned increasingly towards the person whose company had given him more pleasure than any other. It was bad enough to have been suckered by Gross over his job, but even worse was the knowledge that the bastard had cost him Doungjai. Notwithstanding his own complicity. Was it too late, even now, to patch up his relationship with Doungjai?

He tried her apartment, only to be told that she had moved out recently and no one knew where to. From there he progressed to the market stalls along Silom Road in the evening, but the tray of watches was no longer there, neither was Doungjai. A few enquiries of the nearby stallholders elicited no leads as to her whereabouts. Perversely, as the chances of discovering Doungjai's whereabouts diminished, Michael's desire to see her again strengthened until it became almost an obsession.

By now, the bars of Patpong had become a regular haunt. Not because he was hunting for female company, nor because of a weakness for alcohol; what he craved, after Doungjai, was the company of others. Even bar talk with strangers was better than spending the long evenings alone in his small room.

He usually visited two or three bars in an evening,

selecting them at random, so some weeks went by before he happened upon the Black Pussy one night. He had been there about half an hour, had just polished off his third beer and was about to move on when Doungjai burst onto the stage. Wondering if wishful thinking had stoked up his imagination, he sank back in his seat and watched in amazement as she went through her performance.

Amidst a host of conflicting emotions, uppermost was the sickening thought that this magnificent creature had been his and he had let her slip from his grasp. It was beyond belief that he had ever contemplated allowing Gross even to touch her, let alone colluded in it.

His initial instinct, when he had recovered from his surprise, was to approach her after her act, but something held him back. A disturbing thought did nothing to shore up his confidence. The change in his own circumstances was nothing compared to what had happened to Doungjai: from selling watches a few short months ago, and still a virgin, here she was entertaining the customers in Patpong with the most provocative act he had ever watched. It worried him too, that he may have been directly responsible for driving her to this. In the end he decided to wait until the next evening before speaking to her. It would give him more time to rehearse his choice of words.

Every evening following, Michael went through the same routine. Arriving with every intention of speaking to Doungjai, he continued to put it off, afraid she would turn him down again. Privately acknowledging that he would deserve it, didn't help a bit.

Yet he had to know whether there was any lingering goodwill on her side. Ironically, on the evening he decided to delay no longer, she did not appear.

'Doungjai have holiday', one of the girls informed him. 'I think she come tomorrow.'

Her non-appearance brought home to him the possibility that she might one day move on to another club, leaving him the task of finding her all over again. He resolved to speak to her the following evening, come what may.

The Black Pussy had filled up quickly in the few minutes since Michael had arrived. He sat in his usual corner, brooding over his beer, his stomach knotted with tension.

Suddenly there was a bustle of activity at the entrance. Michael drew further back into the corner when Doungjai appeared, followed closely by a big European man and another Thai girl. She passed within touching distance and without a sideways glance. She spoke excitedly to the man behind the bar, before sweeping on through the door behind the stage. Her companions went with her.

Shortly after, Michael became aware of people converging on the same door. He was tempted to join them out of curiosity, but he did not want to chance bumping into Doungjai in such circumstances. Just as quickly, the crowd dispersed and flowed back to the bar. The cause of the commotion seemed to be over.

A few minutes later, Doungjai reappeared accompanied by the two people she had arrived with, plus another European man who was holding a handkerchief to his forehead. The party seemed very agitated. They talked volubly together for a while. Eventually Doungjai left the other three and went through into the back of the bar.

When she had gone, her two male companions headed for the toilet. On an impulse Michael followed and to hell with the risk of running into Doungjai. As he entered the seedy Men's Room, the two Europeans were just coming away from the urinals. He joined them at the washstands, wondering as he did so what he was hoping to achieve.

'It looks like you've got yourself another chance,' the thickset man suddenly said to his younger companion in a gruff Scottish accent. 'Don't go and blow it again.'

He was drying his hands on a paper towel. In a moment they would be gone and the opportunity to strike up a conversation lost.

Michael said lightly, as he ran a comb through his blond hair: 'You guys wouldn't happen to know if the girl who does a dance with fire sticks has been on yet? I've heard she's very good.'

'She'll be on in a few minutes,' the Scotsman advised him, with a sidelong glance at his young friend. 'And she's no just very good, she's bloody *great*.'

'I take it you've seen her before?'

'You bet.' The young man spoke with feeling and more than a hint of pride. 'She does the best act in Patpong.'

The Scotsman looked quizzically at his companion, but said nothing

'You sound very positive.' Michael did not miss the look, though he couldn't begin to guess what it signified. 'You wouldn't happen to know her personally, by any chance?'

'As a matter of fact, I've known her for three years,' the young man stated.

'Really?' The reply shook Michael. Suddenly a huge

gap in his knowledge of Doungjai had opened up. Either that or this young guy was a liar. 'Well, I'd better get back. If she's half as good as you say, I won't want to miss any of her act.'

'See you, pal,' the Scotsman called after him.

The lesbian act was just finishing when Michael returned to his seat. He was not sure what to make of his new knowledge. The young kid could not have been more than eighteen, so how could he have known her that long? There was also something about the way he referred to Doungjai that he could not fathom. It also looked as if she was booked for tonight, so he would have to put off his grand confrontation yet again.

As he sat there, perplexed and frustrated, a fanfare of music heralded Doungjai's arrival on the stage. Her heavily oiled body glistened beneath the leaping flames and every movement seemed designed to emphasise her spectacular curves or expose her intimate bodily charms. She gave a performance *par excellence*, as if she were saying to someone: 'all of this is yours, if you want it.' Perhaps, Michael reflected, there was a message in it for him too; only that message might read: 'all of this could have been yours'.

Michael didn't stay to the end. His resolve in tatters, he got up, knocking against the table and upending the empty bottle. It rolled off the edge and shattered on the floor. Few heads turned his way; to a man, the club's clientele were transfixed by the uninhibited display before them, and it would take more than some broken glass to tear them away.

Michael stumbled down the stairs and out into the teeming streets, resolved never again to return.

*   *   *

Throughout the meal in the Tawana Ramada Hotel, Cully was not his usual ebullient self. His eye had almost closed and a dark bruise was developing round it.

'That bastard had a kick like a mule,' he growled, gently fingering his face. 'I don't mind a kick on the arse, but no on the bloody head, especially when I'm standing up.' He gazed apologetically at the other three faces around the table. 'I'm afraid I lost my temper with those guys.'

Robert placed his arm round Doungjai, who snuggled against him. 'We would never have guessed,' he grinned. He pulled away and eyed her approvingly. 'That was some performance you gave tonight, Doungjai.'

Cully perked up a little. 'I'll second that.' He didn't remark on Robert's change of heart in the last twenty-four hours. Perhaps the boy was growing up at last.

'You think so?' Doungjai looked pleased with the unanimous approval. 'It was special for Lobut. Tonight I feel very happy. Lobut is safe and now I finished with Mister Brown.'

'I'll bet that other fella enjoyed it too,' Cully observed.

'Fella?' Doungjai was puzzled by the term. 'What is "fella"?'

'A man,' Robert explained. 'Someone we met in the Gents. He said he'd heard your act was very good.'

'It look like you famous, Doungjai,' Nang smiled.

'You should have heard the build-up Robert gave you,' said Cully.

'Build-up?'

'He told him you were the best in Patpong.'

'You said that, Lobut?'

Robert smiled sheepishly. 'Oh, er . . . I told him what I thought, that's all.'

'Did you notice the guy looked kind of surprised when you said you had known Doungjai for three years?,' asked Cully. 'I got the feeling maybe he knew her.'

'He certainly couldn't wait to get back to the bar,' Robert agreed.

'What this man like?' Doungjai queried.

'Your usual customer . . .' Cully began. 'No, come to think of it, he was dressed a lot smarter than your average bar hopper. I suppose the girls might think he was quite good looking; in his late twenties I'd guess with longish fair hair. American accent. Anyway, Doungjai, you certainly gave him his money's worth – and the rest of us.'

Doungjai smiled, but a little distantly. Cully's description reminded her of someone she used to know.

Chapter Forty-Eight

It was the first time since she started working at the Black Pussy that a man had paid the bar for Doungjai and taken her back to his hotel.

When they reached the hotel, she waited demurely in the background while he went forward to the desk. The receptionist handed over the key with a friendly exchange, but her eyes were looking past him at Doungjai – appraising, assessing and knowing exactly why she was there. Doungjai was glad when they reached the privacy of the lift and even more relieved when the bedroom door closed softly behind them.

Robert was even more keyed-up. At sport he had excelled almost since he could walk, but with girls he had always been a little reserved. Most of his pals had steady girl friends long before he had plucked up the courage and persuaded a bubbly little sixteen year old to yield to his sexual prowess – only to discover that her love making skills were already well honed. She had taken control right from a sweaty hesitant start and had made no effort to hide her disappointment when he climaxed long before she was ready. He had felt humiliated.

At least he had learnt from the experience. Even if he was not quite Superman in bed, he had always consoled himself that, at barely eighteen, youth was still on his side and one day it would all come

338

together. Today, he was resolved, would be that day. He had never forgotten the first and only time he and Doungjai had gone to bed together. Although three years had gone by since then, he remembered every minuscule detail as if it were yesterday. He still cringed when he recalled that in spite of his best efforts and her full compliance, he had failed to conquer her virginity.

Further reminiscence was dashed from his mind as soon as they closed the door. Without a word Doungjai began to undress. Although she undressed every night for her stage act, her nervousness was all too apparent.

Robert watched, eyes gleaming, until she was naked. She stretched to her full height and did a pirouette on tip-toe, posing for his approval. It was a pose he had already admired in the Black Pussy, but this was for his enjoyment only. She was his private dancer. That brown velvet girl flesh was all his.

Her figure was pure magic and in the bright light of the bedroom he was able to appreciate fully how it had developed in the last three years. From generously curved, early teenage adolescence, her body had become a sleeker and even more stunning physical package. Robert remembered his amazement at the size of her fourteen year old breasts. They had developed in perfect proportion to the rest of her.

She came up to him and her nipples prodded his shirt front. Assertive and yet vulnerable, they seemed to drill into his chest. His arms went round her to grip the cheeks of her bottom. Digging his fingers into the plump flesh, he was mesmerised by their lush resilience.

'I have quick shower?' she suggested, and he reluctantly released her.

Even before he heard the water start to run, he had removed his own clothes. He was already fully erect and sat gingerly on the edge of the bed, waiting. Like Doungjai, he had decided this was no time for coyness and, as soon as she returned, towelling furiously, he stood up and made for the shower, his rampant penis on show. Such was his arousal that his erection remained undiminished throughout the shower.

When he emerged from the bathroom, she was stretched out on the top of the bed, face down. Robert lay alongside her and, propped up on one elbow, lightly ran his hand up and down her back as if stroking a big cat. She responded by raising her bottom provocatively and opening her thighs. His fingers slid between the parted cheeks and she gave little gasps of delight when he began to tease the tight rubbery ring of her anus. 'Oh, Lobut,' she moaned, in insincere protest, thrusting her hips higher and reaching for his penis.

Rolling her over onto her back, Robert brushed the palm of his hand across her thrusting nipples and down over her belly. The absence of body hair excited him even more and he caressed the marble smooth mound before edging his fingers into her silken slit. Easing her vaginal lips apart, a tentative exploration unearthed the tiny nodule of her clitoris. Doungjai squirmed under his featherlight touch.

As her juices began to flow, they both instinctively knew that this was the moment to consummate their love. He eased between her thighs. She guided him into place and, with the lightest of pressure, he slid inside her all the way. The rhythmic grip of Doungjai's vaginal muscles was beyond anything he had ever dreamt of and he was lifted to further sensual heights as he withdrew slightly, and then thrust again and again. Doungjai wrapped her legs tightly round his back, locked ankles and drew him even deeper, while her small cries became ever more shrill and ever more urgent.

Such intensity could not last long. With one long final thrust, Robert grew rigid while his seed jetted deep into her body. His timing was impeccable for she gave a little scream and crushed him to her, engulfed in her own orgasm.

They lay without moving for what seemed an age, while their satiated passion ebbed. When he at last raised his head to look at her, he saw her face was moist with perspiration. She looked tired, but a timid smile said it all.

'Thank you, Lobut,' she whispered. 'You make me happy like never before.'

'Me too,' he murmured weakly. He was still descending from the clouds.

Like that favourite photograph he had taken of Doungjai, on the bridge the first day they met, he had got it exactly right this time. At last they were able to say all the things they had wanted to say before, but had held back for reasons that now seemed trivial.

During a pause in their lover's dialogue, Doungjai said suddenly: 'I think you very brave man, Lobut, and Cully him think so too.'

Robert pulled away and looked at her in surprise. 'Brave? Me? Why?'

'Because you go see Mister Brown alone to help me. In restaurant tonight, Cully tell me he never go like you alone to see him and other two men. He say too risky.'

Good old Cully. Robert could not imagine the Scotsman avoiding a dozen Browns and his henchmen if need be. Yet the accolade was a great stimulus for his ego. More importantly, it had boosted his credit with Doungjai a few more notches, which did no harm.

'For you I'd sort out an army of Browns anytime,' he boasted, adding, more modestly: 'It was still lucky for me Cully showed up when he did.'

She stroked his brow and kissed the spot where he had hit the wall. 'You my big hero,' she purred.

'And your lover,' he reminded her.

He had already recuperated from his earlier endeavors. His penis was once more erect and eager for further exploration. Doungjai, sensing his renewed readiness, maneuvered herself to sit astride his head, facing his feet. As she bent forward, Robert's view was filled with the twin mounds of her buttocks and the yawning groove bisecting them. Adjusting her position, she eased her body further back until her anus and pussy lips were pressing down on his nose and mouth.

As he inhaled the scent of her female arousal, cool finger tips trickled along his inner thighs. Doungjai toyed awhile with his testicles before turning her full attention to his penis. She kissed and tongued the tip, before taking it carefully between her lips and drawing its length into her mouth. Sucking gently but firmly, she only released the shiny mauve head when Robert's panting signaled an imminent explosion.

Yet even in these exquisitely sensitive moments, as she sat nakedly on his face, Doungjai was typically forthright and unpredictable.

'You have lovely cock, Lobut,' she crooned, slowly stroking the object of her admiration. 'Him very big and very beautiful, make me feel horny too much,' With a mischievous smile, she added: 'Just like my friend tell me.'

Robert frowned and tried to move his head. 'Your friend?' His voice was muffled.

'My friend, Lek.' Her smile widened, and it was full of mischief. 'She tell me she play with your cock when you visit bar first night. She say him make her feel horny also.'

Robert sank back, pinned beneath the twin cushions of Doungjai's bottom. That was another problem with girls. They were incapable of keeping secrets from each other.

Chapter Forty-Nine

It was Sunday and Lumpini Park's one hundred and forty five acres were thronged with Thai families. They were glad to escape from the traffic and the choking fumes on their one whole day in the week together, and to enjoy the open spaces away from the small crowded homes that many of them occupied.

Alone, Doungjai stood on the stone bridge, that linked the island in the centre of the lake to the rest of the park, and gazed unseeingly across the sun speckled water.

At the other end of the bridge, children were tossing chunks of bread into the water and pointing eagerly as the surface was churned by the hundreds of small fish rising for the feast. Behind and beneath them two catfish circled lazily, revealing their impressive size when they occasionally moved to the surface to seize a bite. A small turtle paddled furiously on the perimeter of the action, trying to grab its share, but the swifter fish invariably beat it.

Old men played a Thai form of drafts in the shade away to Doungjai's right and youngsters took photographs of each other. Ghost-like and barely audible, the sound of a woman's voice, singing to the accompaniment of an electric organ, drifted through the trees from a small pagoda-style building.

These were just a few of the sights and sounds to be

encountered any Sunday in Lumpini Park, a place that had become a symbol to Doungjai. It would always have a special meaning for her, inspiring feelings of sadness and loss as well as hope and happiness.

Today, though she was sad that Robert had returned to England, she felt more optimistic about the future than she could ever remember. For a start, the crippling financial burden that had dominated her life for so long, looked less daunting, more manageable.

Her mother's worsening health had united the whole family in the realisation that she would have to have an operation if she was ever to recover. It called for a big financial feat and, in spite of everyone's protests, Doungjai's brother, Chut, had declared his intention to quit school at the end of the year to find work. Her sister, Oiy, had made similar noises although her schooling had another year to run. Doungjai's two elder brothers, having married and started families, had both recently changed jobs for better money and had pledged some of the extra to the family fund. This spirit of collective sacrifice augured well for the days, months, and years to come.

With Brown off her back, Doungjai was immediately able to contribute more. She had decided to carry on dancing at the Black Pussy, but only after a solemn promise to Robert that no one would pay the bar for her. Moving into Nang's apartment after her marriage to Cully, would also mean a saving in the rent.

As for Robert, he had promised to be back in Bangkok within the month and to make a modest contribution towards Doungjai's mother's operation.

Another attraction was his invitation to Cully's wedding.

'If you don't show up, I'll send my big brothers to look for you,' Cully had warned with that familiar twinkle in his eye. Far more damaging than this threat was the bear hug he gave Robert before he climbed into the taxi for the airport.

Doungjai fingered the ring on the third finger of her left hand – the ring that said she was not merely Robert's girl, but his fiancée. No date had yet been fixed for the wedding, nor had they the slightest idea where or how they would live. These matters would be settled when Doungjai's mother came out of hospital after her operation.

It had been the cheapest engagement ring in the shop – 'We have to save all our money now, Lobut,' she had cautioned – but to her it was still the most precious piece of jewellery in the whole world.

The innocence of their first flush of love was gone forever, killed by reality and necessity and human frailties. But in its place a far stronger love had emerged. A more tolerant, more durable kind of love, that had already been tested and proved capable of withstanding life's squalid intrusions. It was a love that was destined to survive.

She watched a family of her favourite ducks negotiate the step from dry land into the lake, and smiled wistfully.

If this had been a fairy story, there would be nothing now to stop her and Robert from living happily ever after. But they lived in the real world where happy ever after was for fairy tale characters only. She had already had more than her fair share of troubles in her young life and there were sure to be more in the years ahead.

She had no illusions. In some respects she had been lucky. Michael had been an unhappy interlude and so had the loan, necessary though it was at the time. They were mistakes from which she had learned much. Performing naked at the Black Pussy was a different matter altogether, as far as she was concerned, even if Robert was against it. Her act harmed no one and provided pleasure for some. What really mattered was the money she could earn there to help make her mother well again. She had nothing to reproach herself for on that score, and felt sure that Buddha would understand.

Well, almost sure.

THE END

Aspire Books are available from bookshops, super-markets, department and multiple stores throughout the UK, or can be ordered from the following address:

Aspire Publishing
Mail Order Department
8 Betony Rise
EXETER EX2 5RR

Please add £0.50 PER ORDER for postage and packing, irrespective of quantity.

Aspire Publishing

1 UNIT

No. R.001

SAVE 10 Units

and exchange them for any **1** Aspire
book of your choice

SAVE 20 Units

and exchange them for any **3** Aspire
books of your choice

THIS OFFER IS VALID INDEFINITELY

Redeemable at any stockist of Aspire books
or by post to:

Aspire Publishing
16 Connaught Street, LONDON W2 2AF

For the name of your nearest stockist
telephone, fax or write to:

Aspire Publishing
Voucher Redemption Dept.
8 Betony Rise
EXETER EX2 5RR
Tel: 01392 25 25 16
Fax: 01392 25 25 17

ASPIRE
1 UNIT
No. R.001